MW01169279

# Bind &

# Keep Me

## Pierced Hearts, Book Two

by

# Cari Silverwood

Copyright 2013 Cari Silverwood

Editor: Nerine Dorman

Cover Artist: Thomas Dorman aka Dr. Benway on Deviantart and Facebook

All rights reserved. This copy is intended for the original purchaser of this e-book only. No part of this e-book may be reproduced, scanned, or distributed in any printed or electronic form without prior written permission from the author. Please do not participate in or encourage piracy of copyrighted materials.

This e-book is a work of fiction. While reference might be made to actual historical events or existing locations, the names, characters, places and incidents are either the product of the author's imagination or are used fictitiously, and any resemblance to actual persons, living or dead, business establishments, events, or locales is entirely coincidental.

## *Disclaimer*

This book contains descriptions of many BDSM and sexual practices but this is a work of fiction and as such should not be used in any way as a guide. The author will not be responsible for any loss, harm, injury or death resulting from use of the information contained within.

## Early praise for Bind and Keep Me

"Bind and Keep Me, leads you down a depraved path of dark desires that you know are so wrong, but feel too good for you to care. Cari Silverwood makes losing what we all cherish—our freedom—sinfully erotic."

**Bianca Sommerland – author of Deadly Captive.**

"Enthralling and seductive, Bind and Keep Me brings the taboo into our basements and locks us inside. A must-read for lovers of dangerous erotic fiction."

**Skye Warren – author of Wanderlust**

# *Acknowledgement*

With every book I write there are a bunch of great people behind the scenes helping me. I'd like to thank and give big, huge hug to Sorcha Black, my crit partner and cheerleader extraordinaire. Bear in mind that you will never, ever see Sorcha in a cheerleader costume and if you did she'd be forced to silence you forever. Pom poms are not her thing. Black is. And anything else that goes with black. Most of those things are bad. You have been warned.

I also need to thank my beta readers Mj, Ekatarina Sayonova, Bianca Sarble (a fellow author), Lina Sacher (who did triple duty on the re-reads), and my editor, Nerine Dorman.

# Chapter 1

## Jodie.

"You're sure?" Melissa cocked her head at me while stepping over the splattered pink ice from a dropped frozen drink. The dark waves below slapped and sloshed at the hull of the ferry and the pylons of the jetty. "I know they won't mind you coming with me. My car's just down that side street." She pointed ahead. "Stephanie is an old friend of yours, yes?"

"She is, but…" A very long-ago friend. I shrugged and gave an apologetic smile. I wasn't really apologetic. I also wasn't sure if I should be refusing. Melissa was an acquaintance through work connections, but she knew people in the industry and, hell, she was friendly.

Leon Edante, a wealthy dentist, was celebrating some big thing. A partnership, I thought she'd said. He worked on the mainland and kept a posh house here on Magnetic Island, somewhere on the slope behind Horseshoe Bay. Squeezing in on this party at the last moment, without an invite from the host, seemed wrong, despite Melissa's insistence. I glanced at her.

Even jostled by the herd of tourist lemmings and islanders coming home, she carried herself with elegance. My auburn hair was the same shade as hers and I was just as slim, yet I felt drab next to her. My business skirt and silver-gray knit top versus her strappy dress, and I lost hands down.

"Okay. I'm sure we'll see each other again. Take care. If you change your mind…"

I nodded and she walked away.

Damn. I'd been set to do some networking when Melissa dropped this bombshell. I toyed with my phone. To go home or not to go home, that is the question. A pleasant if somewhat hot fifteen-minute walk up the hill to our place where Klaus was waiting for me, or ask to join Melissa, Leon, and Stephanie for dinner and risk looking like a fool if he stared at me and said no?

I sighed and selected Klaus's phone number.

"Hi. Where are you?" Through the phone, his words sounded distant. Maybe I was imagining the hint of masculine rumble, but my memory brought the words to life and warmed me.

I smiled. "I'm back. I'm down at the jetty. I've got an invite. Leon Edante…you know? The dentist? He's celebrating some business success with a dinner with two other women. Just a quiet thing, but one of them, Melissa, is a producer with Channel Seven. I'd like to go and see if she'll divulge some hot tips on what they're looking for." I bit my lip, and waited to hear if Klaus would okay this. "It's at his place in Horseshoe Bay."

"Oh yeah. The one that was featured in *Living Houses*, last year. Rich then. Good-looking?"

Was Klaus jealous? A devious urge to push took me to the edge. I gripped the phone tighter, drew in a breath, and jumped over. "Yup. Very. And he's got these gorrr-geous bedroom eyes too." I let out a shuddery sigh that made a man beside me shoot a puzzled look.

"Bedroom eyes?" Ooh. Short and harsh-sounding, that reply.

"You wondering if I might swoon, fall into his arms, and check out his bedroom furniture?"

He laughed. "No. I know you won't. Make sure you're home by eight and take your underwear off in the car before you come up, female. I want to try out that new cane—with you, ass up, over the sofa arm."

*Fuck.* "I think I just swallowed my tongue. You're such a romantic."

The picture that had evoked. And *female?* So passionless. My Klaus in sadist mode. My body tightened. I hated the cane. But I loved it too.

"I am, aren't I?"

"Yes, Sir, you are. You'd out-romance a stuffed warthog."

"A what? Care to repeat that? My caning arm is in dire need of a workout."

"Uhh. Strangely, no. I think I meant to say Cyrano de Bergerac had nothing on you."

"Much better. Get that tongue back, won't you? I'm going to expect to use it."

*Where?* I almost asked, but had a feeling I'd already earned a few extra whacks.

"I will. Bye. Love you," I whispered.

"Bye, sweetheart."

I pressed the phone to my chest for a few seconds. This dinner had better not take too long.

I found myself still smiling as I tucked the phone back into my bag. Klaus was my rock, my soul mate, my lover, my man who delivered me delicious pain over his lap, or with his hand firmly clenched in my hair or his foot on my neck. For an independent-brained feminist it had been some earth-shaking revelation to discover I liked both sadomasochism and this…this power exchange. I wouldn't have done it for any other man. But I loved him.

I shook my head. *Be gone, fluffy love-smitten thoughts. Work calls.* I jogged to catch up to Melissa.

\*\*\*\*\*

Crickets were chirping somewhere. I'd lost track of time. Dark, though. The downlights were on and the windows reflected the black of night. I squinted at my watch then gave up trying to focus. The residual heat of the afternoon must be making me drowsy, though the meal and the wine might have as much to do with it. I didn't drink often, not anymore.

From my comfy seat in the corner of the sofa, I smiled lazily across the coffee table at something Leon murmured to Stephanie. Not much networking going on, but I was cool with that. We were all a little befuzzled. I pulled my legs up, tucked them under me, and cuddled up to the big pillow. I could lie down for a minute. Then maybe I should go home.

We were celebrating…something…something to do with Leon. Whatever the fuck it was, the champagne was good. My cheek on the soft pillow, through slitted eyes I watched the bubbles in my champagne rise and pop. The tilt of the liquid, as it approached the lip of the glass, warned of imminent spillage but my hand refused to move. My eyes closed like a bank vault.

Black. Swimmy darkness. There came soft voices. Laughing voices. Something tugged at me, shifted me…the cold glass was gone from my hand. My mouth numb, my heart beating snail-slow, I sank into the sea. I drifted far and deep, though somewhere out there, I knew, I always knew, things were circling me.

Coolness on my legs. Warmth sliding up them, touching me, under my clothes. Laughing and gentle questions.

*No-no-no*, someone said, ever quieter.

*Open your eyes. Open your eyes*, but I only sank deeper.

Delicious shock as the warmth touched where my limbs met and flowed farther, inside…

I was sinking ever deeper.

Shark deep.

# Chapter 2

## Klaus

I was on the phone to Kat when I realized Jodie was really late. I stopped in the middle of explaining yet again that I didn't know if Jodie would be interested in attending another play party. The other one, a year ago, had left its mark on both of us.

"Klaus?"

"Yeah?" I studied my watch. Almost nine. Last time I'd checked it had been ten past eight and not drastically late enough to ring alarm bells. But an hour overdue? My alarm bells turned into a siren for a few seconds. Where had she said she was going?

"Hey, Kat, did you see that house featured here in *Living Houses*? Owned by a dentist called Edante. Very nice architectural design and somewhere in millionaire row in Horseshoe Bay?"

"Um, no. Sorry, I'm not into magazines about houses and shit."

"Okay." I frowned. She had to still be there, yet this late…she'd have called. Our arrangement was for her to inform me if anything stopped her being home on time. I drummed my fingers on the arm of my leather armchair. "Kat. Gotta go. Something I need to do. We can talk tomorrow."

"Sure. Sure. Say hello to Jodie for me."

"Yep. Will do."

Kat was nothing if not persistent and had the tenacity of a cute bulldog. She'd been trying to get into Jodie's pants again ever since that awful night. It *had* started well. For a sometime submissive, Kat had made a great Domme. Whenever I heard she was looking for a Dom who was man enough to dominate her, I raised a skeptical eyebrow. The woman liked to boast of all the potential Doms she'd scared off.

I tried contacting Jodie, only to hear her phone divert me to message bank. My heart did a little screech to a halt before resuming beating. It wasn't impossible that the battery had run out, or she'd dropped it in a fish tank or something. Just unusual and unlikely. But this was a respectable professional, wasn't it? A dentist. She'd be perfectly safe, *if* she were there, at his house.

Maybe I should check.

I had no phone number for him.

"Phone book," I muttered. Nope, not in there. I grabbed the laptop off the table and fired it up. No number listed online either. "Damn."

I needed to figure out if she was there, first, surely. The police wouldn't be interested in a girlfriend staying over late at a party. Nine o'clock? It wasn't even midnight, for chrissakes.

Was I being premature? I swiped my hand down my face. Yes, I was. Nobody was perfect. I should go do something to distract myself. Jodie would turn up soon.

I found a comedy show on Tivo, slumped back into the lounge with a light beer in hand, and flicked play. One of the benefits of having employed a second accountant was getting a full Saturday off. Next weekend I'd make sure Jodie and I shared the time together. This was ridiculous.

It reminded me of one of our differences that really wasn't that different. Jodie and her "I love yous". I grimaced. She wanted me to say it too but love was such a strange undefinable thing. How in the world was I supposed to know if I suffered from it? If pushed, I was happy to repeat to her how she was my one and only. Because she was. Jodie took that as love, but I knew she wanted me to say it. I liked things I could touch, handle, and count. Love was for poets, not me.

Half an hour later, I gave up and turned off the TV. I couldn't stop wondering what Jodie was up to. The least I could do was figure out where the house was. Then…another hour? Yeah, an hour at most. But the six kilometers of roads from Nelly Bay to Horseshoe Bay were tortuous and there was the possibility she'd had an accident.

Stuff this. I had to know.

If she wasn't there, and if she'd left ages before, I'd be getting the police involved. So, plan. Drive to his house and check the road along the way. Except I still didn't know the address.

"Right." I threw down the remote and it bounced onto the floor. I left it there. Where to start? Google?

Ten minutes later I'd narrowed it down to three possibilities from Google Maps. And she still hadn't called and wasn't answering. I practiced wearing a hole in the ceiling by staring at it for another few minutes before I swore, gave in, and grabbed the car keys. I didn't care if I looked a fool turning up at this private party like some forlorn lover.

The drive to Horseshoe Bay must have left finger indentations in my steering wheel. Why was I so tense? Jodie was an adult. Even if we had an almost TPE arrangement, she could, if she chose to, terminate it. Or she could be bloody late and get caned extra hard.

I was getting ever more sure I shouldn't be thinking those thoughts about punishment. Not now…not when something was wrong. But accountants didn't have telepathy, did they? This would be nothing…some miscalculation. I pulled over and stared along the steep, rising road.

As if it would jar loose a brilliant deduction, I scrubbed my fingers back and forth through my hair. Then I resumed driving slowly along the street, trying to decipher numbers in the meager light.

Fuck. Where was it? And why didn't millionaires have good street lighting?

Number twenty-four turned out to be the one. I recognized the house from when I'd cruised along like numerous other rubberneckers, inspecting the award-winning dwelling.

Three levels, crisp minimalistic design, and a color scheme that tended toward chic white and ocean blues and etched, cantilevered glass. From where I'd parked my jeep under the gum trees, I gazed up the slope. The pinpricks of the stars behind the roofline made it seem fairy tale pretty.

Time to go ninja style and find Jodie?

No, first, be polite. I knocked at the front double timber doors with the sculpted wave-patterned handles. Nice, but they were locked. The soft light from the other side of the glass panel showed no flickers that might mean people moved about inside. No one answered the knock. No one called out.

I knocked again. Nothing. Then a few more times just to be certain.

I stepped back and looked up again, surveying the second story balcony. A light was on up there.

The scent of flower blooms sweetened the air. Peaceful, really. There wasn't a domestic argument to be heard anywhere nearby, or even a piece of rubbish on the poorly lit driveway, or out on the street. A perfect, nice neighborhood. The worst bit of violence came from a possum that had clambered up a tree, a black silhouette against the lighter sky. It set to screeching at its fellow tree dwellers. Maybe it was claiming all the mangos?

I tsked at myself, hands in my pants pockets. Indecision wasn't my thing.

I might be at the wrong house. If I went sneaking about, I might get shot, yelled at, arrested. The law said invading other people's houses was bad. Apart from liking to beat Jodie, tie her up, and cause her exquisite pain while making her climax, I wasn't bad. I was a pillar of society. A pleasant, unassuming accountant who was into kink.

Still no voices, no noise from inside.

The sick churning of my stomach when I thought of Jodie, lost or injured, decided me.

I sighed. "Bugger this." Sometimes even accountants got a little crazy. Dancing on tables, tooting party horns, and rescuing lost girlfriends from the clutches of millionaires wasn't just for stock market hotshots. Ninja-ing it was.

Scaling up to the balcony, where the main living area seemed to be, required a leap from a tree stump, and one determined heave of muscle. Then I swung up my legs and shimmied under the steel-and-wire railings. From an overhanging tree branch, some creature chittered indignantly. But as I padded inside through an open sliding door, I heard no man or woman-made sounds.

"Hello? Anyone home?"

Silence.

I made my way past a long, low coffee table cradled between three sofas. On it was a sprawl of wine glasses, platters with the remains of sushi, and glossy books. After checking out a kitchen, a games room, and an entertainment room, I found the stairs and went up to the third floor.

The first door, partly open, spilled a wedge of light into the carpeted hallway. I sucked in a breath. If this was the wrong house, here came my police record.

Some black cloth draped on the floor caught my eye. Underwear. Lacy. With tiny red hearts embroidered along below the elastic.

Jodie's. I'd given them to her a week ago.

Fuck.

I'd eat my hat if she was having a swinging affair with this guy. No, no way, I'd fucking eat his heart. Fair was fair.

Except I knew she wasn't. So, I counted to ten and told myself to relax. Maybe there was a good, plain, simple explanation for this… Nope, couldn't think of one. I wished I'd brought a gun. But I hadn't. Being a second dan black belt in judo would have to do.

"Ready or not, here I come," I whispered to myself then shoved the door open with the toe of my shoe.

Clothes were strewn across the polished timber floor and a brilliant blue rug. Jodie's skirt and gray top were there, as well as other clothes I didn't recognize. The door swung farther. This was a bedroom, a huge one, with another set of sofas and an open walk-in robe, and to the right…was revealed the bed. Rumpled sheets and more blues of quilt. A down-casting lamp stood beside the bed…and a woman's foot poked out from under the sheets. Unmoving. Sleeping?

Dark dread trickled slow as death into my flesh, cooling my chest and pinning me with an ice-sharp ache, right in the very middle.

What had happened here?

I stepped in, breath caught up on some hard lump. My eyes seemed to snag and stop on each new detail as they came into sight. I was a robot with my gaze ratcheting along on cogwheel teeth. *Jerk.* A man's body facing away from me. Naked. *Jerk.* His back. *Jump* again to see her head beyond his. They lay as if spooning. Her auburn hair trailed over the sheet that was pulled up to her cheek.

A memory triggered. Me and Jodie, in bed, cuddling. Her sensuous warmth against my skin. Her scent. Our murmured exchange of lovers' pretty words and soft kisses. And, as always, my amazement that we suited each other so well, and that she loved me.

I could hear quiet wet breathing like someone sucking air in past phlegm.

My legs were distant from me and stiff as I approached the bed and looked down. My body wasn't mine. I was ten thousand feet up, and the bed was down there, far, far away. This was not, *could not,* be real.

The man breathed stertorous and harsh, like a dinosaur inhaling swamp. He was making the sounds. She… I stretched out a hand to move aside some of her hair. The ice cold of her ear and her cheek froze me also. Slowly, I shifted the sheet downward. Loops of her hair clung to the sheet, uncurling. Then I saw her neck, her blue-white neck.

No. Fuck, no. A gasp tore like a red wound from my mouth, ripping a hole in my soul. "No." Tremors took my arm until I had to draw it back before I knocked against the man.

I stared. He breathed through open mouth. She was cold and still. Her hands were tied up to the headboard. A ligature of rope was wrapped loosely about her neck.

I knew fifty ways to kill him but all I could think of was crushing his face into a red smear on the white sheet.

"Bastard," I grated out, gripping a hunk of his hair in my hand. His eyes popped open. Mine fixed on his. I wasn't missing a second of this. My other fist drew back to my ear—there all by itself, it seemed—ready to unleash hurt on him.

His pupils were huge and dilated. Drugs? On the bedside table lay a syringe with no needle, a small glass bottle, and a ripped-open packet.

"No," he croaked, half-turning his head to look up at me. "Nooo."

As I stared into his dark eyes, he coughed, his hands stirred feebly under the sheet, and vomit bubbled from his mouth, welling up like a disgusting fountain.

Logic arrived, late but welcome, and through the rage, I recognized how poorly he defended himself, how much danger he was in from inhaling his vomit. I moved my hand higher in his hair so the vomit wouldn't spill on me.

"If you cough," I told him calmly, as if this was merely some science experiment. "You might get some air. If not, well, I suppose you might drown in your own foul stench. I can't think of a better way for you to die." I narrowed my eyes, lowered my face a little, and I spoke through gritted teeth. "Die you evil fucking bastard. Choke on that shit."

It took a few minutes…of watching him breathe in and out through the sludge in his mouth. Watching him die. Whatever he'd taken, whatever drug, it had slowed his reflexes and his brain and he'd lost all idea of self-preservation. As the last dribble of air sighed out and his body relaxed into death, I added a eulogy.

"I hope you knew what I did to you, you piece of filth. You killed Jodie." I had to halt for a moment. I was so empty inside, so raw, like someone had scraped out my insides. My next words, I whispered hoarsely, "My beautiful, beautiful Jodie."

Tears had blurred my vision by then, and the first of them spilled and ran down my face. But I wiped them away, sniffed them back, and made them stop. I had to take care of her now. I could grieve later. I wasn't leaving her in this fucker's embrace. I stepped carefully around the foot of the bed to her side, and bent to move the hair from her face.

"It's not her," someone said quietly, shakily.

The earth tilted. My heart lost a few beats forevermore. I turned, searching the room. "What?"

"It's not Jodie." Beyond the two red leather sofas, curled on the floor with handcuffs around her wrists and rope on her ankles, was a young woman, naked except for white underwear and bra, with her hair, black as oil, tumbling across her shoulders.

But…her words…

I swung my gaze back to the dead woman, reached, and brushed aside the hair over her face. "My God." An unfamiliar face was beneath—her mouth open as if straining for air.

"It's not—" she began again.

"Jodie," I finished, slumping a little in shock. "Where is she then? Where is she! Is she alive?"

"Last I saw of her. Yes. She's in the next bedroom down."

As I tore out the door, I heard her cry, "Let me go. Please? He might wake up! Maybe he's not dead!"

The next bedroom was dark. When I turned on the light, there she was on the floor, also naked and bound, at ankle and wrist, but looking back with big scared eyes that seemed riveted to me. A scarf was tied across her mouth. I did a quick scan as I strode forward. No one else was here.

I knelt and cupped her face and kissed her while saying softly, over and over, in deliberate reassurance, "It's okay. I'm here. I'm here." Then I drew back and stared at her for a moment to fix in my mind it was really her, alive. My pulse was harder to convince and kept pounding away.

I applied myself to freeing her—undoing the scarf and the ropes. Some sort of stiff nylon rope. Maybe he used it for his yacht, the one he'd never see again. Whatever it was, it was stupid stuff and hard to unknot.

She sniffed and kissed my upper arm as I worked. Her words slurred. "I knew you'd come. Knew it, Klaus." While I wrestled some more with the knots, she closed her eyes as if too tired to keep them open. Drugged?

"Of course I have. I'm yours forever, remember? Just like you're mine." The last loop came off her wrists.

Her eyes opened, blinking, clearing with each second, or so it seemed. "I do. I do remember." There were tears in her words and that squeezed my chest, hard.

"Good. Don't you ever forget. I had *yours forever* tattooed on my heart and it's really bloody hard to get tattoos off of there."

Her hands were cold and trembling. Mine were almost as bad, fucking shaking. Crapitty-crap. Now was *not* the time to lose it. I clamped down on my feelings and drew her hands to her front, kissed them once, and checked them for color and capillary refill.

With my arm over her back and my forehead snuggled against hers, I settled for merely holding her for a while. Just for a few minutes longer, I would be her cocoon, keeping away the outside world. In here, all was warm and safe. I breathed with her and stroked her and made myself calm down too. Nobody in the next room was going anywhere by themselves, or going to come to further harm. Unless…unless… All on its ownsome, my mind started sifting facts and going down pathways. I was in so much trouble. I veered away from that minefield. *First, make sure we're safe.*

"Jodie, I need to know if there is anyone in the house apart from us and the guy in the bedroom and the two women? Are we in danger from anyone I don't know about?"

Again, the tears made her words wobbly, but I was relieved at how clear her thinking seemed. "No. No one else." She shook her head. "But I can't remember exactly what happened to me. I can't. Things are all confused."

Shit. "You were drugged? I'm just wanting to be sure we don't have some guy apart from this Leon who might have done all this."

"I…I don't know. I think it was him. I guess. He seemed so confident and yet something was off about him."

"Okay. Maybe I can ask…" The woman in the room next door. I knew what she was, what the police would call her—a witness to murder.

I'd made a big huge enormous life-changing mistake. No. Now wasn't the time to wallow in that. I mentally took myself by the scruff, and shook myself. Being selfish here was not happening. I focused on Jodie.

"How are you feeling? I'm thinking you need a doctor. How groggy are you? Do you feel sick?" Had she been raped? I wasn't asking that, not yet. That was a definite possibility, even if wondering about it made me feel like going back and killing the man again.

If she seemed to be getting sicker, I'd be phoning for an ambulance.

"My stomach feels funny. I thought I was going to vomit. But not now." She shifted her legs up and closer to me, until her knees bumped my shoulder, then she felt my face with her fingers, patting me like she too couldn't be sure this was real, *I* was real. "I just couldn't get loose. And I can't remember anything before I woke. Only coming here and drinking champagne. I don't think I even finished one glass…" The hitch in her voice was followed by Jodie searching my face. "Klaus, what are you hiding?"

I watched those beautiful eyes take stock. How in hell she'd figured this out, I did not know. I should work on my poker face. Least I knew now she was thinking fine. I had to tell her.

"I killed the man, Jodie. The man on the bed with the woman who looks like you. Who I thought *was* you. There's more, though."

Tiny creases formed between her eyebrows, and I caressed the curves above each brow while I waited for her next words, her next question.

"You killed him…" Fear poured out with her next sluggish words. "What happened in there? It's something terrible, isn't it? That would be Melissa on the bed. What's happened? You can tell me." Her voice quavered.

If I said this the wrong way, would I lose her? I had only one excuse, and it was Jodie. I'd thought it was *her* corpse. *What an ugly word corpse is. But death is damn ugly.*

"The woman is dead. I killed him because he was lying beside her, and she has been strangled by a rope around her neck and her hands are tied. And I thought…he'd killed you." I swallowed. I had to say this. "I thought it was you he'd killed, so when he started to vomit, I held him so he'd breathe it in. I let him die. I *made* him die." The rest. *Say* it all. "And I'm not sorry."

"Ohmigod."

I sighed. "The other thing is there's another woman in there, handcuffed still, but okay, and she saw what I did. I didn't see her until after." When her expression didn't alter, I figured I needed to spell out what that meant. "She is a witness to me killing this man."

"Oh, Klaus. Oh god. I don't know what to say. I shouldn't have come here." She began to rock, shaking her head against the rug, over and over, as if by denying it she could change what had happened. Her face went a smudged red and white. "It's my fault. Now you'll go to jail and it's my fault. It's my fault. I'm sorry." She made a strangled squeak. "I'm sorry."

"What! The hell it is. It's not your fault." I wiped away the tears leaking from her eyes, thinking as fast as I could under the circumstances. "They can't tell that I did this. People do that all the time when drugged, and he was drugged. Maybe she'll stay quiet if I ask her to?"

"I don't want to lose you! I should have said no to coming. I should have known." She wrapped her hand around my finger that had been stroking her forehead and sobbed, her shoulders trembling.

Was it the aftereffects of whatever she'd taken? This was irrational. "Of course it's not your fault. *Shh. Shh.* Let me think this through."

For once though, I was having trouble getting it all lined up in my head. I'd murdered someone. Bad man or not, it was what I'd done.

And I'd been seen doing it. That was, for me, the worst of it. For a man who always liked the moral high ground, I had awful shaky foundations.

I leaned my head in my palm, with Jodie still clutching the other hand. I had to do right for her as much as me. I had no right to drag her into something illegal, to make her a victim again.

I didn't want to go to prison. The police would see it the wrong way. I'd killed a man just because I wanted to. Not in self-defense. We didn't even have the death penalty, *legally*, for any crime here, so this would never be excused. Not completely. I needed to find out more facts though. If it meant only probation or a year in jail, could I do that?

Maybe.

I shut my eyes. The prospect of being labeled a criminal horrified me. I'd been through this moral bigheadedness question already when I discovered the extremeness of my cravings for sadistic activities. If not for Jodie—her compassion, her understanding, and her sheer stubbornness—I might have been forever angry and grieving at what I saw as my depraved self.

What if I had to go to jail? Could I stand having my name dragged through mud?

I didn't *want* to. It was not something I even felt I deserved. The man was an evil bastard, as far as I could tell. I wanted to stay free and I didn't want to be seen as a murderer. Enough. I'd chase this tail some more later.

"Okay. Here is what I want to do. You need to say if it doesn't sit well with your conscience. Because…" I stared directly into Jodie's eyes. "Because I don't intend to be tried for this, *if* I can avoid it. But I am not going to make you my accomplice. There's only one way to wriggle out of this that I can see, and that's to convince that woman in there not to say what happened."

A quiet pause, then she nodded. We were so close I caught her scent and felt the warm movement of air as she spoke. "Yes. I agree."

"Good." Maybe this was the right time to ask the next question. "Jodie," I said softly, "Do you know if you were raped?"

Her lips compressed and she looked toward her toes for a few seconds. This must be a hard thing to contemplate but we needed to know. "I…no, Klaus, I can't be sure. It doesn't feel like it. You know. I don't feel sore or, or messy, or anything. But…" She pulled a face, as if disgusted, then shrugged.

Maybe a doctor was the only way to find out? "Okay. Try not to worry about it. We'll find out. Okay? We *will* figure this out."

Pensively, she nodded. "'Kay."

Even though we'd both like an answer straight away, I couldn't see a way to be sure.

"I need you to do what I say, for the time being. It will make things simpler. But answer me this—the other woman in there, do you think she will she do this? Lie and deny seeing what I did?"

"Stephanie?" Jodie thought awhile, with her bottom lip between her teeth. Her little headshake might have been a *no* or an *I don't know*.

Gently, I held her face in my palm. "You don't know, do you?"

"No, Sir, I don't."

"Then let's go find out."

Later, I could try to find a way to research the law on this. Maybe, if it seemed the best course of action, I could simply front up and confess. Maybe that would be best for Jodie and me…

If only that didn't seem like ripping off pieces of who I *was* and feeding them to a passing dog. If only, every time I considered confessing, I didn't want to scream, *this is not fair*.

All of this mess was because I thought he'd killed her. My vengeance had seemed so right.

# Chapter 3

## Stephanie

My wrists were aching, so were the muscles in my arms. I tried to shift my numb shoulder into a better spot on the rug on the floor between the sofas. Even with the rug over it, lying on the timber for this long was painful. *This has not been a good party.*

That stupid thought had been alternating with terror ever since the big guy had entered the room and let Leon die. Clearly Leon had fucked up in a big way, but he didn't deserve to die, did he?

Not...I shuddered, remembering the awful gurgling, the smell of vomit...no, not like that. That had been awful, terrifying, a whole lot of bad adjectives. I wasn't close to either of them, though I knew Melissa more than I knew Leon, but still. I never wanted to see someone die again.

*Especially not me.*

The trembling took me again. The handcuffs clinked.

What if this stranger found out everything? I wasn't squeaky clean here. A little chemical something to liven up a get together was fine in my books, but this had gone too far...way far out into outer space, like, it was as far as bad outcomes could possibly go. The *Star Trek* of bad outcomes. And yet, not being able to predict something...did that mean I wasn't to blame?

No. I let out the breath I'd been holding and decided again, no.

*I'm not a coward. I'll take the heat on this, except not to this man who kills people that make him angry. No fucking way.*

"It was Leon, mostly," I whispered to myself as footstep sounds tapped back down the hallway. Leon was mostly to blame. Those were too many sounds to be just *him*. Had to be Jodie as well. Who was he? Jodie's boyfriend? Oh god. That would be it. If he found out what I'd done to her. Shit, shit, shit. He'd just *killed* a man in front of me.

Then he came back in. Jodie followed him then she stopped dead, stiffening at the sight of the bodies on the bed.

"Klaus...oh damn, damn, you were telling the truth."

"Yes. I'm so sorry, Jodie. There's nothing you can do for her. Take your time, sweetheart. Don't look...if you can do that?"

"I'll try." She sent him a wobbly smile. "It's hard not to throw up."

He took her shoulders and hugged her to his chest while rubbing her back. His chin rested near her ear and he whispered something.

The love in that gesture fairly radiated round the room. I envied them so much. Dead people, stench of vomit, me tied up on the floor and hurting a little, but for a second all I could see and feel was that love.

Envy. God, how I envied them. Bastards. I smiled inside. Jodie had caught herself a man. I eyed him some more and my situation hammered home again. I was so fucked, especially if Jodie remembered.

The broad, assured masculine stance, the obvious muscles under his t-shirt and surfer shorts made me want to shrink into the floor. I was shit at lying, at faking the truth. Maybe he wouldn't ask me anything important?

After he kissed Jodie's head and murmured something, he walked over and crouched a foot away. I quietly crossed my fingers and tried to look innocent without shaking. But my heart was thumping away so frantically inside me I was almost sure he could see it.

"I'm Klaus, Jodie's partner. You okay?"

Partner? Not husband, not boyfriend? It sounded more permanent than boyfriend, which was not good.

Those words, his presence above me, and the casual drape of his hands between his thighs imparted solidness, control—intimidation too though. I just flat-out knew I never wanted to see this guy again. Not after he let me go anyway. He scared me.

His close-shorn, sandy-colored hair reminded me of the military and he certainly had the build for a soldier.

Was I okay? He was waiting for an answer.

I nodded. Behind him Jodie was collecting her clothes from the floor. She began dressing. Only a mild unsteadiness, when she nearly tripped while putting on underwear, betrayed her nerves.

"Do you know where the key is to these?" He waved his fingers at where my hands were cuffed together before me.

I stared at them for a second like I'd not seen them before. The matter-of-fact questions unsettled me. Like, as if somewhere under that he was ready to erupt into rage again. How could he be so calm with all this around him?

I risked looking him in the eye, shrank, but managed to stay on target despite the urge to look away. "No. I don't know. Maybe on the table next to the bed?"

Klaus frowned. "No, they're not there. I guess I'd better check his clothes."

"Wait." Jodi held up a small metal object, and jingled it. "This it? Found it on the floor."

"Looks like it." Finally, I could tell he'd seen the camera on its tripod where Leon had set it up in the corner. After one long look, he rose, fiddled at the back of it then went over and checked the key.

When he knelt and fitted the key into the handcuff lock, I couldn't stop the shakes returning.

"Hey. Don't be frightened. It's over. See? I'm getting these off. The man over there can't hurt you anymore." The soft rumble of his voice mesmerized me as his fingers brushed my palms.

The cuffs fell away. After I sat up, he started on the ankle rope. "Stephanie?" He cocked a brow at me. I nodded to acknowledge my name. "Can I call you Steph?" A loop of rope slid free.

"Yes." I nodded again, feeling the trembles die away. Maybe he was a nice person, just a bit unhinged by everything? I could see how that might happen if he'd thought Melissa was Jodie. Just like that, tears sprang up, overflowed and dripped from my cheeks onto my leg.

Would I ever get over this? Every time I thought of them, especially her, a vibrant happy woman, dead, the tragedy clawed at my insides again.

Alerted by something, maybe my sniffling, Klaus paused and checked me over. "Heyyy." For a moment, he caressed my lower leg. "*Shh.*"

"It's—" I choked out then shut my eyes. *Dead friends; me fucking up, and everything.* "Oh shit. This is so stupid. How…" Hand to my forehead, I made myself tighten down. The tears stopped. "I'm sorry for swearing."

"Oh? I think under the circumstances it's allowed. There, you're free." He helped me to my feet and onto the nearest sofa. "Tell me where your clothes are. Then we need to decide what we're doing."

"We do?" God, this is where it started. What did you do about two bodies except… "Call the police?"

"Maybe. Find your clothes first. You must see this isn't straightforward?"

My reply came out so quiet. "I guess." I glanced down at my white bra and panties and found my face warming. Dumb reaction. I clasped my knees and cleared my throat. I wasn't normally a mouse. "I guess it's complicated."

Jodie padded over, now fully clothed, and hugged me. Inside I freaked—scared to bits she'd leap back and go, *I know what you did.* "We'll get through this. Just listen to Klaus."

"I am." Despite the guilt, I hugged her back.

My thoughts were clearer now, the drug's effects had lessened, and the bad memory bobbed back up and stayed there. The one that had been haunting me—the memory of me helping Leon hold Jodie down. Would I ever erase that?

I inhaled shakily. "Thank you."

"You're welcome," she murmured.

As I watched Jodie go over to Klaus, all I could hear inside my head was one word, *traitor*. Though *idiot* maybe fitted better. So what if I'd been tripping out, how could I have done that? Or thought it right?

But, thank *god*, she hadn't remembered.

I dressed. As I did so, I deliberately didn't face the bed. From the floor, they might have been sleeping. I didn't want to look at them. Maybe Melissa and Leon would be breathing when I looked, if I just waited a little. Maybe it was all a mistake. Crazy thoughts ran through my head. I knew they were crazy, and yet, when I turned and stared, I was hoping.

They were so still. The reality of their death slammed into me again. I forced myself to keep looking despite the sweat prickling onto my forehead. I bit down on my hand until it stung. Dead. Gone. Nothing was bringing them back.

I literally shook myself.

*Get moving. I'm alive. Nothing I can do. Vile. Awful. But it happened.*

It still seemed impossible.

I helped Jodie check the room for anything that might have fallen from her pockets. There'd been nothing. Then we went out to the other small entertainment room where the mess of sushi entrees and wine glasses still sat, and Klaus started asking all the wrong things.

"I want you to tell us what happened here. Exactly. Okay, Steph?"

"But...they're dead." I clenched my fists. "How can we just *talk*?"

"Yes, they are. We can't bring them back to life. But, I think both of us may benefit from this. I need to know why. Why did he do this? Did you know he was using a drug of some sort? Was this planned in some way? Without setting you on some particular course, I just *need* to know. You can see it's important?"

I nodded brightly. *Fuck.*

Then he stood there waiting, his arms around Jodie's waist. Neither of them had sat but I'd automatically perched on the edge of the rattan cane lounge.

The blue-tinted Doulton goblets were Leon's current favorites. One of them was half-full. The flat liquid glinted in the fluorescent light. Outside in the night, past the wide-open glass doors, the wind sighed and sent tree boughs rubbing on one another and rustling. The pages on a magazine flipped. Leaves skittered along the wide verandah. I was surprised my knees weren't rattling too.

Only a few hours ago *they* had been here, alive. Laughing. Talking. Getting a little high while watching Jodie float away into dreamland. I could see them still.

"Steph?" Jodie was peering down.

"Yes? Um. Sorry." He wanted the story. I stared from one to the other, and began.

I told of how we'd had dinner then come out here and…and how Leon had added something to the wine to get things humming. Neither Jodie nor Klaus said anything, so I ploughed onward. Jodie had flaked out, almost unconscious, and ended up undressed on the spare bed. Leon had decided to try some kinky sex with Melissa while I watched. I remembered giggling as he tied her up. Then I'd maybe passed out for a while and woken to find Melissa had gone blue and stopped breathing. When I screamed and shook Leon awake he'd panicked.

I…

I hid my face in my hands and dug my nails into my cheeks.

"Keep going, Steph. What happened then?" Klaus again, in such a quiet normal voice. How dare he sound *normal*?

Get it over with. In a monotone, I said the rest. "Then, he tried to revive her and couldn't and when I said we needed to call the police, he hit me, and yelled, and he handcuffed me and said he needed to think. Then, he took more of whatever the drug was. That's it. You came."

Klaus frowned. "He got back into bed with her? With the dead woman?"

I shut my eyes a second, trying to erase the nauseating image. "Yes, he did."

"Christ. But, that's it?" Klaus sounded incredulous. "You're missing a big chunk."

"Yes. Steph, what happened to me? Please? I need to know. Was I raped by him? What did he do to me?"

The concern on Jodie's face brought the guilt back. I'd wondered where my conscience had gone up until now. On holiday, maybe. Now it was back.

"No. He went away for a few minutes after he went crazy to tie you up too. After Melissa died. He said that to me. Said he needed to know where we all were while he figured out what to do. I doubt there was time to do anything else…bad. I don't think he was that way inclined right then. I think…" I shook my head. "I'm sure nothing happened to you."

"Okay." Jodie stepped back into Klaus's arms. "You're certain? I need to know for sure."

"As sure as I can be. Leon exhausted himself fucking Melissa. Poor man. Poor her," I muttered.

Now they were both dead.

It had been interesting to watch them make love. Even if I'd wanted it to be me. *Later*, he'd murmured, after I'd crawled and kissed over the top of them. Head in hands, I remembered, and the knife agony twisted inside my gut at the strange mingled memories of life and fucking and death.

"Do you believe her?" Klaus asked.

"Yes. Why do you ask?"

"Because you have no memory of this and I don't know her."

Oh God. Now he was discussing me like I wasn't sitting in front of them. "Hey!"

"Quiet!" His order slammed into me and I nearly bit my tongue. What in hell?

Jodie added, quietly. "I believe her. Steph has trouble with lies. She hates them. Put her on the spot and she spills her guts every time. I remember from when we went through University together. Those parties when we told stories, admitted all sorts of shit about each other. Right, Steph?"

Heart in my mouth, feeling like Klaus had gutted me too, I nodded. Best to admit it. Now, he'd believe me.

"Really?"

"Yes." Jodie laid her head back against Klaus. "We used to tease her about it endlessly."

"Huh." Now he stared at me like I was some new sort of bug. "How inconvenient for you."

I resisted squirming under the pressure of his gaze.

"So, what have you still not said?"

My breathing stopped. My chest plain refused to move because my throat had closed down. Damn him. "Nothing?" I ventured, squeakily. Fainting was a real possibility.

"Bullshit. No. There's more." The flat yet suspicious tone in Klaus's voice skewered me, all the way down to where the truth waited. "Tell me. Tell us. Did you know he was giving you all this drug? What was it? How did Jodie end up naked?"

All of those questions were horrifying. I hid behind my hands, and gulped in air.

"Steph?" That was Jodie, sounding concerned and horribly curious. "Answer Klaus."

"Nooo." I kept hiding.

"Tell us," Klaus growled in an ominous tone. "What did you do?"

Oh shit, oh shit. They left me alone while I cried quietly for a minute, then I sighed and hung my head. "I'm sorry, Jodie."

Silence.

"Why are you sorry, Steph?" Klaus asked. "Spit it out."

"I knew he was giving her the drug. I thought—" I shrugged. "It was just a fun thing to do."

"And?" he prompted.

"I don't know what it was. He said it was something new that only a few people knew about. That it was safe, and made you a little…looser. Less inhibited." I peeked out from under my hands.

"How did Jodie get undressed?"

"No. I don't need her to answer that." This time it was Jodie who had the dead tone in her voice though she was pale as pale could be. "I just remembered something. She helped him. She was helping him. I remember struggling. He told her to hold me. And she did."

"I said I was sorry, Jodie. I wasn't right in the head myself. You know?" Oh hell. Did that sound like whining?

But all I got back was a dark stare from Jodie and a contemplative strange look from Klaus. No one swore at me, thank god. After a minute I relaxed and sat back against the sofa, waiting to see what came next. It was a relief to let that out. Now they knew the worst.

"Okay." Klaus kissed Jodie on the top of her head. "Here is what we are doing. You, Steph, are in hot water too. The cops find out about what you did and you will be in jail for some time. Let's try to avoid any of us going to jail. Okay?"

I nodded. It was good to see him taking charge. I had no idea what to do. The world settled a little, the tension in my muscles ebbed.

"If Jodie and I were never here, the cops won't think to ask you bad questions. We will clean up everywhere Jodie has been." He gestured at the table. "You can say you all washed up after. Jodie and I will wait out on the verandah while you go everywhere. Okay? I'm trusting you to do this. Wipe down door handles, toilet buttons, light switches, taps. Put your own prints on them. One hour and I'll check what you've done. We will get this right. You can say you managed to find the key and get yourself out. But…be thorough. Especially where Jodie sat and lay, you need to vacuum for stray hairs. Anything that might have DNA or fingerprints. I'm pretty sure I've not left anything on Leon, but check there too. Actually, wipe his neck with the sheet, just in case. Vacuum the bed there too. I will help you figure out what to say. Okay?"

Wow. He'd really thought this through. Could I trust him though? I had no choice really. Either blunder my way through this, or let him help. I smiled. "Thank you."

"Not a problem. It's—" He checked his watch. "Nearly ten thirty. We have time. No one will come near this house until morning. Let's get going with this clean-up."

He'd forgotten the camera. Good. I'd just delete what was on it. Except, what if he remembered and got suspicious that I'd done it? Maybe saying it now was better? That would make me seem conscientious and he'd think it meant nothing.

"The camera?" I said just loud enough to be heard. "I'll get rid of what's on there?"

He paused in a way that made me go, oh shit. "Camera?"

The tip of my tongue ended up on my lip as I waited for Armageddon. But then anything he did tonight struck me that way. I was delicate enough to shatter in a puff of wind right now.

"No. I'll get it. We'll take it away so they don't wonder why there's no memory."

Definitely shit. Keeping a frown from appearing was hard work. Sweat prickled to life on my back. I looked down, sure my thoughts were written on my face.

If he watches it…

He won't. Pray he won't. It'll be all right.

*I'd giggled as I helped pull off Jodie's top and skirt. And barely blinked as her bra came undone after Leon fumbled under her back, I was so determined not to miss any of this unveiling. She'd slid, and was half-on, half-off the sofa. I licked my lips, stared some more at the plumpness of her nipples.*

*A woman's breasts weren't something I'd ever gotten to play with before. Melissa wasn't into girls. All those years ago, I'd fantasized about making love to Jodie. Not done anything, of course.*

*"Kiss her," Leon demanded, as he pushed my face toward Jodie's.*

*Though her eyes were lidded, her lips were soft enough to captivate anyone with a latent appreciation of women. When would I get to do this again? After a small hiccup of wondering if this was a good idea, I smiled and seized the opportunity. I didn't protest at all as he guided me down to her breasts, and lower, lower, past her belly button, licking, tasting.*

*"Oh, you're good at this." Leon laughed. "Lick her clit. Make her moan."*

*I laughed too. Shuffling her panties down over that curve of her butt, until they curled just a little way down her upper thighs...mmm. Must be my birthday. This was one amazing present.*

*"Lick her," he repeated.*

*I did as he suggested, and she did moan and sigh. I felt the vibrations of her noises filter deep inside me. She tasted different from a man. Sexy. I so fucking wanted to do it until she came.*

*"Put your fingers inside her. Put your tongue in even."*

I coughed and wiped my sweating palms on my white dress. *Go away memory.*

Klaus returned, camera and tripod in hand.

It was going to be okay. He'd never look. Please, god. But if he did, I was emigrating to the North Pole, because I would for sure be hunted down and exterminated by this man. Going down on his girlfriend while she was out of it...he'd never accept that I was messed up too. That hadn't been rape, had it? Technically?

# Chapter 4

## Jodie

I copied Klaus and aimed for serenity, at least on the surface. I knew his mannerisms so well by now. He was angry but concealing it. After giving Steph his spiel about everything, I let him take my hand and lead me out onto the balcony.

My stomach was a little unhappy still, but much better than it had been. A few times earlier on, I'd almost vomited. If Klaus hadn't been here, if I'd been left alone, I would have been a quivering, sobbing mess. I'd been yo-yoing from numbness, to recalling Melissa and Leon lying cold and unmoving on the bed, to this dreadful certainty that somehow, *somehow*, I'd caused the whole mess. I hadn't, but they were dead. How could anyone have died here, on Magnetic Island, one of the most beautiful tropical islands off the coast of Australia?

*Inconceivable.* Unlike the movie, no hero was coming to rescue the princess from the Sicilian with the poison, or from the other evil guy. No magic pill existed to bring everyone back to life. There was only Klaus. I smiled to myself. Klaus was my hero, always had been.

"Here will do." To my surprise Klaus set his back against the house wall and slid down it then beckoned to me to join him on the floor.

I barely hesitated. Sitting between his legs, with the quiet night sky out there, and the breeze brushing my face, finally, I could feel a little safe. The prickling, cold sensations running over my skin slowly ebbed. My mind cleared. I sighed, and reached back over my head to slide my palm through his short hair, to caress his face.

In the summer sun, on the beach, his hair was golden.

That was enough to break the moment. I sobbed, once, before I caught it. He only clasped me tighter against him and slowly the rise and fall of his warm body against my back made me relax again.

"Thank you, Klaus."

"For what, sweetheart?"

"For coming here. For being you."

Beneath my hand, I felt the stubble on his chin scrape on my skin as he shook his head. "Tonight, I didn't do so well. I'm sorry."

I opened my mouth to deny that, but he continued. "How are you feeling?"

"I'm..." I took stock. "Stomach ache. *Everywhere* ache. Confused." I slowed down my listing. "Terrified. Sad that this happened at all." Even if she was at fault, Melissa had died. Leon, I didn't know him. He'd died but anger at what he'd set in motion was all I felt right then. "Angry and lost too."

He offered a humorless, cut-off laugh then kissed my nape. "Yeah. I understand. We'll just do what we can to make things right. I can't bring anyone back from the dead, though. Wish I could."

He rarely admitted fault. We had an almost Master/slave arrangement when at home. I liked it that way. Without Klaus my world was shakier, and lacking. I loved his dominance, his assurance. I loved placing my life in his hands, and knowing how much he cared about me.

"Jodie, there are decisions we need to make tonight that I cannot decide for you. I can't and wouldn't do this anymore than I would command you to have our child without consulting you. This is just me and you."

"Okay."

"First off. This big idea of mine of pretending you weren't here, it won't work if you can be connected to this party in any way. Did you phone anyone who is here? Were you on CCTV together with Melissa down at the jetty? Some of those shops might have it though the jetty itself doesn't."

I thought a minute while picking at the thread on my blouse. "No. We separated. I caught up to her at the car she'd parked on a side street. No to all those. This was a spur-of-the-moment thing."

"We should clean her car too then. But, good, we still have three options. The first—run away and leave Australia."

What? "Leave our home? Here? The island? Our whole *country*? All because someone else involved us in their crazy party? No. Fuck no."

He shifted behind me then went on, "Second choice is for me to admit everything to the cops. I don't know how much jail time that would involve, but it would be some. Steph too, she'd have to take her chances."

"You in jail? That really makes me even sadder." I cleared my throat, feeling that heaviness in the center of my forehead that came from building tears. But, we were thinking this through. "How long would that be?"

"I don't—"

"Do a search on your phone? There must be cases like this? The police can't tell you've been here, can they, if you do that?"

"No. I doubt it. Only in a Hollywood movie. Wait. I'll see what I can find." He pulled out his phone and started tapping.

The smell of the sea was stronger up here once the night fell into the later, deeper evening close to midnight. Maybe because any traffic pollution lessened, or because it was cooler, or maybe the wind changed? Whichever, it was beautiful. I loved the sea. It was why I lived here on Magnetic Island. From this height, in daylight, you would be able to see the big crescent sweep of Horseshoe Bay. Klaus loved the sea too. Thinking of him in jail for a couple of years... This was all so ridiculous that now and again, I almost felt reality jump, like my brain had to re-engage to catch up.

From his movement, he'd tucked his phone back into his pocket. "Well? Find anything?"

"I can't be certain. We need a lawyer, really. But, I'd say, possibly fifteen years jail."

I gulped. "Fifteen?"

"With good behavior, I'd get that reduced. I'm guessing here, but five to ten?"

"Holy fuck. No way! No way. Uh-uh."

"I agree."

"What's the third option? We're doing that aren't we?" I strained to listen and could hear the vacuum starting up somewhere in the house. "I'm amazed you got Steph to agree to this so easily. She's as allergic to housework as me. More so. I only had a thing about doing yours. You poor baby." He growled at that so I hurried on. "Her room at college merited a bomb disposal crew."

"Yes. That's part of why I think I might be able to work the third possibility."

"It's not this?" I half turned so the side of my face was on his shirt and inhaled. "Mmm. You smell good."

"No, not this. This is not going to fool the cops. All this cleaning will only make them suspicious. And if they interrogate her, we're screwed. I don't trust her to lie well enough. I don't trust her, full stop."

"No?" I tilted my neck to look up at him. "She was my friend, back then, at uni."

"That, you call a friend?" Now the anger showed in his voice. "She held you down so a man could strip you and god knows what else they did. Do you believe she has told us everything? I don't."

"No," I whispered.

"He might not have physically raped you, but I'd call that sexual assault."

I slumped, staring at the timber slats on the floor under the chair next to us. "I know. I couldn't understand that either. Even if she was under the influence of whatever drug he had, she never warned me he was giving me anything. I—" I looked up again, swallowed. "I don't trust her either."

"Right then, moving onward. Option three, the real option three, is this. Think hard before you answer. I'm not involving you in anything illegal just because I lost my temper."

"But you didn't *just* lose your temper. You thought I was dead. You don't need to explain that to me. The man was a prick and deserved it. And I don't care if people would judge me badly for saying that."

Klaus studied me. Those eyes of his were so intent, so dark, like when he was hurting me with a cane or needles, or a flogger, and he needed to watch closely to make sure he didn't cross the line and go too far. I didn't remember my safeword sometimes. Once only, he'd forgotten, but that was long ago, now we both knew better.

"You get to safeword this one if you want."

I blinked. Had he read my mind? "Tell me. But, Klaus..." I searched for and found his hand, gripped it tightly until he fastened his hand on mine even tighter. Good man, he knew I'd needed that. "I trust *you*. I doubt I'll say no."

"Just listen. Then think. The last option. If we can't trust her. We need to silence her."

I waited. I knew he didn't mean murder. He searched my eyes.

"No comment? Good girl. You know I don't intend to kill her. I could never do that. If it came to that, to truly harming her, I'd take option one or two." Klaus squeezed my hand for a second. "I mean to take her to our house. To put her in the room. To keep her there, indefinitely. Until, we can trust her enough to let her go."

Flaws. I could see there were flaws. My heart thudded so fast it hurt my chest. "How can we ever trust her that much? This is kidnapping."

"Yes, it is."

"So how could we ever trust her enough? She'd have twice as much damaging information. Murder, as well as kidnapping. I..." My mouth stayed open. He'd said to think.

"I don't know the answer to that, but I see no choice. She seems impressionable, guidable." His focus flicked toward the glass doors.

"You think she's submissive enough for you to do that? I mean I know you're dominant Klaus. Hell, do I know that. But this? It's not BDSM."

"No. Submission is a consensual thing. Dominance though, has possibilities. I can do things; see who she is deep down. Though I find it hard to imagine ever trusting her. But I'd rather try this, than be jailed for something I barely see as my fault, or to leave my life, my country, or you." He brushed his fingers through my hair, cradled my face.

"Oh, Klaus." I sniffled back more of those dumbass tears.

"Jodie, this has ripped a huge hole in our lives. We cannot be the same after this. I can't tell if this is me rising to the occasion, or descending into Hell. If I could take back what was done tonight, to you, I'd sacrifice myself to whatever fucking god I could find, but I can't.

"Two wrongs don't make a right, but I want to make a better wrong—one where we can live and laugh and love again."

I drew in a breath so deep, then put my free hand to my mouth, and held that breath for a while. Time to jump off this cliff. Though really, I'd been on my way down all night. I hoped we figured out how to fly very soon.

I let my hand fall away. "Yes. My answer is yes."

"Good. Now, rest. You've been through a lot. Rest, beautiful."

Rest? "Hell is going to turn into a ski resort first."

"*Shhh.* Don't be a bad girl. Rest."

I grunted in amusement at the hint of his normal dommy self.

Of all the things he'd said and done, oddly, that gave me hope.

"Just remember this for me, please? That I never wanted to be the bad guy."

"Man." I rolled my eyes, even if he couldn't see. "You never were and never ever will be. You're my hero."

"Rest."

"I am!"

"*Shh*."

It grew cooler but with Klaus cuddling me, I would have stayed until my ass went completely numb. Besides, the island in autumn was balmy, even at night. Half an hour or so later, all the sounds of cleaning had stopped and we heard Steph in the corridor, approaching the room behind us.

"It's time." He stood and helped me rise to my feet.

"How are you going to do this?" I murmured.

"Jodie, just stay back and keep out of my way. You'll see."

Pity surged in me—pity for Steph. I knew just how fast Klaus could move. How strong he was. She wouldn't have a chance. "Don't be too hard on her, will you?"

"What?" A puzzled expression appeared. "I will be as hard on her as necessary. You are something special, Jodie. Sometimes I wonder how I got so lucky."

"Meh." I shrugged. Strangely, I also feared for him. When did anything ever go off without mistakes? Maybe after tonight, nothing would scare me again? If only. I dug my nails into my palm. He'd be okay.

Soon, we'd have a prisoner in our basement. Damn.

I was going to make an effort to become Stephanie's friend again. It was for the best—forgive, forget. I could do that. What she'd done, yeah, forgivable, probably, with time. Klaus could be the big meanie.

If one of us didn't befriend her, she was going to fall apart.

After Klaus said we needed to clean Melissa's car, we girls trooped down the stairs to the closed-in garage where Melissa had parked her silver Mazda sedan. Trying not to think of what we planned to do with her, when Steph was finished, occupied me. I pretended to be fascinated by the BMW next to this one, and wandered around it. Klaus arrived a minute or two later with the rope and handcuffs.

Eyebrow raised skeptically, Steph swung the vacuum cleaner and wiggled the hose end toward the cuffs. "Hmm?"

"You need to decide how you want us to leave you," he said casually. "Tied up so you can do a convincing attempt at getting free by yourself, or not."

"Ahh." She seemed convinced and switched on the machine.

The Mercedes, the BMW, and the jet ski in this huge garage, were just more evidence that Leon had succeeded in life. What a waste. Being rich had drawbacks, like wanting to blitz your brain on drugs when you partied. And not giving a damn about who you dragged down with you.

Again, we let Steph wield the vacuum then she wiped down the door handles and dashboard. There was nothing else I could recall touching.

"Done." She climbed out of the car backward, and set down the vacuum.

Kidnap time. Yah, I'd named it. You didn't do this every day. Seemed like it needed naming.

Out the corner of my eye, I saw Klaus moving in—medium strides, but he was three yards away at most. *Don't stare. Don't.*

From the startled look on Steph's face, I must have seemed about to explode. I wasn't staring at him, I realized, but I was sure as hell staring at her. My eyes felt like they were bugging out.

Slow motion? No. Hell no. He reached her, wrapped a hand around her arm, spun her, stepped in and hooked her ankle, and went down with her to the concrete. She hit with a slight thud as the whole side of her body contacted then was face down. The *oof* sound made me sure she'd lost the air in her lungs and was winded. He leaned on her with his knee.

Though she kicked once, with her heels, all that followed was a firm "Stay," from him, a double click as the handcuffs engaged, some muffled screams as he wrapped a knotted scarf over her mouth......damn. Then the rope went round her ankles while he half-sat on her butt.

As I moved in, slow, and ready to flurry backward if she somehow got loose, Klaus was finishing off with some turns of the rope around her wrists below the handcuffs.

I stopped, openmouthed, a little stunned.

One hogtied woman blinked and squeaked back at me. Her attempted wriggle and scream when Klaus stood was met by a hard slap on her ass and a growled, "No fucking around. Shut up."

She did. The scarf wouldn't be that good a gag but Klaus was intimidating.

"You okay?" he asked, putting his hands on my shoulders.

Was I? I gulped, nodded. "Are we leaving now?"

"I'll carry her to the front door and back our car up closer. Don't touch anything unless it's with the rag she was using to wipe the car." He picked it up off the ground. "Here."

I took it. My hand fell to my side as I looked at Steph. Her chest rose and fell, rapid and deep, and every so often a small moan broke from her gagged lips. Her brown eyes were dark.

Scared. Who wouldn't be? What must she think we meant to do to her?

I squatted, feeling a strange need to reassure her. "You're coming home with us. We're not going to kill you or anything. But you need to behave."

A tiny spot of blood stood out on her white cotton dress. There were two simple loose pockets at the front. The shape of a small pair of scissors showed in one of the pockets.

"Crap." I reached in and fished them out with a finger in one of the handles.

"I didn't see those." Klaus took them from me. The dryness of his words said he wasn't amused. I wasn't either. "Didn't trust us?"

From the angry twist of her face, he'd got it in one.

Yes, I'd been right to wonder if something might go wrong. How dangerous was this going to be?

On the drive back to the house, that thought rambled round and round in my head along with a whole flock of others. Klaus had put Steph on the floor in the back with me.

We'd left that shitty house behind us. The house of dead people. People who had thoroughly fucked up my life and theirs in one fell swoop. Was I sorry now? For this? What we did to Steph? Yes and no. My chest was so tight that sometimes it ached. I was scared right down to my toes. The horror of what I'd seen tonight could never be erased, and yet I was also, in direct contradiction, exultant. We'd done it.

So curious. I was excited, of all things. Triumphant. Some sort of odd over-reaction from fear? I had no idea as to that.

After a few minutes, she wriggled about and I wondered if she meant to try getting up. Not easy with her hands at her back. Though Klaus had put down a pile of blankets from the boot, and she was on her side, it couldn't be all that comfortable.

I frowned. So long as her hands weren't irreparably damaged, I was definitely okay with her not feeling one hundred percent comfy. The wriggling, though, was getting bolder. I had my knees up and my feet on the seat. I slowly slid one foot off the seat and lowered it until my cold toes touched the side of her neck.

She stopped and stared up at me—her eyes glasslike orbs that said nothing in this flickering darkness. I could empathize with almost anything and anyone, Klaus had told me. I knew what she must be going through. I did sympathize, and yet…

She writhed again, away from me an inch, as if escaping my touch. I moved my foot in and, keeping my eyes open so I missed nothing in her response, I pressed harder, ever harder, onto her neck until she stilled. Then I leaned down, and let my other foot slip also, to rest lightly on her ribs. She stayed there, quiet, and I thought her throat moved in a swallow.

"Good," I whispered, and I smiled, I fucking smiled, and a thrill shivered through me from my groin. A sexual thing. I could tell.

Damn. I would have to be careful. This was a little creepy, even to me.

With my foot on her neck, she couldn't do much, but as we drove past streetlights I got to see the frightened glares she fired at me.

One cross lady. I was content though. We'd done it.

When I flexed my toes on her neck and saw her glare some more, my smile stayed. *Bitch.* Klaus had been correct. What sort of friend did what she had? Anyone normal could see in a blink that helping a strange man strip your unconscious friend was wrong. She'd wanted us to believe the drugs had made her do it but right now that excuse didn't make the grade. I pursed my lips. My anger was too fresh and raw.

For the first time that night, since I'd awoken, I truly studied her. Her soft, calf-length white dress had a cute bodice front that wrapped over her breasts. It was feminine and had rucked up to mid-thigh. She was pretty. Fit certainly. From memory, Steph liked her swimming, and she had a brain when she bothered to use it. Hot even, with that figure and her pure black hair. I recalled how it washed about her shoulders like a wave when she turned. Would Klaus find her attractive? A tiny twinge of jealousy peaked then flowed away.

He was my man. That would never change.

This person was going to live in our house, eat our food, and maybe…try to do everything she could to escape. I would. If I were her.

The other side of the coin? I sat back a little, thinking. We, Klaus and I, got to say precisely what she could, and couldn't, do. That rocked my brain.

The next streetlight showed her glare had drained away to be replaced by an unreadable flat expression. Then her mouth wobbled and she whimpered, just once, with her gaze fastened on me.

I bit my lip and swung back into worried mode. This was a real girl. What were we doing? I'd never gotten anything worse than a parking ticket.

# Chapter 5

## Klaus

As I carried the girl down the stairs to the room, I had a bad case of déjà vu. This was how my own introduction into the world of BDSM had begun; only I'd been asked to help Jodie enact a capture fantasy. From that had come our relationship of Master and slave. Though we'd evolved a little since then, and become more comfortable in our roles, and often I think we dropped into merely Dom and submissive, it had begun in the Room.

Capitals seemed right for this place. Nah. I downgraded it to small letters. Pretentious bullshit.

With her weight on my shoulder, my shoes made big hollow thumping sounds as we descended. The one muffled protest she made I settled with a smart thump on her behind, and a "Quiet!"

As behinds went, hers was a nine out of ten. Soft, bouncy, well-formed, and not mine.

There was going to be no leeway for her being petulant or rebellious in this enterprise.

Down here, in the room, was our collection of BDSM toys and equipment—cuffs, chains, ropes, spanking bench, and rings bolted to the walls and floor and ceiling. Our dungeon that was soundproofed and mostly underground, and inescapable, as far as I knew. What would she make of all this?

More importantly—would we ever be able to let her go?

I went along the corridor, reached the door, and fumbled to open it while steadying the woman with one arm over her back. It snicked open and I booted the door to send it swinging inward. I clamped down on a shudder. This was so Hannibal Lector. Jodie and I—serial killer one and serial killer two.

No way. No bloody way. I eyed the derriere of the girl, of…Stephanie—I chastised myself for forgetting her name—as I strode to the left hand wall where I'd long ago set up multiple bolted-in rings. Many fun times had been spent here while I kept Jodie pinned against the wall so I could torture her. She liked to hear Nine Inch Nails blasting out of the speakers while I flogged or cropped, or did whatever struck my fancy to her. Sometimes I'd played her *Raindrops on Roses* or a sugar-sweet Christmas song to add to the torture.

But this girl wasn't into BDSM, or us. This wasn't an agreed-upon scene of fake forced seduction. I had to keep my dick in my pants. No matter how pretty or enticing she was. And, yes, she was enticing. My appreciation of the divine female form refused to go away and hide in a dark corner. I could control my voluntary actions but not my involuntary ones, like the hard on that had already arisen.

There were reasons, good ones for what we were doing. I had to keep that in mind. Yes, and the best-laid plans of mice and men often blow up in our faces.

Carefully, I went down on one knee and laid Steph on her side on the floor. I slipped my finger between the metal of the cuffs and her skin. The cuffs might leave a bruise, but the gap was correct and nerve damage unlikely. They'd be removed in a minute anyway. Since handcuffs were illegal in Queensland, I made a mental note to dispose of them ASAP.

The ridiculousness of that—worrying about the handcuffs when we had a kidnapped woman in the basement. *Be daring*, I may as well hang onto the cuffs.

By the time I heard the patter of Jodie's footsteps on the stairs and she entered the room, I was busy collecting the bits and pieces I needed from the big timber toy box we kept down here. Cuffs, collar, leash and ball gag, just in case.

"Close the door."

She obeyed, though without taking her eyes off what I was doing. The girl lay on her side where I'd left her, shivering and whimpering a little.

Ignore that. She needed to know we were serious and now, right now, was the crucial introductory phase. Though I had to admit I wasn't sure exactly how we were going to somehow get to the stage of being able to trust her.

I massaged my forehead. Yeah, no idea. We had to wing it. Stockholm Syndrome? Plain ol' brainwashing? Logic…mmm, no, cross that one out. And me, an accountant. Haha. What I really wanted, really, *really* wanted, was to see a business plan before we went a step further.

One labeled, maybe, *The Gentle Persuasion of Stephanie*? I rejected that one. *The Mean and Nasty Persuasion of Stephanie*? Better. Gentle was for non-kinky accountants. I'd graduated. I had unplumbed depths and a great capacity for being mean and nasty. I was fairly sure I could even crack my knuckles in a pinch.

I glanced at our scared victim—our victim in the cute little white dress that showed a peek of white underwear and butt cheek due to how the cloth had collected under her. I rose, unfolding my legs and taking stock. Fast and efficient might be best. I'd talk once I had her in place.

When Jodie looked about to intervene I pointed at the floor and waited for her to kneel. The world might have been knocked off course but some things could stay the same.

Stephanie was still shivering. I took a step toward her, thinking how I would fasten her to the wall, make her understand this was how it would be from now on—we held her reins. Her next whimper was even more pitiful. So terrified. And why wouldn't she be?

Fuck. Was this the way? How could you make someone trust you, which surely was needed before we could trust her, if all you did was scare them and order them about?

Rapport. The word sprang up. We, Jodie and I, needed to form a bond with her so that trusting was part of the relationship. I stood there awhile, not sure how long, thinking, tapping my back teeth together in a habit I'd had since childhood but didn't often do anymore.

I crouched on one knee next to her and began swapping the handcuffs for the thick leather ones. I snicked each padlock in place to lock in the buckles—you'd need heavy-duty shears, a knife or the key to remove these. Once the ankle cuffs and collar were on I lifted her so she stood with her back against the wall. With her hands linked behind her, her virginal white dress, and her downcast eyes, Steph looked suitably chastened.

I wasn't stupid, though. She'd possibly knife us and run if she had the chance. Rapport, we needed that so badly. I knew what my mind was hinting, but going there was so wrong...

"There." I drew her chin up, gently, as if she was made of glass. "Eyes on me. Understand, Steph. You're no longer in control of your life now. I am." She cast a worried glance at where Jodie knelt, then at me, then at Jodie again. "She's not going to rescue you. Jodie is my partner as well as my submissive. You'll learn what that is. Jodie, get me a pair of scissors, please."

The scissors I'd taken from Steph were in the car along with the vacuum cleaner. More evidence to dispose of. When I'd first seen those shiny scissors, and the blood on her white clothes, I'd envisioned those scissors plunged into Jodie. What if? What if she had done that?

Nothing, *nothing*, would stop me protecting Jodie. I'd do what I had to.

I put my hand around Stephanie's neck and thumbed her skin. "I'm not going to say much more tonight. Tomorrow we can sort things out correctly. Your duties, your position here. How I will punish you if you do wrong. It's late. We're all tired. You're terrified."

She flinched and her neck moved in a tiny suppressed swallow.

"It's obvious that you are. You don't need to hide it." I leaned against the wall next to her. "I'm not going to murder you, or torture you."

"Are you going to rape me?" The flutter in her voice—more desperate nerves. She might crumble into a hysterical heap if I did the wrong thing, said the wrong words.

"I'm not into rape." So true. But…but, but, but. There were other ways. My badass conscience whispered to me. *We need this. We need a relationship. Unless you want to go to your deathbed with a woman's skeleton in your fucking basement.*

God. I focused on her. For the first time, she looked back at me squarely.

"Thank you for that."

"Just one of my weaknesses." I gave her a bland smile. I might not do rape, but maybe I was contemplating seduction of a woman tied up in my basement—a small yet significant difference. But what if it was the best, the least traumatic way to achieve results, for all of us? I was not going to try beating her into submission. No fucking way would I try that.

Jodie arrived and gave me the scissors. Watching the subtle change in Steph's face, the relief as she saw Jodie had returned…

As a way of cementing in place my dominance, I was going to strip her of the dress. But I had a small epiphany. Both of us were needed here. My sub or not, I could see a role for Jodie, maybe. It should be both of us.

I fished the leather leash from my pocket, clipped it to the collar then to a ring on the wall. It was long enough so Steph couldn't hang herself.

"Come with me, Jodie."

Outside the room, I shut the door and cornered Jodie next to the door jamb. With my hands around her ribs beneath her arms, I bent and kissed her well. God, the warmth and swell of feeling. "It's so good, being able to touch you again. So good." With my nose buried in the hair above her ear, I breathed in, enjoying her scent and just being near her.

"Me too," she murmured shakily. "Me too, Sir."

After a minute I drew away. "We can't leave her too long. So, here is what I've decided. This isn't going to work, scaring her into doing what we want. We'll end up with a woman who will maybe seem complacent, but underneath it all, she'll want to do us damage. We need to make her want to be here. We need to make her like us."

She nodded, her eyes serious. "I guess. That sounds so incredibly impossible, though."

"If you're agreeable, beautiful, I'd like to get close to her emotionally…maybe even sexually. Are you happy with that?" I kept my hands firmly on her body while I waited, content to feel the rise and fall of her chest.

If she said no, I wasn't sure where to go after that.

"Sex? You're talking maybe sex? With her? Us, doing that with her? After what she did to me? That's so odd. So, maybe, wrong? You're not talking force?"

I shook my head and Jodie looked away at nothing for a few seconds.

A fleeting hardness crossed her face. "Good, because that's kind of what they did to me. I'm okay with this. On one proviso." Her eyes narrowed and she prodded my chest with her finger in a "you're-my-bitch" gesture I hadn't seen for months. "You said this was just a you-and-me decision?"

I grinned and captured that finger. "Careful. You might get that bitten off."

"Sorry, Sir. But, may I ask if, if we ever make it into bed, that I be allowed to…" She faltered. "I don't know how to say this."

I waited. I wasn't sure where she was going with this either. "Try me. Say what comes to mind."

"I feel really awful when I think of submitting when she is around. Like I don't want to be seen as on her level. I want to grab her and rub her nose in this *mess* we have to deal with. It's… No, I'm tired." She rubbed her face. "I'm tired and I'm not sure what I mean."

Interesting. "I understand, I think."

This had potential. I nibbled and nipped a few of her fingertips while I thought. Her gasps while she attempted to pull them from my grasp were sad reminders of what we were missing. I kissed her palm. "We can try this and see where it goes. We'll make sure you're above her in the pecking order. Just don't forget who is charge of *you*."

She hugged me. Her reply was muffled against my shirt. "I won't, Sir."

"Here. Take the scissors. Just follow my lead."

We went back into the room and, as if we'd not left, I settled in beside Steph and put my hand to her neck.

"Jodie, I want you to cut off her dress. No slave of ours is going about dressed on her first night."

"Slave, Sir?"

"For the time being. Yes. Cut from bottom to top to reach, here." I tapped the top of Steph's cleavage and smiled inside at her jump. "Then the shoulders so it slides off."

"I'm not going naked!" Steph squirmed against my hold, and her shoulders shifted as if she tested the cuffs.

"Stop!" I tightened my grip on her neck a tiny amount, felt the tension in the cords of muscle there. I was leaving her panties on but I didn't think that would win me any points. "You will do as you are told. It is our dress, and this is not your body anymore. You belong to her, and to me. Understand that?"

The stiffening of her body signaled the first defiance I'd seen since we'd arrived here. It was good to see feistiness being aired. Slapping it down was easier this way.

"Understand?" I asked in a growl that spiked more fear in her eyes.

I didn't look away in the age-old challenge of one animal to another. The one who broke first lost. It was that simple.

She dropped her gaze. "Yes."

"Cut the dress, Jodie."

"Okay," she answered quietly, and she began.

The central cut wasn't really needed to get the dress off, but psychologically, when the dress parted, yes, I thought I'd like that. That revealing would be somehow more sexual. The mind was a big part of this process, of subduing Steph. For a second, just a second, I clamped down on my desires.

But, I sighed, damn it. This was a new part of my life. I couldn't afford to be squeamish. We'd set our course for immorality to preserve what we had. I had to embrace this, or give up and go under. If I wanted Jodie to end up with a pair of scissors in her back, go down the *good* road.

No. Not me. I never gave up. I could be bad if I had to be. And if I was going to be bad, I would do it right.

"Good work, Jodie." She had reached the waist and I could see a hint of the smooth tanned skin of Steph's thighs. "Keep going." I stroked Steph's neck some more, this time as deliberately and slowly as I would the neck of a woman I owned in every way—body and soul. "I want to see all of you, Stephanie."

After a moment, her lips seemed to part and the tiniest of shivers ran through her. I smiled. Maybe this was going to work.

# Chapter 6

## Stephanie

Sometimes fear can be solid—it can be something that clogs your lungs and invades your blood vessels until you wonder if the next pump of your heart will see you dead.

I had to stand there while my dress was cut, dead center up my body, with those scissors heading toward my breasts while *he* held my neck and Jodie looked up at me with a strange smile. Yes, I was terrified. And sickeningly, I was aroused also. This was like some strange erotic dream. Was I half-awake, trapped in a nightmare?

His words, "I want to see all of you."

*Shudder.*

His voice, a breath away, adjacent to my ear. He was still there. When he spoke, my hair stirred. Fuck. Go away. Leave me be. I just want to lie down and cry.

I let my head go back until it tapped onto the wall and I shut my eyes, trying to keep out what was happening. But her fingers kept touching me. My thighs, my stomach, her hand touched, light as air, and moved on as she steadied herself. Or was her touch deliberate? My clitoris arose, unbidden. Those cold metal scissors kept advancing, and the hold on my neck was unrelenting.

I was sick. I must be. Why else was my underwear dampening? Why else did I have to breathe in fits and starts while I prayed he was blind and didn't notice?

His words had made this happen. They weren't going to kill me, or torture me, and he wouldn't rape me…and that, I had believed. Why would he bother to lie? And then, god friggin' damn him to Hell, he'd said he wanted to see all of me.

There was no way I could escape the sexual context. I'd never before felt so helpless and yet also so very much the center of anyone's attention.

What the fuck was wrong with me? Maybe it was the drugs? My legs were quivering from the prolonged tension. I needed him and her to go away, and leave me. I needed them to…

"Go away!" I whispered forcefully. "Please. Go away! Stop this, please!" I wasn't sure why I was being polite, except that, really, I was still very afraid.

"No." His hand tightened, a bar across my throat. "Do you really think we obey you?"

Jodie with her scissors, kept snip-snipping through the cloth of my dress, and reached just below my breasts. "No. We don't."

Her open hand slid up over my mons and I stiffened, my thighs tensing at the invasion, my mind stalling in place as silently I swore one word over and over. Then her hand came farther, and I could breathe again. She paused with her palm on my stomach before slipping higher.

Even a second before she reached my breast I anticipated the pressure of her warm fingers, cupping me there, gently. Was I dreaming this? People had died tonight, hadn't they? Leon and Melissa? This could not be real.

As the blades snicked to within an inch of the neck hem, I choked out, "No. Please. Don't." I pulled at the wrist cuffs, testing them, though even if I were loose what would I do? Where could I go? I'd seen how strong and fast he was in the garage.

"Don't?" Jodie straightened and faced me, almost nose to nose. Her brown hair swung across her face. Her hand came up, and settled on top of his. The two of them held me. Her body came in. Her soft breasts pressed against mine.

I could smell her, feel her. This was real. As if I could doubt. A chill cloaked me. Real. People were dead. This was real. Oh shit, oh shit. I sniffled.

"Don't, Steph? Is that what you said earlier tonight? Did you say don't? To stop him taking off *my* clothes?"

I'd been trying not to look at Jodie but some small variation in her tone made me look. Were those tears wetting her lashes? If so, they mirrored mine. Was that regret I saw? Fear even? Crazy as a circus clown on crack, my emotions swung about. I sorrowed for her, deeply. For that minute flicker of time I felt it for both of us, maybe even for Klaus.

"I think I did, Jodie," I whispered. I thought it was true. "I did try."

I think I'd hesitated, before I had let go of my inhibitions. I wasn't completely sure what was true though, not anymore. The night had become so surreal and so wrong, and I doubted *everything*.

But this was now. They'd kidnapped me. My sympathy evaporated. Lifting on my toes and squirming, I struggled to go somewhere. Up, sideways, down—I tried them all, but his hand on my throat didn't budge at all. I lifted one knee and bumped Jodie.

"Stop moving." He shoved my chin higher. "Stop struggling. If you kick Jodie you will find out *now* how I punish."

I crumpled.

"Fuck. Please, please stop? Please?" I went up on tiptoe again for all of a quarter of an inch before his hand prevented any farther movement.

"Uh-uh. No." He smiled at me. Bastard.

Then Jodie moved back in and snipped away the last shred of cloth that parted my dress. It swung free to either side. The cold air brushed my skin a moment before she pressed her body again onto mine. "You need to understand that you are going to be ours. You gave up your rights tonight when you gave away mine."

Her eyes were like little worlds before me. I could sink into them, and if I did, I had an inkling they might eat me up and spit me out in small pieces. What had happened to my old friend Jodie?

*Fierce* was the word that sprang to mind when I saw how she looked at me. I'd never thought of her like this. I quailed, trying to shrink even farther back against the wall.

"I'm sorry." And I was. "I'm so sorry. Let me go. I won't do anything bad. I promise." I curled my toes, suddenly aware I was barefoot. Where had my shoes gone?

"You're sorry?"

Oh fuck she was ignoring the *let me go* part. "Yes."

"Let you go because this has happened? Because we are stronger than you? Because we have the upper hand?"

"No," I sobbed, looking aside at Klaus, as if he might help. Calm down, say what needs saying. Maybe there is hope. "I am truly sorry for everything. No one should have died. Or…or what happened to you. If we are careful, we can still do this the right way. We can go to the police. I *can* say what you need me to. I can."

She stared with the scissors raised. I swallowed and felt the hardness of his grip on my neck. Her eyes squeezed shut a moment before opening to that light blue vista again.

Uncertainty? Maybe? I prayed hard.

"No, Steph. It shouldn't have happened to me. They shouldn't have died. But it has. They did. And we all have to pay. Think on that. Also," she added, inserting the scissor blade under the middle of my bra, "This should go."

Then she cut through my bra, as efficiently as if it were nothing, and next she snipped through the shoulders of the dress and the shoulder straps of my bra. Then she stripped me and tossed all the pieces of dress and underwear aside. I simply stood there, letting it happen. For the time being, my tears had run out. I was numb. Devastated even.

I was mostly naked in front of two people who hated me like no one else ever had.

So much had gone wrong tonight. I hadn't really thought they would listen. I'd just hoped. While I was coming to terms with that, she put her whole hand over my breast and clawed her fingers in. The shock made me jerk.

"What now, Klaus?" she asked. Her fingertips seemed to screw in even more and my nipple, treacherous thing, bumped hard into her palm. I hissed at the pain.

"Now we leave her here, alone, for the night."

I had shut my eyes again and I listened in that self-imposed darkness. *Thank God, they are leaving me.*

"You can't get out, Stephanie," he added. "I'm leaving all the cuffs on and the collar. They will never come off again, unless I replace them with other restraints. Or unless we decide to trust you and set you free."

Free? I clutched my aching breast after she let go. But I kept my eyes closed. Go a-fucking-way!

Once he'd locked on a small chain to join my ankle cuffs together, they did as he'd said. I stayed there at the wall, letting it hold me up. I opened my eyes to watch them leave.

He pointed out a camera, and a door that went to a toilet. Then he packed away the leash, some rope, and some sort of red ball, into a chest then locked it. They walked out and the room was blissfully drained of energy and empty.

The door shut. The light dimmed to a soft glow. Near the door, a camera light blinked green. They could watch me even in my sleep.

Ohmigod, I was alone.

When I summoned the energy, I dropped to my knees and crawled to the small mattress on the floor. There was no blanket or sheet but it was a warm night. It must be late. Time seemed irrelevant when my world was disintegrating.

After lying there a while, I realized I needed to pee and managed to rise and walk in small steps to the toilet, the ankle chain catching every few steps when I got the cadence wrong. I closed the door and checked for a camera light. None.

"Fuck." I collapsed for several minutes, sitting there on the toilet, crying. They couldn't see me in here. Afterward I stayed there crying some more. I didn't want them to see my tears.

Only exhaustion made me leave. I rinsed my face and went back to the bed. Sleep claimed me, washing in and out like a tide before I succumbed completely.

I gasped awake, torn from a dream about someone sobbing in a dark shrinking room. The overhead fluorescent light flashed on and the door creaked. Jodie was framed in the doorway, bleary-eyed and dressed in a pink tank top and panties. She rubbed her hand across her face.

"See. She's okay." Klaus moved in behind her. The man was taller by a foot or so.

"No. She was crying for ages."

He sighed. "You want this?"

"Just for tonight? Please?"

"Okay. For you." He patted the top of her head.

"For her too." Her mouth twisted. "I guess."

To my burgeoning horror, Klaus strode toward me.

"What? What are you doing now?" I struggled backward and hit the wall behind me. I covered my breasts with my hands.

"Stop worrying." He stopped to unlock the chest and collect the leash he'd used earlier then he came and stood before me. "You can come upstairs for the rest of the night." His eyebrows rose. "Jodie wants to pamper you. She thinks you'll feel safer in our bedroom."

"Safer?" I gasped out, while still futilely protecting my assets, as if he'd not seen them earlier.

"That's what *I* said when she suggested this." His small smile seemed so wrong. "I told you, I don't do rape. You will be on the floor, on a mat I have there for Jodie when she's being bad. Or when I just feel like keeping her as my pet."

"Pet?" I realized I had my mouth open and shut it.

"It's nothing. A part of who we are. You'll learn soon. I'll make sure you do."

Ah. God. The assessing look he trailed up my body sent ice-cold tingling through me, closely followed by a rush of warmth. I dropped my gaze to somewhere less challenging—the floor. The man was lust incarnate in the way he talked, walked and carried himself. Also, he was my personal horrible nemesis who scared the crap out of me.

But I accepted this. I couldn't do anything else, and I let him lead me like some bedraggled pet up the stairs to their bedroom. The leash was clicked onto a ring in the floor, he fluffed up a blanket on top of a small mattress, and I crashed again and fell into darkness.

For the next two days they fed me, kept me in the room downstairs during the day and in their bedroom at night. Sleeping on the mat was agonizing at times. With the ungiving floor beneath the thin mattress, my shoulder went numb every few hours, and I was forever tossing and turning, and red-eyed by the morning. Sometimes that was from crying. I tried not to do it if I thought they could see, but I couldnt control what I did in my sleep.

Was I cramping their style while in their bedroom? I didn't give a shit. After two days I was still swinging from angry to sad to terrified so often that sometimes I just curled up and tried to think of nothing. Despite his promise, they'd not given me any tasks, or sorted out anything really. I'd forgotten it was a long weekend.

If anyone had discovered the bodies, I hadn't been told. Whenever that thought hit me, I felt ill. We'd left them there dead and cold, on the bed. By now, they'd be rotting, and no one knew except for us. That was so callous. They'd made mistakes, like I had, but someone out there would want to grieve for them. Often I'd awaken from the memory of me standing in the middle of the room, watching Leon and Melissa on the bed, waiting for them to stir and breathe again. I'd awaken to find myself staring at nothing. That memory was wearing a groove in my mind.

From the way Jodie and Klaus were walking on eggshells, I doubted the bodies had been found.

Irrational hope surfaced, just a shred, a glimmer. Maybe, they would let me go?

Tuesday. Early morning light filtered in through my eyelids. I lay there, thinking through my options. Klaus would be back at work today, I'd gathered. Jodie would be alone. Could I appeal to her to free me? Could I even dredge up the courage to attack her with something and demand she let me out?

I opened my eyes a fraction. Their murmurs and noises had woken me. He had her mounted on him and both were naked. But her soft sounds, that I'd thought were moans, were not, I realized. She was crying.

"What is it beautiful?" He reached up and placed his hands either side of her face, cradling her. "Tell me."

"It's—" She sighed. "Everything. How can you just carry on like this? I mean, what we are doing is…" She glanced at me.

"She's still asleep," he murmured. "And if she's not, so what? Say what you want to."

The sag of her shoulders and slight lowering of her head said anguish. It bothered me. They were the ones who had turned this into a nightmare, weren't they?

"I don't know who I am anymore. I'm afraid the police will still discover some evidence that points to us. I'm lost, really, damn lost." She played quietly with his fingers. "I don't think I can go to work anymore even. How can I? I love what I do. Filming. I loved it. But now, one of us must stay home, with her. Klaus, what are we doing? We're keeping a woman captive…it's just so, *so* wrong."

"You know why we are doing this, what the alternative is. Say the word and I'll give myself up. Or I'll get you, or both of us, out of the country. Say it if that would make you happy again."

*Yes! Do that! Do the right thing.* I ran a finger around the leather edge of the cuff on my wrist, and hoped.

Jodie choked out a laugh. "No. Hell no. Okay. Okay." Hand on his wrist, she smiled down at him. "I'm sorry for being all stupid. I know it's the best we can do."

"Not stupid. But yes. I believe this is the best option. That woman is not blameless."

*Fuck you, Klaus.*

"Yes. I know."

"The police," He seemed to just stare for a moment. "I can't say for sure, but I think we have a good chance at not being found out. And so, we will stick to our plan. But right now, I want to make love to you. I need to. I think you need this too."

Then he drew her down and kissed her.

"I love you," Jodie whispered.

"Jodie, remember this, I will never love her. No matter what. You are mine."

"I wish you could actually say you love *me*, though." Even I could hear the desperation in her words.

"You know that you and only you are truly mine."

How fucking romantic. So they were in love. And, damn, how I envied them. I'd never had that amount of love from anyone—man or woman. I was pretty sure he loved her even if the idiot had trouble with the word. Even bad people could be in love. But were they the only bad ones here? What was I?

Fascinated, I watched them make love on their rumpled bed a few yards away.

Soon her soft moans arose along with, I assumed, Klaus's cock that must be inside her.

My eyes still open merely to slits, I watched avidly.

My mind's appreciation of their lust didn't seem to care about what they'd done to me. He gripped her wrists at her back in one hand while he drove up inside her. When she tried to match his strokes by undulating her pelvis he slapped her breasts hard enough to make me wince.

I swallowed at her blatant moans as they climbed in loudness. Seemed as if she liked that.

His thrusts grew even more powerful, smacking wetly into her while his free hand worked at her between her legs. She threw her head back and arched then screamed as her climax ravaged her.

I shouldn't be watching. I shouldn't be getting aroused, not when they planned to do god knows what to me.

Despite my misgivings, I was…I was stunned at the raw beauty of this, and beneath the blanket I reached between my own legs and began to massage my attentive little clit. Already it was hard and sensitive and it throbbed awake, rising even more as I stroked it.

After running his hand over her breasts and pinching both nipples until she gasped, Klaus laughed then flipped her over onto her stomach. With one hand clawed in her hair and the other holding her ass cheek he started fucking her in earnest. I moved finger and thumb up and down on my clit, faster and faster. The tension of an orgasm built to imminent explosion level so quickly I prayed they wouldn't notice my own gasps. His violent thrusts buried her face under the pillows, buried her choking gasps and squeals.

The moment he came every muscle in his body seemed intent on driving his cock even deeper into her. They were a montage of fucking sculpted in lust and groans and straining muscle.

I shouldn't be doing this. This was so twisted. I ceased moving my fingers and just held them there, thumb and forefinger a fraction of an inch, a fraction of movement, away from my now supersensitive throbbing clit.

*Stop*. I hissed in through my teeth.

Too late. His orgasm triggered mine. Waves of pleasure shook me. My legs clamped in on my hand. I shut my eyes and bit down on the blanket, striving, at the same time as I enjoyed the last ripples of my orgasm, to contain the roughness of my gulping breathing.

The shudders as he came down from his climax were mine also. Then, as I quietly removed my masturbating hand from its warm burrow between my thighs, he looked across at me, and at the movement of my blanket, and he winked. I blushed, and still couldn't stop the harsh rise and fall of my chest. Fuck him.

I glared back and his smile faded into a narrow-eyed calculating study of *me*. Crap. I chickened out. I pulled the blanket over my head.

The thud of him getting out of bed then the subsequent thump of his footsteps approaching made me oscillate between an urge to throw back the blanket and tell him to fuck off, and a need to hide away forever. My heart hammered madly.

"Come out, Stephanie."

"No," I said, quiet yet defiant. What a good start to the day.

"I think you just earned your first punishment."

I quivered and stared into the dark under the blanket. What the hell did that mean?

A few seconds later the blanket was ripped from my grasp.

"What a surprise," he said dryly. Then he unlocked the leash from the ring and tugged on it. "Crawl to the bed." The jerk on my neck made me glower up at him.

"I am not an animal." And to his bed? As if. When I went to rise he put his foot on the leash so I was unable to get up.

"If I say you are to crawl, you crawl. Come." He tugged again.

"Damn you," I muttered under my breath, but I went to hands and knees and crawled. A few feet from the bed he stooped and picked me up around the middle then carried me the rest of the way half-draped over his arm like some sort stuffed toy he'd rescued from the floor. He plopped down on the bed with me head down over his lap.

"Fuck! Put me down, you cunt. You have no right!"

If it wasn't for his hand also gripping my hair, I'd have done a far better job, but I squirmed anyway and tried to bite his thigh. Between my cries and cursing I heard him tell Jodie to get a ball gag. The bed rocked as she went to do as he asked. Thinking he was distracted, I sank my nails into his thigh but only managed one deep scratch before he shoved my face into the bedclothes then wrenched both my wrists behind me and linked them together.

I didn't have any idea what I was really doing except delaying the inevitable.

"Bastard," I spat those angry words into the sheet, inhaling the scent of their sex. "Fucking let me go! Let me go!"

"No," he said calmly. "You are going to learn to obey without all this nonsense. The consequences of disobedience…" He slammed his hand down on my ass. The slap jolted me forward and seemed to echo. The sting nailed me to the spot. Each phrase from then on was punctuated with another smack of his hand. "Are. Immediate if possible. Painful. If possible. Or otherwise appropriate. You will not. Swear. At me or Jodie." One side, then the other. Harder and harder, like some robot on a mission to obliterate my ass. By now I was gasping in a choked, high-pitched fashion. "Gag, Jodie."

With him holding my hair tight enough to make me wonder frantically if he was going to pull it out by the roots, a smooth ball was wrestled into my mouth and a buckle done up at the back.

"Bastard," I coughed weakly around the ball.

"What?" *Slam*, he hit me again.

I found more energy and kicked backward with both legs, and the side of one foot slapped flesh.

"You okay, Jodie?" His tone was clipped.

Oh fuck. I'd kicked her.

At the same time as asking that, he'd pinned my upper body down, and now he managed to rearrange me so he could put his leg across the back of my knees. My wriggles did nothing. I was completely trapped. Just his leg seemed heavier than a ton of bricks. Panting around the gag, I slumped, turned my head sideways so I could get more air, and gave in. Staring blurrily out at the room and the mat where I'd slept, I trembled, and waited for the next blow.

"I'm okay," Jodie said. "Just winded."

In all this time, he'd left my panties on, but now he tugged them down below the curve of my ass. I closed my eyes as his big fingers slid down into my crevice and between my lower lips. I was wet down there still. My whimper sounded pitiful even to me.

*How dare he touch me there!*

"I see you were indeed having fun. Do you think she deserved punishment for swearing and refusing an order?"

Stupid. This was *my* body. Yet there was nothing I could do that wouldn't make him punish me more. So I waited, humiliated, for them to discuss what to do with me.

"Yes," Jodie answered.

"And how many more for kicking you?"

I heard her sniff. The bed rocked a little. "Ten?"

"Ten it is." Then he shifted, leaning over to pull out a bedside drawer at the same time as keeping me in place.

I heard a scrape then the drawer shutting.

"Klaus? Isn't that too harsh?"

"No." The croak of that word speared a chill into me. "And an extra five to put behind us what happened on Saturday night. I think that's fair."

He touched me with something hard and thin down there, pressing it onto my buttocks. Then he drew his hand back and began again, only this time it was some sort of stick, making a lethal swish in the air before it connected. I curled my hands into fists, grunting with each blow. Then instinct made me stretch back to protect my ass and he grabbed my wrists and pushed them higher.

Over and over, licks of molten fire flared across my skin. He didn't stop at fifteen and, by then, I was shrieking non-stop in the back of my throat. I thought Jodie was saying something but all I wanted to do was to get away from the relentless scorching pain.

# Chapter 7

## Jodie

He wasn't going to stop hitting Steph, or not any time soon. He was scaring me, and Steph...he was turning her ass bright red. The last hit had broken the skin. There was blood. When he got to eighteen—I'd been counting—I put my hand on his shoulder and spoke loudly to get through to him.

"Klaus. Stop, please. You're frightening me, and Steph will never see you as more than an ogre if you keep this up." I shook him, feeling the almost granite hardness of his muscles as they flexed under my hand.

The crop clattered to the floor. Then, without looking at me, he untangled himself from Steph and got to his feet.

Outside birds screeched and wings flapped. Our house was close to the beach, though atop a cliff, and sometimes the compost heap that we kept for the garden enticed seagulls. A fresh breeze sent the light blue curtains billowing in above the bed. The serenity of world outside contrasted with what had just happened.

Klaus stood with his back to me; his hands were loose at his sides, but from the tension in his muscles, I knew he was upset. He'd not lost his control before like this, not even at the play party when he'd nearly let Kat put a needle into my nipple. Kat had given us advice on how to approach his sadistic drive, as had Moghul, and he'd been so careful to restrain himself since then. He liked causing me pain, and I liked that pain, to a degree. We matched up so well.

But now...I looked from him to Steph, who lay quivering and whimpering on the bed. There were bruises already, big bright blotches, and the leak of a tiny trickle of blood down into the cleft of her buttocks. They both needed me. I didn't understand why, but I was torn between consoling her and hugging him. I had never thought Klaus was perfect. I could forgive him, but could she?

I put a gentle hand to her back and leaned in quickly to whisper in her ear. "It's over. I'll take care of you. Okay? Nod if you heard me." When she nodded, I leaned over and placed my other hand on Klaus's hip. "Sir?" I was lost as to what to say. I wanted, needed, to talk to him, but knew he might not take it well if I instructed him in any way. "Klaus?"

Then he turned and took my hand in his, entwining his fingers through mine and raising them to his mouth to deliver a kiss. He went to one knee before the bed to undo the gag, slipped it from Steph's mouth and placed it to one side.

"We're done. We're square now. Okay. Done. I was angry at you, Steph. I never do this. I promise I will not again go beyond what you can take. You're going to have some nasty bruising but you're not badly hurt." He looked at me. "I'll get some ointment from the medicine cabinet. Stay with her. Do not release her."

"Okay." I smiled then let it fade as I turned to our captive. Crap. I sure hoped we could get past this. This was *not* beating her into submission? Oh my, Klaus. Oh my.

Gingerly, I sat on the edge of the bed beside her and stroked my fingers through her ebony hair. So glossy and heavy, like stroking cool black water. I let the rhythm of that caress calm us both, doing it repeatedly for a few minutes. Her choked sobs settled. Then she sighed and looked up at me. Her mouth moved as if she meant to speak but wasn't sure how or maybe what to say.

"I'm sorry." The apology slipped out before I could stop myself. I couldn't quite figure out why I'd said it. I *was* sorry, but did that mean I should tell her so? "What he said, it was true. He rarely gets angry, and he almost never loses control."

Steph coughed and licked her lips. "Almost never? I think once was enough."

I raised an eyebrow and smiled crookedly. "Mmm."

"I think my ass is broken."

That made me snort. "You have no idea. That's mild compared to what I can take, and like. The only other time he lost it, I nearly had a needle straight through my nipple." Was that TMI? Maybe. But then, I needed to get her seeing things in a better light. I needed her to see who we were and that what he'd done wasn't...oh hell, yeah, that was too much. The startled expression she wore seemed frozen on. "Umm. Too much that? The needle thing? It was, wasn't it?"

Steph only blinked at me.

Right. No more mentions of needles.

I shifted to survey the damage to her ass. The welts...I ran a fingertip across one and jerked as she hissed. "Sorry. They are nice though. He's marked you up good." Was this what Klaus saw after he beat me? I had to resist touching her again. I'd love to see that delightful flinch when I hit a sore spot. And speaking of sore spots, there were definitely lots of those.

She groaned. "I'm not a fucking work of art. Did he mean that? We're even now? You're not going to blame me for the other night from now on? I'm tired, so tired of feeling bad about all this. Tired of being angry too."

What was this? She'd had the biggest ass whooping ever and she was what, feeling guilty? I searched her face.

"If he said that, then he means it. He won't do this to you again. Not like this. Klaus may be a sadist, but he's my sadist." At last I could hear him returning. From the time he was taking, he'd been dithering on purpose. I placed my hand on her back where her spine curved into that alluring dip at her lower back.

So warm, and soft where the mounds of her ass began. A man's ass was hairy and nowhere near as nice as a woman's.

Klaus stalked in, a tube of ointment in hand. He came to the bed and studied her. "How are you? Recovering?"

As if his concern stunned her, Steph bit her lip and hesitated a second or two. "I'm…" She frowned.

"Answer me." Now I saw his Dom side returning. He went to one knee and laid his hand over her nape, but lightly.

"I'm sore." Her lips twitched. I figured she was chagrined at her own acquiescence. She'd learn. Klaus could be so very persuasive. If he tried, really tried, she'd be putty in his hands.

"Thank you for answering, Stephanie. Keep still while Jodie applies this." I moved away until I knelt near her bottom. Klaus handed me the tube and a square of gauze, sat on the bed beside her shoulder, and patted her.

The man was still naked, and for the first time I saw her remember. Her gaze traveled to his groin. Her eyes widened. My chuckle was only half-suppressed. Though he didn't have an erection, it was getting there. Way to go Klaus.

Well, I was naked too, but with all the screaming and struggling, who'd had time to dress?

With a good dollop of ointment on my hand, I got up higher on my knees and inspected her butt again. Her first whimper when I put my finger to her skin, made me smile. She had her face hidden by Klaus's thigh so she couldn't see me. I could smile all I wanted to. Klaus cocked an eyebrow at me but I only shrugged.

I used the gauze to dab up a few spots of blood. I let my fingers follow a wheal over the round hill of one cheek then down toward the split of her ass. I went a little farther, perhaps, than the end of the welt. Applying this was going to be fun. I stared at her engorged sex, at the sheen of moisture. The temptation was there—to slip my fingers inside her. Wow. I hadn't thought of her this way much before. Something about having her tied up, freshly beaten…I was going to have to think this through.

"This might hurt some more, Steph. But it'll help you to heal."

"Thank you." Her speech was hushed, but distinct.

The warmth that grew from hearing her gratitude surprised me. I blinked. "You're welcome, Steph. Maybe you should bite down on something...like Klaus." I flashed him a grin.

Luckily he was occupied with stroking her hair and only growled a little at me. "You wish, woman. I'll make sure you choke on something of mine yourself, later."

"Yes, Sir." At last though, the mood had lightened, just as the morning sunshine was lightening and warming the room. Struck by some weird impulse, I leaned in and kissed Steph on her lower back. "She has a pretty ass, Sir."

He nodded and said quietly. "Yes, she does. Though my marks improve it."

From the odd noise Steph had made, she was struggling not to make some cutting remark.

"Good girl," Klaus patted her again. "Just remember in future, this is our ass. Jodie's and mine." He winked at me.

Easy to say. Too easy. I examined her, from head to toe. All tied up and compliant—collared, wrists bound at her back, ankles cuffed, and her ass colored up like a blossoming rose. Time would tell if Stephanie agreed with that statement of ownership, but I reached down and pinched her skin enough to make her jerk. I was beginning to like this idea.

When I was finished, Klaus rose and declared he had to shower and get ready for work. Then it struck me—I was going to be alone with Stephanie for the first time. The prospect both scared me and intrigued me. I'd get to have a say in what she did all day until my Sir returned.

After the shower, Klaus drew me out into the kitchen and leaned me against the counter, his hands either side of my hips. Steph we'd left in the bedroom, chained up near the mat. A chain, this time, I wondered why he'd swapped the leather? Was he worried she'd chew through it?

Most of our kinky gear was tough, but none of it was meant to be indestructible.

"You be careful." He kissed my forehead then stirred his finger around in the curls of hair at my shoulder. "She's a thinking, breathing human being who isn't predictable. The house is secure. Keep your phone on you always. It's passworded like the laptops and PCs?"

"Yes." I rested my hand on his at my shoulder. "And I know where the house key is. On top of the fridge in the fruit bowl and the other copy is in your study."

We'd played so many games of captured slave and I'd never known where the keys were. This was new. I was the slaver; Steph was, in a way, the slave. To me, it had added to the excitement, to the utter dominance of the role-play, if I knew I was locked in with Klaus. All our glass was double-glazed and tinted—a good move in the tropical sun. With the air-con on and windows shut, with all the uncuttable security screens, no one could spy on our kinky frolics. Though this was no longer a game. This was so real it tied my stomach in knots now and again when I thought back.

As if he read my thoughts, Klaus added, "Time to move on. We cannot worry about discovery anymore. I am shutting that down. We take precautions. We make her like us. We progress toward building a relationship. We aim for letting her go, one day."

"Okay." But my forehead wrinkled up anyway.

"What?"

I breathed out all the worry then attempted to address his question. "I don't think I can stop worrying by order. I'll try though. And I still can't see how we can let her go. Won't she be recognized? If the police pick her up...no matter how much we trust her—that will be it. We'll be done for. Arrested. Jailed." I shook my head.

"I'm still thinking on that one. If we help her relocate...that's my best thought so far. Give us time to figure out options."

"Sure. I will, Sir."

Easy to say. He was right though. There was no point in bringing up details now. I'd think about it by myself. Maybe I could see this from a new angle.

"Chin up, sweetheart." After kissing me again, he pushed away. "Keep the phone handy. Contact me if you need to. And—" His stare was level, serious, sobering. "Be a good jailer."

As often happened, my gaze dropped to trace out the hints of his scrumptious musculature that showed under his dark suit. Broad shoulders, thick neck…solid man in every way.

Years of judo had honed a body that looked capable of stopping a small tank. Heck, Klaus *was* a small tank. I'd once tried lifting him under the shoulders and hadn't budged him an inch. He'd just given me that evil laugh of his and taken me to the floor. Stomach down, with my arm locked at my back, the side of my face to the cold tiles, I'd smiled as I heard the tinkle of his belt as he fumbled one-handed to unbuckle it. Then came the slide of leather through the loops. He'd given my butt an impromptu belting and spanking then he'd gone out, leaving me to poke and stare in the mirror at my new throbbing red marks. How I loved this man.

"Breakfast?" I asked.

"I'll pick up something on the way to work."

"Something healthy?"

"Sure. Is a donut healthy?"

I groaned. "Not in this universe."

Before he left, he gave Steph a little talk about the consequences of misbehaving. Having him staring down at me, lecturing, I would've been toast. I wondered how it affected her.

"Behave for Jodie. This house is secured and locked. You can't get out even if you escape the restraints. You have seen what I'm capable of. I am a sadist. If you even attempt to harm Jodie or escape, I will make sure you regret it. Be good."

Then, to my surprise, he'd bent and patted her head. I almost swallowed my tongue at her shocked pleasure and the following dramatic frown. She put her head down as if to hide her thoughts. What a little storm he'd provoked.

I searched myself for jealousy and, no, it wasn't there. If anything, there was a sort of delight. Was it because I liked seeing him dominate another woman? This was all as new to me as it was to her.

When the front door closed behind Klaus, I locked it, put away the key in the kitchen then I ran through the facts. He'd be back at five thirty or so. A day to fill. What to do with Stephanie? Again a curious interest spiked in me. There was a certain appeal in this. A certain illicit, kinky appeal. I had someone to both care for, and to order about.

Do this, do that, bend over and lick the floor with your tongue? I snorted. I'd never been into playing with dolls, but a person? A woman? Seemed like it could be a yes.

She could be so dangerous. How was I going to deal with that every day for however long this took?

I padded back into the bedroom. Ignoring Steph, I headed for the en-suite shower. Being naked all day was nothing for me, but not with her here. Not that I was embarrassed…

After putting on black panties, I changed into my boot-cut blue jeans out in the bedroom. The way she tracked me had me wondering at her sexual orientation.

I sorted through my cupboard and drawers for a cute black bra. The t-shirt I chose was just a red one with some sporty slogan across the breasts, but it hugged my curves like glue…like kinky ass glue that had naughty designs on my tits.

As I slid it on and tugged it into place, I also watched Steph in a casual way. A "nothing unusual here, just your jailer checking you're in the right spot," sort of way. Except I was really checking her reaction to me. Though her perusal was done sneakily, I'd bet a million she liked women. The last two days, and during that trip in the car, I'd sensed this vibe off of her—past the terror and the temporary hate, there had been a latent sexuality.

I stalked over to her. Sitting there naked, with her legs to one side, and with that chain leading to her neck, she looked so pretty. When she shifted on her knees and sent me an inquisitive look, I tsked. "You need a shower too."

"Yes. That would be nice."

Nice. Such a cautious word.

There was no point in taking chances. "Give me your wrists." I pointed. "We're going to have a talk after. You can shower, then we'll sort a few things out."

For a few seconds, wrinkles flickered into being on her forehead, vanished, and reappeared. Was she doing it, or not doing it? I didn't want to resort to falling back on repeating Klaus's threat this early.

Be assertive?

"Now!"

After a last disgruntled noise, she held up her wrists.

I nodded. What small hands women had—this was what Klaus saw when I gave him mine. Funny. The world had brightened somehow with her offering her wrists. I'd focused down, locked in. I'd liked her doing that.

"Thank you." I linked the cuffs, feeling odd in this reversal of roles.

"You know this is wrong. You can't keep me here forever."

"Ya think? You have no idea how determined Klaus can be once he sets his mind on something."

"Huh." She looked disgruntled, as if she'd expected me to go, *hallelujah, you're right*, and free her all of a sudden. "Aren't you worried you'll go to Hell, as well as jail?"

"And you won't? You're no angel either, Steph." I wasn't getting into the philosophy of this with her. Mainly because I hadn't got the right and wrong of this straight in my head yet. Maybe I never would.

"A friend once said if you can't tell your mother about something you're doing, you shouldn't be doing it."

I snorted. "There's a lot of things I do I'd not tell my family. You can scratch that argument off the list."

She shrugged. "Worth trying."

Still shaking my head, I unlocked the chain then I made her walk into the en-suite where there was both a toilet and a shower. I let the leash dangle down to the tiles. "Now, shower." And I leaned on the open door.

"I need to pee," she muttered.

"Oh." So many little things to consider. Damn. How safe was it to… "Go, then. The door stays open. I'll be just outside."

Every second of every minute I half-expected her to jump me and try to strangle me or something worse. Whatever was holding her in check? Uncertainty of the outcome? Klaus's threat? I was not ever going to carry a gun or a knife. If it came to that I may as well let her go. Klaus had seen some submissiveness in her, but no one sane would do anything and everything you told them to, just because you said it, no matter how dominant you were. We needed more to hold her with.

However, the prospect of the shower made the anxiety worthwhile. My imagination had been poking at me.

"In." I gestured.

She turned it on, adjusted the taps, and stepped under the flow. I loved women's bodies—and that one scene we'd done when Kat had dommed me with the men present too, them fucking me, Klaus domming me as well—an incredible experience.

The water ran down Stephanie's back, making her skin shiny, dripping off her bottom…the rearrangement of all those pretty muscles as she turned under the water made me swallow. Then she hissed and went to step aside.

"What?" I moved to steady her with my hand on her hip. The shock of touching a woman's flesh echoed inside me.

"My ass stings," she growled, head down. "Let me out. I'm only washing off that ointment."

"No. You need to clean up. I'll re-apply it after. Stand still and I'll soap you. You can't reach here, on your back." My tongue tip sneaked onto my lip as I waited, praying that she'd do this. When she said nothing more, I picked up the bar of white soap and smoothed it across her shoulders, then lower. But skin on skin tempted me, so I lathered soap on my hand then reapplied myself to diligently moving bubbly soap on her slickened back from point A to point B.

When I'd dreamed of a ménage, I'd never gone further than what I'd already done. A limited scene, limited contact, me being ordered about. But, wow, a woman's curves beneath my hand was a symphony of sensations. I daren't shut my eyes for fear of missing something.

I guess my jeans were getting wet. So was I.

"Stephanie." Then I recalled what worked for me. I moved in until my mouth was within licking distance from her ear and said hoarsely. "Turn around."

She had braced her cuffed hands on the shower wall. Her inhalations and exhalations seemed labored, and her mouth, oh my, her lips, they were so kissable and swollen looking, so lickable.

I settled instead for the slow curl of my tongue across her ear lobe, plus a tiny suck. "Turn."

After a bare moment, she did so.

When her eyes met mine…the *zing* that act of obedience gifted me with.

Soap drip-dripping from my fingers, I looked her up, and down. "You're so beautiful." Annoying, how raspy my voice had come out. "Don't move. I'm going to soap up your…" *Breasts.* The word caught in my throat. "…front."

A man was a feat of strength and engineering and dominance. A woman, I decided, was a hot bundle of sex, elegance, and beauty.

Without asking, I placed the flat of my hand on her stomach and urged her a half-step backward so the water ran over her raven-black hair, then over her breasts, curling like a sumptuous river.

"Jodie, it's not… This isn't—"

I laid my finger across her lips. "*Shh.* Say nothing."

Words might ruin this, so I soaped her body while I watched both her and her eyes, enthralled by the signs of her arousal as I circled and cupped the heavy mounds of her breasts, and by her hastened breathing and parted lips. Playing with her nipples, first in a pretend accidental way, caused no protests. Delighted at her response, and bolder, I took each nipple and squeezed them, over and over. They shrank into taut little buttons.

I imagined how they'd feel sliding under my licking tongue.

"Jodie—"

"*Shh.*"

I played some more until her hips gave a little sideways wriggle.

When I ventured southward and allowed myself to slide a finger straight down the middle of her mons, over the bump of her growing clitoris, and farther…oh the bliss as she closed her eyes and moaned just a little. I smiled. She tilted her hips forward onto my hand.

I kept it up. Being a woman, I knew the rhythm that would get me off. This time, simple was best. Next time though… Sliding, slipping, up, down, I let the soap wash off and went in for the kill, my finger went up, up, up into her cunt, while I watched her arch even more and the flutter of her closed eyelids.

As I used my thumb on her clit, I felt the clench and unclench of her thighs on my hand then she came with her walls spasming down onto my finger.

"Fuck, that was glorious," I breathed. I moved in, jamming her into the tiles of the shower, flattening my clothed body against her naked one. "I made you come didn't I? Say it."

Her reply was a bare weak "Mmm."

I shut off the taps.

"Good." I bit her lip a few times then I worked my way down to her neck in nibbles and licks. I was now completely soaked but the result had been so worth it. "Let's get dry," I murmured to her neck while tasting it yet again.

Rapport, Klaus had said. I was doing this part well, wasn't I?

I decided not to put on more jeans. Last time hadn't worked out so well. After we'd dried ourselves, I ended up sitting on the bed in shorts and a new t-shirt, with her leash in hand.

"Lie across me and I'll redo the ointment," I said softly, patting the bed beside my thigh. She'd not said a word since that orgasm. Maybe it had shocked her as much as me? Maybe she hoped it had miraculously not happened?

She shifted from one foot to the other. "I could put it on myself?"

"No."

Stephanie grimaced. "No? I'm not a child, you know."

I merely raised an eyebrow. I was getting the hang of giving orders. Besides, this one had good consequences.

"Okay." After a petulant tweak of her mouth, she let me help her to lower herself until she was across my lap, wriggled once then lay still. "Do it."

That sounded wrong, defiant even? If a submissive instructed Klaus, what would he do? Hmm. This I could fix. I slapped her hard on one ass cheek.

"*Ssss!*" She tried to sit up but I pushed her down.

"No telling me when to do anything. Understood?"

"Eh. No? I mean…"

I slapped her again.

"Shit! Look—"

"More?" I asked.

After a few seconds the tension in her back ebbed. "No. I guess…"

"Sorry that you swore? Or do I have to inform Klaus?"

"You wouldn't!" Stephanie sniffed then sighed. "I'm sorry."

"Good." I unscrewed the tube of ointment. "We have to talk and maybe this is a good time." I began to rub in the ointment. Not a hardship at all, relaxing in a way, attending to this well-formed, though bruised bottom. If only the shower activities hadn't left me madly wanting Klaus's tongue, or someone else's…like Steph's.

But I had topics to cover. I thought for a while. Where to start?

"You understand, Stephanie, that we intend to let you go once we trust each other?"

"Yes," she whispered.

Seemed the orgasm or the massage had relaxed her. That amused me.

"So," I moved some ointment onto a bruised area. "So, it would be in all our interests to get this trust thing worked out sooner, yes?"

"Mm-hm."

"We need to get to know each other...very well." We needed, perhaps, to see things from her perspective. If I were Steph, what would I be worried about? Really though, there were things I was worried about too. Things I needed to hear twice before I moved on.

That familiar obstruction clogged my throat. I tried, maybe failed a little, to keep my words steady.

"You said Leon didn't rape me. Are you sure?" I hurried on. "Klaus isn't here. Is there anything you were scared to say?"

With her lying on me, the tightening of her muscles was obvious.

"Steph?"

But she shook her head then turned and gave me a solid unwavering look. "He didn't rape you. I swear it." She turned away again. "You didn't find anything did you, that made you think he had?"

I managed to swallow. "No. I didn't." The relief that swept me then was palpable. I hadn't realized how much that had bothered me. I smiled. "Okay. Moving on."

I thought of Klaus, and of Baxter, our here today, gone tomorrow cat who'd adopted us.

"Have you family, Steph? Pets? Is there anything we need to fix for you? I mean we can't do anything about your job."

Or about mine. I'd already been ringing everyone concerned over the weekend to excuse myself from projects and suggest they find a new producer/director—my previous job description. I was a little nervous asking her about pets, as what would we do if she said yes, she had a Great Dane back at her house or apartment that needed attention. No way could we cope with that. The cops would pounce on us.

"You want me to tell you about me? You're joking."

"No, I'm not. We need to trust you, and it follows that we need to know about each other."

I could almost hear wheels turning in her head.

"I guess that makes sense." Her doubt stood out in flaming red letters.

"Steph, if you try violence or to escape, and fail, Klaus will be so bloody angry."

She stiffened.

"Why bother? If we will let you go anyway, why risk anything that might hurt you too. Do you really want to hurt me, Steph?" I reached and stroked her nape and soon her muscles relaxed. "This whole situation is beyond us all. We're all in danger of criminal charges. Adapt. Do what we ask you to, and you'll be free sooner."

Time edged past. But I waited, patiently. This was so important.

"I…" She paused again. "Fuck. I don't know."

Emboldened by her hesitation, I let my hand find its way into the beginning of the cleft between her ass cheeks. I toyed a little there until her breathing deepened.

"You like this, Steph. You like me, yes? Sexually."

"God." She put her head deeper into the sheets. Her toes nudged into them at the other end. I waited some more. "Yes."

"Good. Then this will work." I stooped to kiss her bottom. "I like you too. Klaus wants you also. Did you know that?"

"No. Not exactly. Um. He does? I don't know if *I* like that."

I took the plunge. I didn't want to be an equal submissive in this. "Be ours for a while. Why not? Learn to trust us. Show we can trust *you*."

"He scares me."

"You'll find that's part of his attraction."

"It is? No. No. I don't know still."

I had a feeling Klaus had made up his mind that the three of us together was the only option. I'd leave it to him to convince her. Besides, we'd run way off track. "Back to my questions. Family? Pets?"

"Huh? No. No pets." Her head wobbled in negation. "Family? Damn them. No. Mum died five years ago and my stepfather went back to Switzerland and a UN job. My stepbrothers went with him. Maybe Thom would worry, that's it."

"Thom? One of your stepbrothers?"

"Yes."

For a second, I stilled my fingers. Sad, in a way. I recalled her at university as a very crazy party-goer, but happy. Scatterbrained sometimes, but she breezed through subjects I'd had trouble with. I guess she had that odd sort of smartness that just didn't carry over into everyday life. And Leon and Melissa—how had she gotten mixed up with those two?

"How long did you know Melissa and Leon for?" Dear god I hoped she wasn't going to say anything bad. If they'd been close…

"Not long." She sighed. "I met them both at a swingers party a month ago. Melissa knew him better. I had coffee with her a couple of times after. That, the other night, was the first time I did, that. Fuck." I heard her give a little cough like she was having trouble getting words out. "I'm sorry, I… Why am I saying that to you? I'm not sorry. Just, yeah, I'm dumb. Sad. She was a nice lady, really. Really she was."

There wasn't much I could add there. I knew they had been living people but I couldn't connect. Not when so much bad associated in my head whenever I thought of that night. Maybe one day I could. Not now. I felt nothing for them except anger. I was, oddly, grieving more for Steph. But then she was here, lying over my lap. So I patted her until she seemed to relax.

I steered us back to calmer waters.

"So, you work where? Last I remember you were doing the journalism course, but you dropped out."

She shifted, her bottom wobbling a bit. Funny how enticing a butt was. Well, to me it was, and to Klaus. He would like hers. The idea of both of us messing about in bed with Steph… I had to focus sharply. Thinking of sex right now was too distracting.

This bottom under my fingers is severely unattractive, I told myself. I bit my lip and drew an eensy-weensy circle on her with my finger. I sighed. Not likely that argument would take.

With her cuffed hands beneath her chin, she turned to peer back at me. "I did a nursing course after that. Dropped out again, did various jobs. I've been working at a car dealership for a year now. I'm…I was planning on joining the army. Even got my physical done."

"You? In the army? Never." I couldn't figure that one.

"I guess I'm a bit of a wanderer. I've tried everything at least one time."

Now that was the truth. Stephanie seemed to have trouble sticking faithfully to one thing for very long. Was that bad, for us? What if we let her go because she vowed to keep quiet, but then she reversed her decision?

"I'm done." Lightly, I tapped her behind. "Let's go find some breakfast."

I'd have her help me. Maybe let her wash and dry dishes. There were knives out there, in the kitchen. It could be a test, of sorts. I think I had her figured out, but I would rather know now, not later. I'd count the knives. Though if she were naked, where could she hide one? In my back was about her only choice, and I somehow didn't think she was that sort of girl.

My thoughts went to dirty places.

If instructed correctly, Stephanie seemed far more likely to cave in, kneel and lick me precisely where I told her to than to want to put a knife in my back. I wanted to test that theory out, soon.

# Chapter 8

## *Klaus*

The big square window in my office overlooking the Nelly Bay road and the beach beyond was suffering the usual seaside ailment of getting all blurry from the salt deposits on the glass. Not that I was enjoying the view. Disgusted by my procrastination, I shoved back my chair from the paper-assaulted desk. No matter how high tech we got, the paper documents piled up.

The office was the opposite of where I wanted to be. Leaving Jodie home with a woman who had reasons to hate us seemed the stupidest thing ever. Yet the alternative was to do something that would draw attention to this day if suspicion were to fall on us. Plus we had to earn a living and Jodie had little chance of matching my income. The practice was surging forward and my partner, Chris—well he was not a partner yet, though I had great hopes—Chris was turning out well.

Four reasons had gained him the job. He was a great accountant, innovative at times when it came to promoting the practice, and friendly. And the fourth reason, that he was into kink and one of Kat's previous Doms...that was why I'd first noticed him.

I glanced at my watch. Almost two PM, we'd both had lunch in the office a while earlier but, with the lunchtime rush over, we could afford to have a break. Marjorie could take over. She been with me long enough to know the place back to front. I went out to reception and set it up with her.

After a single, unintelligible grumble at me about losing potential clients, she resumed typing.

I knocked on Chris's office door.

"Come in!"

No matter how often I saw him, his neatly trimmed, pure-blond hair drew my eye. I doubted he bleached it. It was so close to white I felt like reaching for my sunglasses.

His desk looked a tad neater than mine, but then I'd been flinging a few docs about like Frisbees today. Not my usual manner. I guess having a kidnapped woman in my basement wasn't too normal either. I doubted Marjorie would dismiss that excuse with merely a huffed look over her silver glasses.

"Think you can stand giving me that lesson on fling-dong-doo, or whatever martial art it is that you practice?"

He grinned. We had a running joke about judo versus more *practical* branches of fighting. I knew he was correct but that didn't stop me ribbing him every chance I got, and since he happily taunted me back, we got along famously.

"Now?" Half-disbelieving, he looked from under his brow.

"Now. If you've got a change of clothes? We can go up to the park. I have a sudden desire to learn from you, oh wise one."

"No worries. I've got my running gear in my bag. Give me five minutes to change."

It was the truth. This predicament we were in disturbed me. Learning a better way to kill someone, and defend myself, seemed a good idea. Why? Who knew. I wasn't about to fight the cops, and Steph…I could take her out with one finger. Maybe it was a male instinct of some sort, buried under millennia of evolution. When threatened, pick up a big stick so you can beat your enemy's fucking brains out?

Maybe. Besides, I could then teach Jodie myself. She'd had lessons from Chris for weeks. Time for me to do the same.

Once we'd both changed into shorts and t-shirts, we strolled up the hill road to the park. A few tourists sat on picnic blankets and benches eating ice creams and other crap. We ignored them, though once we started sparring most of them looked our way.

Actual kicking and punching wasn't the strongest part of judo, since it was more a grappling-style martial art incorporating ways to throw someone or, in the groundwork, ways to choke, pin, or lock them down. From how Chris moved and responded to my combinations, he'd blended several martial art disciplines seamlessly.

After twenty minutes we were both running with sweat and we needed time to shower and change, so I called a halt. To cool off, we sat on the grass swigging from our water bottles. I plucked at the chest of my t-shirt and waved it to and fro to help the sea breeze dry the sweat.

"That was…" I looked for a good word. "Enlightening."

He swung to face me. "A compliment? What brought that on?"

"A brain aneurysm maybe?" Grinning, I shrugged. "Take it while you can get it. You're a good teacher. I should know. I used to teach at the club."

"You've stopped?"

"Yeah. A month ago." I swigged down more cool water. I looked about to see who was nearby. "Kink and doing things to Jodie to make her scream, even if she wants me too, it made teaching judo seem strange. That's the best I can explain it. I stopped before I got to the stage where I was forever self-analyzing and gazing at my navel. Life's too short for getting hung up on hang-ups."

"Truth. Here's to that." He waved his water bottle at me and chugged down a few swallows, then wiped his mouth. "I know just what you mean, man. Some days…" He shook his head and grimaced. "Some days I feel so fucked up. Some of my kinks I could follow down a rabbit hole forever and never come up for air. You get me?"

"S and m? That power rush you get?"

"That, yeah, sort of."

"Yes." I nodded. Chris was a sadistic Dominant too. "I understand. Kat's helped me sort out when to pull myself back, but I'm always having to double-check myself. I don't want to hurt Jodie more than she needs me to, or more than is wise."

"Yup. Though Kat?" He shot me a quizzical look. "That woman is so confusing, so enigmatic. Bouncy, bubbly, mean too when she switches. Says she's a sub, but naaah. She never really submits. If she did, though…" He pursed his lips. "She's damn hot. I'd have kept her."

"You too?" I smiled. "She's left a trail of perplexed Doms in her wake. I don't think she understands herself either."

Fate likes to mess with us humans—to run us over and then come back for a second and third try. When I got back into my office, I clicked to the local news update before getting stuck into work again, and there was the report on two bodies being found at Leon Edante's mansion. Nothing as yet revealed by the police except that the deaths were suspicious and homicide detectives were handling the case. Any members of the public with information regarding the incident were urged to contact the police.

I sat back in my chair and gnawed my lip. Shit. Well, it had to happen. Now to hope none of the evidence led to us.

My cell phone rang, I picked it up, and Kat was there.

"Klaus?"

"Hi, Kat."

"Have you seen the news? About Leon Edante?"

Fate was backing that truck over me as we spoke. "Yes. Just now."

"Probably another case of too rich and too many designer drugs. Fucking painful how many idiots can't handle being well off."

I grunted.

"Say, Klaus. You rang me Saturday night about him, remember? About where he lived?"

Keep calm. She cannot know. "I did, yes. Jodie and I were thinking of going looking at some of the nice houses on the island and I remembered his."

"Ahh. I see. What an awful coincidence, hey?"

"Yes. I imagine there'll be a ton of police around the house by now."

"Yes. Did you not end up going then?"

"No, we didn't."

Her pause was a little too long, but we chatted for a bit more before saying goodbye. I put my phone down on my desk and arranged it with my fingertips so it was perfectly square on to the edge. Did it matter if she suspected anything? Perhaps…if she told the cops. I'd just have to pray she didn't. Nothing we could do. She was a friend of sorts. Most likely she'd say more to me or to Jodie, before she went that far. We'd have some warning.

I decided then and there to put together an emergency escape plan. Fake passports, cash, and maybe see if I could find out how people went about leaving Australia without going through customs. Boat for sure, up to Papua New Guinea, then there'd be a way. We needed to end up someplace with no extradition.

# Chapter 9

## Stephanie

All we seemed to be doing was frigging cleaning. Now it was washing up after lunch. What next? And this wasn't even my house.

I tried not to scowl as Jodie passed me yet another plate. Only us two, how had we used so many dishes? And not using the electric dishwasher was criminal. Their cat, Baxter, wove around my feet, looking up at me, purring, and no doubt hoping I'd give him some more of the canned food Jodie had scooped into his bowl.

"Sorry, cat. We're all out."

"He's gotten inches fatter in the last six months." Jodie searched under the sink water and froth for more dishes. "Klaus will be home soon." The sideways inspection she gave me sent anxiety burrowing into me.

Klaus…I pretended to be absorbed in drying a bunch of spoons. Was he going to expect sex? This was surreal. Ninety percent of the time he and Jodie were friendly even if there was that expectation of obedience. The rest of the time they seemed to regard me as some sort of a sexually available captive. But I was me. This was my body. I didn't care if he was attractive, or if he had three heads, letting him fuck me was not on *my* fucking agenda.

He was a sadist too. I had no need for floggings or spankings or whatever evil things he did to Jodie. Why couldn't they just accept that I would help them and let me *go*?

After breakfast and cleaning up those dishes had come and gone, Jodie had smiled at me, undone the link between the wrist cuffs, and let me dress in a short lacy and strappy dress of hers. The pastel blue suited her more than me, but I was happy to not be parading about naked. Though she'd clucked her tongue and ordered me not to wear panties.

But... Frick. I was growing tired of these orders. I didn't want to be Klaus's latest second-best woman to kick around. I didn't want to be hurt. She seemed to think I was some creature that had proven its loyalty, and so she'd rewarded me. Her praise had, oddly, pleased me. I couldn't deny that, no matter how silly my reaction seemed.

But then my mind *had* been totally fuzzed out after the shower...after she'd cornered me there. That had been so taboo, so hot, so unexpected. Jodie had made me come with her fingers inside me. I clutched the plate I had been drying for a few seconds as I ran through that in my head.

God. Sure, once upon a time at university, I'd drooled over her figure from afar, and on Saturday night I'd stupidly done other stuff while she was passed out, but I'd never *ever* imagined she felt that way about me.

An orgasm though, it wasn't like she could buy my soul with one. She'd need a trillion of them to do *that*.

Now, I got told to clean and they expected me to somehow destroy my life and be their little sex robot so that they could keep their life the same? Crap. Jodie's dismissal of my intelligence and my need to be me, and not a *thing* she and Klaus could manipulate, was contemptible.

Oh. Fuck me dead. I stared at what I was drying. A bunch of cutlery, among them a steak knife. Not just any steak knife. This was extra-long and extra-pointy. My ears rang; I had such an urgent need to use this. To use this and get Jodie to open the doors and let me go.

Then Klaus could go stuff himself.

I swiftly thought through what I should do, what might go wrong, and I waited until Jodie had let out the water and there clearly were no other knives near her. Important, that part. No point waving a knife at her only to have one waved back at me.

The door to the outside was the other side of her at the far end of this kitchen. Locked and solid, just like the long kitchen window that looked out over the ocean far below. But she knew where the key was.

I could do this.

Heart thudding, I stepped up to her, put the point of it into her side enough so she'd feel its sharpness. I croaked out my demands as fast as I could so she'd hear it all before she had a chance to react. "I've got a knife, Jodie. Show me the key. Don't do anything stupid. Just the key. I'll go. I promise I won't tell about you and Klaus. Okay?"

Silence.

"The key." I sucked in a breath and poked her harder.

She leaned into the sink a second with her palms on the counter top. "What the fuck are you doing, Steph? Didn't you hear what Klaus said?"

"What?" What the hell was she on about? Was she trying to fool me? "I have the knife, girl."

"Think. Did Klaus tell you that you would be punished if you did this? Yes. Did he say the house was secure? Yes. Are we going to fucking let you go when we trust you?" She swung her head and stared at me through a fringe of her auburn hair like some tiger in the grass.

"Um." I gulped. My grip on the knife became sweaty.

"Will this make us trust you sooner? No. And last of all, am I going to give you the key because you threaten me? No."

"What? Listen, bitch. I'm not a pushover—"

She tapped her finger on my shoulder and went on quietly. "I obey Klaus. Not you. I know you, Steph. You're the girl who had to carry the baby spiders outside our unit after we sprayed bug spray. I was half expecting you to do CPR on the damn things. You're not going to stick that in me."

"You don't know me that—"

She pushed my hand back and made as if to step away, but I was cross and pushed toward her. When her hand slipped along my wrist, the point ran forward and jabbed into her.

"Ow!" She leaped away, her hand at her side. "Oh, fuck. That went in."

I'm sure all my blood ran away to my toes. I'd hurt Jodie. Klaus would come home and kill me. A bunch of swearwords did a traffic jam in my head. When she took away her hand, there was a grape-sized splotch of bright red blood on her cream shirt.

"Shit. Shit, shit, shit." Tears pricked my eyes. "Did I hurt you? I'm so sorry! Let me see. Please?"

"No." Frowning, she backed away a step.

When I followed, I made sure the knife was pointed floorward.

My only warning—a stern, "Steph." Then she pirouetted and rammed her foot into my side. Pain exploded in. The room went hazy and I dropped, clutching my hands to my stomach. While I was gasping and retching, she plucked the knife from my fingers. I stared up at her and attempted to speak without spewing up lunch. "What. The. Hell?"

She placed the knife out of my reach on top of the fridge then stood, hands on hips, studying me. "I mightn't be a black belt in anything, Steph, but Klaus is like the nitpickiest of men and once he found out I was clueless about self-defense he made me do lessons. I can kick your ass, girl. Do not mess with me again. Got that?"

Anger spilled. "No, I do not *get* that! Let me go. Look…" I was sprawled on my ass still, with my legs askew and tucked under me. I stared at her feet. "I'm not your puppet. Let me go. Please?"

She merely shook her head. "I can't. You know why. And you've just set our trust of you back ten steps. What am I going to tell Klaus?"

Shit. "Nothing? I'm sorry. You know I never would have hurt you…except by accident."

"You don't understand. I won't lie to him. I never do. Now, give me your wrists, Steph. I'm going to tie you up downstairs until he comes home."

"Look. No. No, no." I held up a hand to fend her off, and scooted backward until I hit the kitchen cupboard behind me. "Can't we—"

With no hesitation, Jodie took a stride, grabbed my waving hand, and twisted it until I had no choice but to flip onto my stomach. Feeling like my muscles were tearing, I was shrieking as she clicked the cuffs together. "Hurts! Hurts!"

"It's done." She released the grip. I heard her panting and I put my nose to the cool tile and shuddered through the residual pain. "I'm fair, Steph. I'll tell him it was a mistake. I know you wouldn't hurt me. That's why this was stupid though…wasn't it?"

I sniffed then felt a kick on the sole of my foot.

"Steph. Answer me."

"I guess." Humiliation at my position and how easily she'd subdued me was vying with a draining despair. What would Klaus do to me? I'd hurt Jodie and I knew that was one of his triggers. Last time he'd been so angry. And I was so frigging dead.

"Hey, pet. It won't be that bad." I heard the rasp of cloth. When her hand stroked my back and then meandered down to pat my ass, I'd guessed that she'd squatted behind me. "I'll help you as much as I can. Okay?"

Defeated, I breathed a few times and closed my eyes before I replied. "Okay."

# Chapter 10

## Jodie

I smiled ruefully down at Stephanie, getting my pulse rate to settle before I tried doing anything else. I'd been all gruff and authoritarian with her, but hell, I'd never kicked anyone for real before. I hadn't wanted to hurt her either but she'd left me no choice. This was getting so fucked up.

My gaze tracked to where my hand was resting…the little dress was so short that half her bottom peeked out from underneath. Pale skin, gorgeous, biteable ass with a distinct view of everything between her legs. As I examined her, I became aware of my clit throbbing in time with my pulse. Seemed I had a thing for her lying down showing me her ass. Bewitching view. I'd love to see her get off again, right now. I *so* wanted to be the one to make her.

Such a submissive posture. And incredibly wrong, staring at her. Though it pained me, I took hold of the hem and started to pull it down.

"What are you doing?" she whispered.

"Making you decent." But my hand stopped moving, almost before my thoughts caught up. "Oh, baby," I breathed. "You so tempt me."

I think I heard her make a tiny noise. Though I listened, she was silent, but her thighs rocked, once. Did that idea stir her?

I stroked her again, struggling to remain…to become calm.

Why had I never felt this way before? Klaus, ass up before me…me dominating him. *Uck*, no way. Ditto when I thought of Kat. I had zero desire to do that to either of them. It was just Steph then? Or this whole fucked-up situation? If it was that, oh my, I was a closet psycho.

"Jodie?"

I looked up. She had her face to the other side and couldn't see me. Did she not want to see? Afraid to? Was there something in her that matched my own desires? I fucking hoped so. I squeezed my thighs together and kept on looking at her…her everything. The posture, the peekaboo baring of her ass, her lack of protest… It fairly screamed at me to do her.

I swallowed and stood, despite the tractor-beam-like pull that made me want to touch her again.

"So…you won't let me go?"

The plea in her voice was so pitiful yet also so ridiculous considering what had just happened that I chuckled. "No."

"Can you at least tell Thom? That I'm okay? Please?"

What the hell? Thom was her stepbrother. Was she insane? Tell him and he'd do what? Ignore us? Though my gut twisted at the idea we were causing her family grief, this had not begun with *my* bad choices. I shook my head. "No. Hell no. Get through your head. You're here now, until we decide to let you go. Us. Not you. Not anyone else. Us."

I caught my breath, staring down at her, cuffed and subdued. This was power. Having a girl at my feet I could do all this too. And wrong, surely, to get a thrill from it?

"I'm getting your leash." I bent and clicked her ankle cuffs together. "Don't you dare move until I get back or I will cane your ass myself, pet. Understood?"

Her yes was tiny and inaudible; it might have been a mouse squeaking.

As I walked to the bedroom, my groin was aching so much that as soon as I went through the door I had to press my hand against myself down there. I sucked in a huge breath.

Surely, wanting to do this was wrong. I recalled feeling the same guilt back when I used to read erotic BDSM romances and capture fantasies by the truckload—before Klaus and I worked out our relationship. I'd felt dirty and ashamed, like I was a freak. I'd been wrong about myself, of course. That was completely normal.

Was this normal then? Wanting to sexually dominate a woman who…was tied up and couldn't get away. Who couldn't say no?

I covered my face with my hands, sagging against the doorframe. This was freaky. But I still wanted her.

If she was screaming *no* at me, I'd not do it. I frowned. That would be so ugly. That would horrify me. So, I guess I had limits. I knew I liked seeing her get pleasure from my touch. That was at least half the enjoyment for me. Thinking of making her climax sent my thoughts racing for that memory. Yeah, I liked that, a lot.

So, maybe this was just slightly wrong? I groaned. Fucked if I knew. Long as I knew my boundaries. Long as I had *that*. Yes. I pushed off from the wall and went in search of the leash.

Getting her down to the room had been an exercise in safety. I wasn't game to cuff her hands at the front. But we'd made it, and I chained her wrists to a wall ring with them still at her back. She had the mattress to lie on and could shift and turn if she wanted.

"What if I need to go to the toilet, Jodie?" She pleaded with those big brown eyes.

"You can hang on. It's two o'clock."

As I marched back to the door, I ignored her protests about it being three more hours. Then I shut the door behind me, and leaned against it to gather my composure. I was so horny I wanted to use the vibe, but Klaus had long ago forbidden me to do that by myself. I too had to wait. Damn her for making me like this. And yet, I also loved that she could arouse me.

I shut my eyes and relished that heavy aching feel between my legs. It made me so aware of being a woman.

"God." I whispered. "I *have* to get you to help me with this soon, Steph." Her tongue down there…

I roused myself from my lustful stupor. I should go do some sweeping and stop having wet dreams about getting her to…" *Stop, stop, stop.* "Fuck. I'm such an idiot."

It was going to be a long three hours. I think I'd found the definition of delicious agony.

Klaus arrived home at a quarter to five. The crunch of gravel and the engine sound from the front of the house gave him away. He must have left work early—an unheard of occurrence. Guess he was worried. Though he did have reason to be. I'd texted him and said there'd been a small incident. His reply: *Be at the door. I'll get Chinese for dinner.*

And so, I waited at the front door, kneeling, head down. He loved me doing this, waiting submissively, and though he hadn't ordered it, I felt the need. Steph had wrecked my idea of who I was. At work I was perfectly capable of ordering people about. Was happy to, really. But here, at home, it didn't fit so well. Besides, I'd been thinking about what had happened, and I'd been at fault too.

After the door closed, I greeted him and waited. From the plastic bag hanging from his hand came the aroma of Chinese take-out.

"Look at me," he demanded.

I peeked up.

"It was more than a small incident, wasn't it?" Klaus's eyes narrowed. Uh-oh. Mr. Mind Reader had arrived. I missed the evil though amused tweak of the corner of his mouth that often accompanied that sort of loaded question. The man looked as if a rock wouldn't dent his face.

"Yes, Sir."

"Where is Stephanie?"

"She's cuffed and secured in the room, Sir." Saying Sir a lot seemed wise considering the thunderstorm brewing.

"Right. Let's go. Downstairs."

"Wouldn't you like to eat first?" Unease unfolded, creeping darkly. This was so unlike him. Plus, I figured if he was hungry he might get an urge to bite way more off than I was comfortable with. Klaus had control in his bones, but sometimes he still nudged close to the danger zone.

"Now, Jodie." Oh my. No "sweetheart" or "love" or "gorgeous". I sighed, climbed to my feet and after putting the take-out in the fridge, I followed him down.

The excruciating look on Steph's face reminded me of her last plea. Klaus hefted a chair inside then shut the door. He arranged it so it faced the mattress. When we'd arrived, Steph had struggled up onto her knees. The bodice of my blue dress made her bosom look about to spill any second. No wonder Klaus liked me wearing it. She looked warily out at us from under her dark mess of hair. Hard to control where your fringe goes when your hands are stuck behind you.

"May I speak, Sir," I ventured.

"Yes."

"Can we let her go to the toilet? I wasn't game to uncuff her before. Not after…" I cleared my throat.

His eyebrow nudged upward. "She can wait. Tell me what happened."

He reversed the chair and sat, his forearms resting along the back. Though his dark suit and shirt were tidy, the lines of weariness on his face shocked me. This was worrying him as much as it had me. More than me, today. I'd had Stephanie to distract me and talk to and ogle. Guilt niggled at my conscience.

"Would you like a drink, Sir? A beer? Scotch? Surely you need food?"

"No. Was that all you wanted to say? I think it best I'm sober. I want you to kneel, Jodie, and tell me what happened today." He took off his coat and folded it over the back of the chair.

Steph hadn't said a single word. She must be dreading what was coming.

I kneeled, thought for a few seconds then launched into my account. I didn't hold anything back. We were always honest with each other. I knew he might get angry, but I valued his decisions. He wouldn't go too far, or not so far that it would horrify me. Part of us, our to and fro, was him pushing. I liked that. When I was done, he studied both me and Steph, then swung his leg off the chair like a man dismounting a horse and headed straight for her.

Before she could do more than stiffen in fright, he spoke. "I'm just freeing you so you can go to the toilet. Jodie will be coming upstairs with me. When we return, be on the mat, kneeling. I already have very good reasons to punish you. Don't disappoint me. Clear?"

She nodded. I think both of us expected harshness, but he freed her, took her hands and drew her to her feet. The difference in their build and height even made me blink. Nothing set off my submissive genes more than seeing a man dwarfing a woman. They were both so lust-inducing I was ready to lick them both all over at the slightest prompt. If only I could get them in our bed, together.

Whatever Stephanie thought of this, he'd certainly stunned her. When I looked back into the room as Klaus locked her in, she was still standing there, staring after us.

"Living room." He pointed upward.

Nervous, I went first. What did he think about Steph sticking a knife in me?

On reaching the living room, he sat on the couch and beckoned to me to stand between his legs. "Show me the wound."

I lifted my t-shirt. "I cleaned it and used antiseptic. It scared her more than me. The bleeding stopped quickly." I peeled back the square bandage. The point of the knife had only slid in under the skin on my side and left a small bruise. The tiny cut was dark red. Clean. I inspected it myself as he gently manipulated my skin. "See. It's nothing."

He pursed his lips, shook his head. "You're sure it's shallow?"

"Yes."

"Lucky. Damn lucky. She could have tripped and put it inches into you, then where would we be? Hmm?" He looked at me. "Should you have uncuffed her?"

Sadness hit unexpectedly. My mouth wobbled. "I'm sorry. I know you said to be careful and I wasn't. It's my fault, isn't it?"

He put his hands to my waist, and on the uninjured side, he rubbed his thumb back and forth. "Partly, yes, sweetheart." His thumb stopped moving. "I need to punish you. Okay? More than her. She's stupid and at fault but if I do to her what I would like to... It wouldn't be good."

Ah. I blinked. I didn't know what he intended, but if the alternative was him hurting Steph. That bothered me. "I can take it."

"Good girl. You were wrong, yes, and I'm going to use you as an example for her. Be brave."

"Sure." I sucked in my lip. The familiar zing of excitement had me. Pain...I liked him doing what he wanted to. Even if it hurt me more than I wanted.

"First." He held up two fingers and his mouth curved in a cautious smile. "Two things I see here. Good things. If you're sure she didn't mean to hurt you, that's a step forward. Sounds like she was trying to help you after even." I nodded. "And what happened in the shower...Jodie, I think you have some switch in you. I wish I'd been there to see that."

I lowered my shirt then added shyly. "Yeah, I think I do. I got *such* a rush."

"Whatever it is you did to make her like you, keep doing it." With his hand over my shirt material, he smoothed the bandage, eyeing me in a calculating way. "Ready?"

I trembled a second then caught it. "Yes."

"It's the rattan cane. I'll have a quick shower then we'll do this. Remember, be brave."

I wasn't sure what he meant to do. He often strung me up by my wrists and beat me since he liked seeing me squirm.

This time…once we entered the room, he barely acknowledged Stephanie where she obediently knelt. He took me to the wall, made me strip all except for my bra, and used leather to strap me to the wall, flat and spread-eagled. I studied the gray paint before my nose— shade of mountain peak, I recalled. I could move my fingers and my head and my toes and not much else.

"I need you still, Jodie. If you move too far, I might injure you badly."

Eep. Be still, or else, huh?

He started with taps of the cane to warm me up to the pain, which was more considerate than I expected. The way I was bound, my mound was pressed against the wall and, as the familiar buzz from the pain insinuated into my body, I couldn't help grinding forward a few times. I half-expected him to tell me to stop but all he did was step to the other side of me and begin the pummeling of my lower ass in earnest, with a few landing lower on my thighs. The hurt rose, the effects fuzzed my head, but he still hadn't gone to anything super intense. This was just my speed. I gasped and swore softly as three swift strokes surprised me.

"Four more. Hard ones."

I curled my toes, but made sure to stay relaxed as those four seared my skin. I screamed on the fourth strike across my buttocks and at that, he stopped.

"Done."

I turned my head in disbelief. Though his gaze was fierce, he stepped aside to lay the cane upon the chair. For some reason the colors impressed on me. White shirt, black pants, golden brown cane. From the way my skin shrieked at me, I'd have good bruises.

As he undid the straps across my back, he kissed the sweat on my neck. "Thank you. I went easy on you today, for her. Okay?"

I shuddered out my words. "Thank you, Sir."

Again, his words were quiet. "Another day, I want to try the barbed wire flogger. Not today. It would freak her out."

Oh fuck. He'd never used that. Though it wasn't strictly speaking barbed wire—because Klaus had decided real barbed wire was impossible to clean in the twists of wire—it was a nasty steel flogger with tiny spikes.

God. I wanted to know what I could take. That would surely make me bleed. I wanted to drift into subspace to the sting, but, yes, another day, another time when Klaus was ready and so was I. Before he released all the straps, he checked my skin and massaged in ointment.

When I was free, he let me dress again in my white panties.

"Steph." He crooked a finger.

Though she shuffled on her knees, she didn't get up.

Uh-oh. There was terror in her eyes.

I was busy drawing my underwear gingerly onto my ass. If asses could talk, mine would've been screaming, *don't*.

"Klaus, you need to tell her what you mean to do…that you aren't doing to her what you did to me. Remember? Sir?"

Rationality slowly surfaced in his eyes. "Of course. Jodie is in charge of your punishment."

*I am?*

He waited, looking at me speculatively as if wondering whether I'd sprout horns or wings.

Fuck. I didn't know which either. The chair looked good.

I removed the cane from the chair and gave it to Klaus, feeling like I was handing him something that might bite me at any moment. He smiled and took it away.

The chair. I inhaled, shakily.

"Over here, Steph." To my rising delight, once she scrambled to her feet, she almost jogged to the front of the chair.

Intimacy was needed. I stepped up to her, turned her with my hands on her hips, and gently pressed her back, so she bent over and had to grip the chair to keep from falling.

I looked to Klaus. "May I crop her, Sir?" I couldn't help myself. Asking him was ingrained. Especially after what he'd just done.

"You can do what you like. She injured you, not me. I'm giving you this. Just make sure it hurts a bit or I might get overcome with an urge to turn her white bottom redder. Oh, one addition. After we've had dinner, you're going to spank her until she comes."

Stephanie gasped. "What?"

"No speaking unless you're told to." Though his voice was flat, her mouth clicked shut. "You've been bad, Steph. I'm letting Jodie punish you, don't make me add my punishments. You're allowed to speak to answer this next bit. From what you told Jodie, you've been through blood tests for the army's admittance exams. Correct?"

"Yes."

"How long ago?"

"Two weeks? About?"

"And they tested for STDs?"

She paused for a few seconds, holding onto that chair as if it were a life jacket. The front of my summer dress heaved as she took some long, deep breaths.

"Were you clear? Negative?"

Oh yes, I knew why she was upset. Klaus had just told her he intended to have sex with her. I wanted to wave pom poms and cheer, but I only tried to open my eyes and ears wider…if that were possible. I didn't want to miss a single morsel of this exchange.

"Uh. Yes," she said, directing her reply to the seat of the chair. "I suppose. But—"

"Shush. Enough. Jodie?"

I grinned. If she'd been fast on the take and said no, that she had AIDs, herpes and crotch rot, she'd have gotten Klaus to back off. But now…

"Jodie? Daydreaming?"

Me? "Sorry, Sir." From the hint of amusement in his eyes, he'd guessed the gist of what I'd been thinking. My man was an evil bastard, definitely. I chugged back into gear. This had to hurt? I wasn't exactly practiced in any of this, but I did have a mean wrist flick when playing squash. The crop was the right length for a racquet.

I went to the unlocked toy box and removed the crop, came back to her swishing the crop through the air to get a feel for the balance.

"If she doesn't squeal at least once expect me to take over." He grinned. "Then we will go have Chinese."

Right. I twisted up my mouth and raised an eyebrow in query but his grin only widened. Okay. He was serious but happy. Okay. I eyed my victim's bottom. Squealing required?

With my palm on the small of her back, I murmured to Stephanie, "Incoming. I'm giving you ten strokes of the crop."

I lifted up the dress to expose her scrumptious ass then rolled the fabric higher to the small of her back. I bit my lip, pausing as I looked at that enticing area between her legs.

Somehow I got through those ten strokes and even, on the last two, made her hop from one foot to the other and squeal.

"Finished," I declared.

"Oww." She scowled back at me but it was all I could do not to chuckle. Petulant little thing. I didn't care that she'd accidentally cut me. The darkening red rectangles and stripes on her bottom...the way she'd plain leaned over and waited for this. I was sold on domming her. Who needed crack? And such promise for the future. So much more I...we, could do to her.

As we went up the stairs, with Steph second and myself trailing last, I was still humming with residual amazement at my new power. I eyed the sway of her ass under the blue fabric. Mine. And Klaus's soon too, no doubt.

# Chapter 11

## Klaus

The microwave hummed in the kitchen across the hallway. With Stephanie sitting quietly next to me on the padded footstool while Jodie heated the take-out, I had plenty of time to think and to study her.

Right or wrong, there comes a time when you have to stop second-guessing and wondering if what you do is moral. Self-preservation was a strong instinct in me.

I'd worry when or if some new aspect called to me. We had the facts. The cops were investigating. People had died. We, Jodie and I, had crossed into this murky zone of what-the-fuck-am-I-doing.

I'd have to tell Jodie about the bodies being found later on. We watched little TV and she'd not turned on the computers all day, so she couldn't know unless she'd taken a call from someone who mentioned it.

But...the deaths, the party, were old news. After I was beaten up as teenager by a gang, I'd applied myself to getting good at judo, and months later, I'd tracked down two of the ring-leaders who'd still been bullying me. I wasn't over-confident, I'd made sure each was alone first, then I'd beaten the shit out of them. Perhaps I'd gone too far? But I hadn't worried about it since then. Done is done. My actions had produced the effect I'd wanted. They left me alone after that.

From now on…I shifted on my chair and observed Stephanie some more…I'd only concern myself with her and us. Because she was the weak point in this.

She wasn't talking to me, but I figured she was scared of me. I had to lessen that somehow, without making myself seem made of sugar and sunshine. Though, considering I'd just caned Jodie and made her scream, I doubted she'd ever see me as quite that kindly.

I smiled. Which was good. As a sadist, I had an image to uphold.

Besides, Jodie had done something incredible today. Something I hadn't expected and it seemed as if Stephanie had been, to some degree, her willing victim.

Jodie came in with the last of the plates, set them down and waited. I eyed Stephanie, and her. I planned to play this mealtime like a game of cards or chess. Whatever hints I was given, I'd use those to decide the next step. My balls tightened. This was more exciting than anything I'd done for months. Even BDSM had become slightly…less exhilarating.

When one door closes, another opens…how apt that might be.

Move one.

I kept my voice at a monotone despite how intense the mood had become. "Stand up and take off your clothes, Stephanie, then give them to me."

I zeroed in on that tiny clench of her throat when the rest of her had frozen. This new opening door had great possibilities.

"I…" She looked to Jodie.

I leaned over and touched her chin, then moved her head so she was facing me. "No. Me, Stephanie. Not Jodie." Though she trembled, she obeyed.

"Good. No talking from now on. If you have something you desperately need to tell one of us, you may pat our leg. Pat, not smack or tap. Use your palm only and be soft."

I had her utter attention. Such pretty lips on this woman. Fuck. Already I was seeing the onset of blue balls tonight. "Nod if you understand."

Though she cleared her throat and frowned, she nodded.

"Good. If you break those rules, I will be putting a gag on you."

The image of an underwear gag wedged in those lips arrived in my mind. A standard ball gag just would not meet the grade tonight. If she spoke at all, I was going to be on that one in a flash.

*Please, whatever gods are listening, make her talk when she shouldn't.*

"Now. Undress."

Slowly she stood then reached to either side of the dress. Before she did anything else, she glanced at Jodie. I caught the slight nod and smile Jodie gave her but let it pass because a few seconds later she was pulling the dress off over her head. Interesting.

The tantalizing reveal of female flesh and the unintended undulation of her hips as she tugged at the cloth had me stiffening in more ways than one. I adjusted my pants.

Once she was fully naked I put out my hand for the dress. Her fingers brushed mine and I swear I heard a sharp little intake of breath.

"Stay there." Though she screwed up her mouth as if something tasted bad, I took my time studying her body—travelling from her neat little toes up to her breasts, where the perfect pink-brown circles of her areolas had me lingering. Her hair tumbled darkly past her shoulders like a waterfall of night. Such an innocent-looking face. An angel turned bad. "You're beautiful, Stephanie. Isn't she, Jodie?"

Those neat toes scrunched up.

"Yes, she is." There was a strange harshness in that word. Jodie was my true partner. Was I overstepping what she could handle?

I glanced across and almost chuckled. No. That was barely concealed lust on her face, not jealousy.

"Sit." I took Jodie's hand and drew her to sit in the chair next to mine then squeezed her fingers. "Our captive is going to stay under the table while we eat. And since we can't trust her with a knife and fork, she's going to eat with her fingers. Happy with that?"

"Yes. Sounds good." Where I'd rested her palm on my pants leg, she curled her fingers and dug nails into my thigh. I smirked. The number of times she'd done this for me—eaten at my feet—and now she got to do it to a woman. My little Jodie definitely had hidden potential.

The stew of frantic emotions sweeping Steph pulled me up fast. Tears threatened. Her mouth quivered. Anger sparked deep in her eyes. I sensed an oncoming impasse. I'd given her no direct threat of spanking or pain if she didn't obey, but I didn't want to do that to gain her compliance. This, *this* very moment was so important. She'd undressed in front of us before, or at least we'd undressed her. If I could get her to take this next step without me…without us directly threatening her, it would be a whole new ball game. It would be like her handing over a part of herself.

Giving her some facts might help? Yet I'd silenced her. She couldn't ask questions.

I sat forward. No threat. No growling. I wanted to see her cave in, apparently, all on her own. So she could see, feel, taste, her defeat against a nothing background.

"Stephanie, this is not simply to humiliate you." Though of course it would, and I *loved* that. "I need to know you can obey orders. After the stunt you pulled today, I *really* need to see that in spades. You're going to kneel and crawl under the table and eat your food from the plate we give you. Jodie? Put the plate down."

She picked up the plate and slid it onto the floor just before our feet.

Stephanie sucked her lip in. An indecisive frown decorated her brow.

*Make it a little easier?* "But first, come here to me. Jodie kicked you and I see a bruise on your stomach. I need to make sure you're okay." I beckoned.

She took a step toward me.

Yes!

*One more step, girl, just one, and then I have you in the palm of my fucking hand.*

# Chapter 12

## Stephanie

*Breathe. The man is being reasonable, for once, isn't he?*

*Be calm. He hasn't said he'd do more than gag me if I talk or, or if I stick a damned fork in his leg.*

I stared at him. After putting out his hand, he'd sat back and was just waiting again. Like a crocodile in a pool waiting for a victim. *And I'm standing here naked, getting, admit it, wet, thinking of him touching me, or even near me.*

I couldn't deny it. Something about this whole stupid, upside-down situation had triggered my most disgusting desires. Didn't mean I liked this, though. I was simply reacting like Pavlov's dog—dribbling at the smell of a man. Gah. This was as welcome as having hot dreams about some random guy on the street who then turns around and gets all up close and personal. Not welcome. Full stop.

But…standing in front of him was better than groveling under the table. So I stood there naked before him and I let him put his hands, ever so gently, on my hips while he examined the bruise on my right side. When he prodded it, I hissed. Though I swayed, it wasn't from the pain. How close he was to me, down there. The steady look he gave me invoked even more heat below.

You just did not hold someone like that, so intimately, unless you knew them well. But I had no idea what to do.

I was certain he knew the effect he was having. The bulge in his pants said I was affecting him as much as he was me.

"Thank you, Steph. It looks sore but not bad. You'll live."

I bit back a thank you. When he used those same hands of his to urge me to kneel, like some hypnotized rabbit, I did exactly that.

I wasn't staying there inches away from his cock. Self-conscious, aroused, and ready to run for the door just to get away from his masculine presence, I crawled under the table. I tried not to display more of my sex than I already had and kept my legs together. Embarrassment and horniness wrestled for upper position in my head.

If I couldn't escape from them, what in the world was I going to do? Mucking around at a party when you could go home afterward and laugh about it was completely different from this continuous assault on my sexuality. I was a person not a place for Klaus to put his cock or Jodie to—

Okay. Face it, I already liked Jodie. I wasn't sure how much of all this was purely because Klaus was telling her what to do, but I liked her. If it had just been her and me, I'd have been sold. I'd have jumped into bed with her and I would have...I would have done almost anything. Wrestling with Jodie in bed would be glorious fun. But again, this was different...wasn't it?

A strange thought bumped its way uppermost in my head. I had tried to get into her bed all those years ago, and I'd been unsuccessful. She'd shown no curiosity about me at all. Now though, it was almost scary how intent she was. Not as scary as Klaus, but then who would be?

A scenario played out on the inside of my eyelids—I imagined her going down on me. I'd never think of a shower the same way from now on.

I sighed and stared at the plate with the small pile of Chinese food. Beef and black bean? It smelled delicious. I was hungry but using my fingers would be giving in. No. This much I could do. I'd starve if I had to. Sucking up food with my tongue or fingers was the bloody last thing I was doing. No fucking way.

For ten minutes, I listened blackly to the sound of them eating and stared at their feet. The ting and scrape of cutlery against china made me glower even more. At least they left me alone. I was rearranging my legs and finding a more comfy place on the chair behind me to lean, when Jodie spoke up.

"You need to eat, Steph."

A trick. I wasn't allowed to talk, so I couldn't answer. I practiced making subtle rude gestures instead, hiding them under my other hand. I wasn't stupid.

When Klaus leaned down and looked at me, I jerked. Fuck. Like a sea monster arriving in your swimming pool. Go the fuck away.

"If you won't eat by yourself... Come here." Then he put his hand down and grabbed my hair in a grip tight enough to make me want to bite him.

I emerged from under the table shuffling on my knees, making *ow, ow, ow* noises and glaring.

"I think we should make this young lady consume some food." Klaus studied me. I glared some more back at him. Not talking was hard. It wasn't that I wanted to obey him; it was that I didn't want to give him an excuse to punish me.

"Yes, you need to eat, Steph." The softer, rational voice of Jodie made me relax a little and lower my gaze to Klaus's leg. "Can you let her go, Klaus? She might sit on your lap to eat?"

What!

"Good idea." Then he hauled me up there. Within seconds I found myself sitting on the man's lap, without clothes on, and with Jodie smirking at me from the other chair. His forearm fastened across below my breasts as he adjusted how I sat, shifting me higher on his lap.

This was going too far. I fumed, wanting to smack someone. At the last second. I remembered what to do, and patted his leg.

"You can speak, Steph." Damn unfair—having him talking, all bass-note-male, inches from my ear.

Men who did that should have to register their voices as deadly weapons. I'd felt the warmth of his words on my neck. In an attempt to get my reaction under control, and to keep my private parts private, I clamped together my legs. What had I planned to say?

"I can eat by myself. Let me go, please." I figured politeness was advisable when someone had the power of life and death, or spanking and not-spanking, over you.

"Let you go?" He put his nose to my neck, and breathed in. My eyes crept shut and a shiver ran through me. "No, I need to make sure you eat. So…" With one arm still across my waist, he bent and retrieved the plate and put it on the table. I watched as he selected a piece of the sliced beef with his fingers and held it to my lips.

"Eat. Now."

Feet away, I could see Jodie being amused. I shut my eyes, blocking her out, him out. Not, this was absolutely not, fair.

The now-cold meat prodded at my mouth.

"Open," he demanded, voice in rumbly beast mode.

I firmed my lips, while thinking some more. He'd banned talking, and I sure wasn't going to kick Jodie, or him. Especially *Him*. Ugh. The consequences of kicking Klaus would be worse than the Spanish Inquisition and probably feature spiky things and spiders dropped in my eyes.

"Open." The tone he used for this simple command was getting harsher.

I rallied my rational self from the fog of mixed horror and lust that only Klaus could summon in me. But Jodie… I checked her out. If I could show her that this was going too far, maybe she'd convince Klaus to rethink. Passive resistance then. Sit him out?

Klaus swiped a gooey fingertip along my bottom lip. "I promise you, Steph, I will get your mouth open soon whether you do it voluntarily or not."

Crap. I panicked and tried to surge to my feet only to find that his arm beneath my breasts was far stronger and snugger than any seat belt. I growled and tried to shove harder with my feet, tried to throw myself sideways, tried everything. I kept it up for two or three minutes before I stopped, gulping in big swallows of air.

At some point he'd trapped both my arms against my body. The man was like some freaky octopus when it came to wrestling.

"I'm far stronger than you." This time he bit down on my neck, twice and painfully, leaving teeth marks and bruises I was sure.

Fuck. I shut my eyes, mortified at not being able to get loose. He hadn't even used both arms. I'd never before pitted myself against a man like this. Never realized how much stronger he might be.

"You won't win. Last chance before I get the spider gag. Open."

Neck stinging, muscles burning with fatigue, and my heart thudding hard, I eyed this now horrible symbol of my defeat—a piece of meat, and then I opened my mouth. He slid the food into my mouth.

"Chew and swallow."

A tear slipped down my cheek as I chewed and swallowed.

"Now that—" Starting near my hairline above my ear, he kissed a line down my neck sending the most awesome vibrations directly to clit central. "—was the best behavior yet."

I opened, and chewed, and I swallowed some more, feeling myself sinking ever deeper into whatever trap this was.

"She's crying." As if in awe, and sadly quiet, Jodie sat forward and ran the back of her finger down my cheek, capturing a tear.

"Is she?" With his hand wrapped hard over the side of my face, Klaus turned me so he too could look. I managed to summon a minor glare. "I think that's more angry tears than sad ones. Yes?"

I growled deep in my throat and attempted to shake my head as much as I could while held. And got nowhere.

"Don't growl, girl. Naughty things happen to growly kittens."

His assured smile sent a prickle of delicious terror into me that I now recognized as a Klaus specialty. Dissected by his gaze, situated naked on this man's lap, and subject to whatever experiment in pain he might choose to do, it was a moment of scalding understanding. I was his victim, whether *I* chose to be, or not. I also knew that I found it arousing.

I melted then and there under the watch of those gray-green eyes. Moisture leaked from my cleft and I shuddered.

His smile deepened, he examined my face for a few more seconds as if memorizing me then released his grip. Desperate, I swung away.

"Are you sure she's okay, Sir?" Jodie's eyes were large, her mouth crooked as if she nibbled in worry.

"Yes, I am. Not only is our girl aroused by this, I can feel her cunt juices soaking into my pants leg."

Oh God. Was that true? Was nothing about me to remain a secret? If I'd been mortified before, now I wanted to sink into the floor and be one with the fucking dust. Eyes down, I waited and did nothing.

"I see." Her voice was rich with amusement.

"You need to eat more, pet." Without further comment he resumed feeding me.

This time I said nothing, did nothing, that might encourage him to say any more horrible things. And I tried to forget what he'd just said.

At the end, Klaus wiped my lips, not with a napkin, but with his fingers. "Lick them clean," he instructed.

I stared at his fingers.

"Lick."

Mesmerized, stuck in rewind, unable to figure out what else I could *do*, I curled my tongue out and licked, tasting the black bean sauce on his skin, tasting him as well, and when he inserted that finger into my mouth and murmured, "Suck." I did that too. I was so fucking lost.

When I was done, he shifted the bowl away from the edge of the table, and kissed my nape. "Now, what can we find to do to our toy?"

*Our toy.* A tide of electricity swept me—all the hairs on my neck arose and the tingle spread down my back to all those secret sexual places, my nipples, my groin, inside me.

"Do you like being called a toy?" He shifted so my legs fell to the outside of his, spreading me apart as he spread his own legs.

What would Jodie see? From the rapt fascination in her eyes—a lot. I went to close my legs but he wrapped his other arm under my breasts and tsked. "No. Bad. Stay as I put you."

I stilled, afraid.

"Let her look. I want you to touch her, Jodie. I missed seeing what happened today and I think I need to catch up. I need to see her come. Can you do that?"

She chuckled as she rose to her feet. "Of course, Sir." I watched her look over my shoulder. "Thank you, Sir. For this present."

"Next time we'll wrap her up together with some kinbaku, some breast bondage, and a few clamps here and there."

"That would be awesome."

I opened my mouth to…to… And shut it again. Damn, still afraid. What was I? A *thing*? Their toy? I inhaled deeply, and didn't blink at all as Jodie moved in on her knees, to kiss first one of my breasts, then the other.

"Be good," she whispered.

My arms were clamped to my sides by Klaus, but taken by some delayed wish to remain inviolate, I raised my lower arms and spread my fingers, shaking my head the tiniest amount as I did so.

Jodie hesitated, wearing a frown that sketched a tiny cute wrinkle on her forehead. Strangely I wanted to kiss her there. I sighed. Totally fucked up, was me.

Then, slow as an incoming tide, she leaned forward mischievously and nipped one of my fingertips hard. When I flinched, she nipped another while fastening that hand in place by holding my wrist. Switching over, she nipped the fingers on my other hand until I hissed and hid it away.

"Mmm!" I shook my head again.

"Don't you like me nibbling on you?"

Torn enough to consider speaking and saying no, and finding I'd forgotten to breathe, I watched her approach my nipple with her finger extended. Concentrating, with her tongue tip on her lip, she circled it with her nail and the lightest touch. My nipple crinkled and the nub stood up hard.

I wanted her to suck it. The *need* that simple act had evoked.

Klaus seemed content to watch, though his erection pulsed under my bottom as she finally, *thank god*, put her head down and engulfed my nipple with her hot mouth. When she bit me delicately, I gasped, unable to stop myself trying to arch toward her.

"I think she likes that," Klaus observed.

"Mmm. She does."

Enraptured at the sight of her mouth moving on me, I clenched my fists. The no I had meant to say seemed stuck in the back my throat. "Bitch," I whispered.

"Oh my. She talked, Sir. What will we do?" She wrapped her hand around my breast and squeezed. "Bitch? I don't think you mean that, Steph. I think you want to be our toy tonight. Hmm?"

Klaus hugged me closer. "A naughty toy. After Jodie makes you come I'm tying underwear across that dirty mouth."

Oh fuck. Though appalled, that had turned me on even more.

An alluring siren, Jodie rose to my level with her hands braced on the sides of the chair seat. Then she cupped each palm on my face and said softly, "I'm going to make you come now. Maybe I'll put my tongue in you." Her eyes were bright, her lips soft and full.

Shocked at how she was reveling in this despite my reluctance, and Klaus holding me down, I opened my mouth. What would they do if I spoke again?

"Have you wondered how her tongue would feel going inside you? I can tell you it feels good on my cock." In a sneaky sexual prompt, Klaus stroked his palm on me, right over my mound. Deep firm strokes.

I breathed out a strangled moan, and clenched, imagining her there. Already she'd pressed her body in close and I sensed her warmth through her shorts.

"Now I'm going to make you pay for that *bitch*." Her smile was wicked, and I couldn't help writhing a little against the iron bar of his arms. I was trapped tightly and she was waiting, wanting me, inches away.

What did she mean by I'd pay? I dreaded finding out.

"Hold on," Klaus said. Then he dragged my arms back and linked my wrist cuffs together. "Done. Now I can play too. Go down on her, girl."

"With pleasure, Sir."

The slow descent of her toward my groin became a painful trail of bites from the nipples and undersides of my breasts, while I screamed a little at each, down across my belly, to my mons. I couldn't stop myself squealing, "Don't, don't, don't," when she bit there too, and hung on.

"Is she allowed to swear if I bite, Sir?" Jodie murmured with her teeth nipping above my clit.

He was laughing, I realized from the movement of his chest. "I think we'll allow that, yes."

"Okay."

My fuck, fuck, fucks became a rising tide of shrieks as she applied bites to my clit and labia. Then she licked me once, hot and slow, with the flat of her tongue up along my swollen lips to my clit, and I subsided, moaning.

"That's good," Klaus murmured at my ear, before he put thumb and finger to my nipples and squeezed.

My eyes rolled back with the climbing pleasure from what Jodie did with her tongue.

"Here?" she whispered, settling on simply sucking on my clit and rolling her tongue across now and then. I looked down for a moment, watching, before a swell of sensation made me arch and flop my head back against Klaus's shoulder. Despite his hold, I'd slipped down his body as I spread my legs more, aching to reach toward where I was being fingered and licked and sucked effortlessly toward ecstasy.

"Or this?" And she slipped her fingers into me, pumping them in time with the rhythm of her exquisite sucking. I looked down again. Her mouth on me, fingers inside, and Klaus handling my breasts and pinching. The worst of it was how my mind continually flicked back to the knowing that they had me at their mercy. I was bound, held, caught, and couldn't stop them, and that repeated thought alone sent me soaring higher and higher. Her tongue, her mouth…my captors.

I shuddered, squeezed my muscles in, and came while gasping a quiet chorus of *no, no, no.*

The aftermath left me struggling for air. Jodie climbed up and hugged me.

"No?" That was Klaus. I opened my eyes to see that enigmatic smile of his. "I think that was really a yes, little toy, wasn't it?"

I shut my eyes, refusing to answer. Something of me could remain an unknown. The man would never have all of me.

"Not answering? Too late for that. Go get the bondage tape and a pair of panties, Jodie. I'll keep this one occupied until you come back."

That sounded ominous. Klaus had let me fall forward onto his arm and wasn't paying attention while he spoke. I wasn't at all keen on having anything done to me in this post-climax lull except maybe sagging to the floor and curling into a ball. As if I hadn't learned how futile it was to resist, I tried to wriggle myself upright, and got to my feet, only to have him grab my cuffed wrists.

"Where are you going? Such impetuous behavior."

I glanced behind me. His grin was lopsided. Fuck. Guess the man liked it more when I didn't give up. Didn't change me. Damned if I was going to sit still for him either. Especially if he was getting a gag no matter what I did. Anger ripped through me.

I let each following word roll off my tongue, savoring them. "Go fuck yourself."

Imagining that he'd leap up and do something bad, I froze, but instead he stood slowly and loomed over me a minute just looking down, not quite smiling. I chilled. Maybe telling Klaus that had been unwise.

He walked around me once, while I kept my trembling to a minimum and scowled.

"You're trying to fire me up? Brave, if foolish. You're the one who is getting fucked, Stephanie. Slowly and with force, until you understand exactly who is in charge."

Not willing to let him out of my sight, I turned my head to keep track.

"No." He grabbed my neck, his fingers wrapping more than half way round. "Move when I tell you to." With that hold he drew me to the chair and made me kneel then unlinked the cuffs. "Shut your eyes. If I see them open, I will hit harder."

I almost swallowed my tongue as I heard the distinct threatening noise of a belt being unbuckled and slid through loops.

"I like seeing a woman with a red ass. I like seeing her flinch at the pain. I love it when my marks last. But you should know this— I'm scaling myself back with you. I'm not hitting you any more than I think you can take. Grab hold of the chair legs."

Oh fuck, oh fuck. Where was Jodie? I wanted her back in here, but I grabbed the bottom of the chair legs and hung on for dear life.

"Though, truthfully, I'd love to see you grow to like this."

To make me like pain? He had to be joking. His calloused palm caressed my ass, gently, heading toward where I didn't want him to go. Jodie…I responded to that, to her touching me without me saying it was okay to. Even if that was weird in some psychological dark way I really did *not* want to analyze. But Klaus, I didn't even like him.

"So beautiful. Nothing better than this view of a woman, waiting for me to do something to her."

My nipples shrank to points and ached. He intimidated me. The room itself trembled when he entered. Or maybe that was just my knees. Fuck, what was he doing? He was big and masculine and…and imagining him back there… Okay, no lies. No point in lying to myself. The thought of him looking at me was hot.

Then his fingers slid into my wetness and he played with my lips, shunting up and down, dipping a half-inch into me, while he kept talking in that deep deliberate way that was as nasty as swallowing pure scotch. So good. So bad.

Another slide of his fingers, so close to my upright clit.

"Uh." I squeezed my eyelids shut even more and put my head down. Already I had that despicable urge to stick my ass in the air to beg for more…from him, from this man I detested.

"Are you our little whore, Steph? Does that label make you hotter and wetter, closer to coming?

Hot? I swear I'd just melted. I sucked in air through my lip that twisted under my teeth. *Don't answer.*

Then he shafted two fingers straight into me, like he owned me, like he could do it when he wanted to.

"Fuck." I gasped and arched a little. Not much, but I heard him chuckle.

"You are, aren't you?" His next finger thrust ended deep then he lifted my butt in the air with just those fingers, stretching my walls, making my knees bounce when he let my body back down. He removed his fingers, slammed them back in, eliciting another grunt from me.

"You're so wet, little toy."

I hated him in that moment.

I heard the shuffle of cloth as he stood.

"Let's try some small doses."

The whip of the belt came too fast for me to stiffen. The smack of it across my pussy shocked me as well as sending a flood of pleasure through the lower part of my body. He laid another five or six strokes over my butt. Though harsh, I was so aroused they seemed to blend in, leaving me enveloped in a fog of hurt and conflicting lust.

If I'm wet it's just because of his fingers. Or so I told myself.

Then he fingered me some more, and used the belt some more.

By the time Jodie stepped back into the room, I was quivering and wanting him to fuck me for real.

"Oh." Her footsteps halted. "She looks—"

"Ready for more?"

*I'm not*, I wanted to protest. It wasn't fair that he knew how to do this. I wanted him to go away and die and I wanted his cock in me so bad.

Jodie's swallow was audible. "Yes."

"Tape."

"Here, Sir. And the panties, I brought both clean ones, and I took off mine. I thought you'd want to choose."

"I do. Good girl."

At that I had to put my head up. As he approached, I battled the stupid impulse to get up and run and the other stupid one—to defy him. It must have showed.

His mouth tensed and he handed a pair back to Jodie. "You have the clean ones."

"Don't you dare." I showed teeth. Yeah, that impulse won. Yet I'd not let go of the chair legs. My courage only went so far.

"Don't?"

Behind him I saw Jodie put her hand to her mouth as if shocked.

"Oh, I dare, all right." With a last stride he reached the chair where I'd finally decided it was prudent to get up and run, but he swung his leg and sat across my back so I was squashed stomach down across the seat.

All the air oomphed from my chest and I struggled to drag in another lungful.

Before I could do more than cough, he'd reached down and was halfway through wrapping my wrist to the chair leg with tape. When that one was firmly trapped, my other clawing hand was treated the same way. Then Klaus sat up and used the tape to bind each of my legs to the other side of the chair just above where my knees met the floor. With fingers jammed into the sides of my mouth, he made me open, and he pushed in the panties.

"Spit them out and I'll do far worse to your pretty pink butt. Understood? Nod?"

Tears blurred my vision. With him leaning over me, his fingers in my hair, and all my limbs tied to the chair, what was the use in getting in more trouble? None. *Don't do it.* I could hear that voice in my head. I tongued the panties, tasting, smelling Jodie's arousal on them. If they'd been his, I'd have spat them out and taken the consequences.

He waited. Patient as a fucking demon with a soul to harvest.

I swallowed around the panties. Saliva was already building. I lowered my gaze, hearing the urgent beat of my heart, and I nodded.

"Thank you." Then he leaned in and kissed me hard, his lips all-encompassing, devouring mine, his tongue forcing my lips apart. The presence of him in there, inside my mouth, with the panties in there too—that undid me, unraveling what last resistance I had. I gave in and tried to kiss him back.

"You. Are. So. Fucking hot, girl."

When he rose, I let my head hang down again, and heard him say, "Undress," to Jodie as he also shed clothes. Zips unzipped, clothes fell to the floor. They were coming for me. And all I was doing was waiting, and aching for them.

"She's a little low for what I want to do to her." He picked up the chair and me as if we weighed nothing much. I gasped as he carried me over to the coffee table and settled the chair legs on it. "Cock level. Much better."

The casual tone in that rattled me—as if I was no more than a piece of his furniture. I gulped, alarmed at what would happen if the chair shifted. My tongue moved against the panties. The floor was an extra couple of feet away and I was on hands and knees strapped to the chair. If it toppled off the coffee table, I'd go with it.

"Stand at her front."

"Sir, she can't do much with the panties in her mouth."

Klaus laughed. He was behind me and he slapped his hand once on my bottom.

"I made a small error there. I want to see her lick you while I fuck her. You can take out the panties. Spit them out, Steph."

Steph? I wasn't toy anymore? Shit. Progress. I moved my tongue and pushed them out of my mouth, a thin thread of drool hanging from my lips as I stared at the floor. Jodie squatted before me, naked, her legs parting as she did so. I couldn't help looking at her. She was pretty. She was also a part of this. And I still adored her, or at least, her body. I wasn't sure what the hell I really thought of her.

The distinct sound of a condom packet tearing made me tense.

"You okay?" she asked me. And yet she also had me in Klaus's favorite grip, with a hand in my hair, and slowly she lifted my head higher so we could look in each other's eyes. There was, strangely, compassion there, as well as an intense expression that said she wanted me.

Klaus used both thumbs to pry apart my ass cheeks, then he dug those thumbs into me next to my labia, exposing me to him. Opening me. I tried to fight how that made me feel, like I was *his*.

Jodie looked up and seemed rapt in whatever he did. At the soft prod of the head of his cock against my entrance, I knew what fascinated her. From that blunt, unwelcome, yet possessive touch on my sex, the heat of lust unfurled.

"Oh yes," she whispered. "Oh fucking yes. I so want to see you enter her. That's just...*fuck*."

"I'll get there." He stroked my butt with one hand and drew a slow line on me. "She welts up good."

I was being discussed like some object when I wanted him inside me. Involuntarily, I clenched down there and heard an appreciative, "Hmm," from Klaus. God, he noticed every-fucking-thing.

"As good as me?" Jodie challenged.

"Better. A pristine ass is best. Jealous, gorgeous?"

She chuckled then looked back down at me, shifting her grip in my hair. "Yes, and no. No because…" She traced my lip with her finger and fed it inside. "Suck on me, Steph."

I shuddered at the want in her voice and at what he was doing. At the same moment, his cock had moved an inch farther in. Deeper. God. As I sucked, my eyes rolled up.

Jodie laughed again in that pretty way of hers. Though keeping her hands anchored in my hair, she stood. Her pussy was an inch from my mouth. She added softly, "Now lick me. Get me off, girl. Get me off like I did you."

As if to make me lose the thread of what she instructed, Klaus slid all the way in. Though I groaned at the immense swell of sensation, I licked her. I wasn't missing this chance, no matter how well he fucked me.

"Ohh," she breathed. In that one lick, I knew I had her, and I smiled as I set my tongue and lips to working at her clit and pussy. I couldn't go far, not with her hold, but I made my tongue do wonders.

The noise of Klaus shunting in and out of me escalated. The wet thuds against my butt, the feel of his balls gently touching between my legs, and Jodie's climbing moan. God, oh fricking god. It seemed never-ending this assault on my senses, this climb of ecstasy. I moaned and breathed huskily along with her. I arched my back to him, as she tilted her pelvis at my lips, and as Klaus sped up in his thrusts. He went in, deeper, harder, louder, thumping me forward in the chair, scraping my knees on the table. The chair legs screeched across the timber.=

Within the mess of thoughts, I surfaced and managed to be delighted that I could do this to him, my supposed controller. At that moment, I had them both caught in *my* trap.

Then fuck, I lost it again—the spearing drive of his cock inside me became too much and I burst into an orgasm, somehow still sucking on Jodie, still breathing through my squeals as she jammed herself onto my mouth.

But I licked, I tasted her moisture, and I triumphed—I'd made her come.

The twitch and pulse of Klaus coming hit me next and I gasped in a tiny climax. The condom he wore limited what I felt, but I knew. I smiled. Then I let my lips slide across to the very top of Jodie's thigh and I kissed her there, panting, with my eyes shut. Though my mind was half lost in the brain-scrambling fuss of an orgasm, I still wondered where this was going. If this was messing me up, what was it doing to them?

And, I wondered, in a macabre way, if next time he'd make me give him a blowjob, because then I could bite his dick off.

So easy to be courageous inside my head. I wasn't superwoman. With my mouth resting on Jodie, I felt him withdraw, and I kissed her skin again, breathing her in.

She let go a little, her hands relaxing in my hair, though she trembled.

I wasn't mean enough, was I? I reconsidered biting his dick off. Still, there might be opportunities. I didn't have to sit still and take this.

# Chapter 13

## Jodie

Though Klaus had made us all get into the shower to get clean, with Steph between us, getting bitten and licked and soaped up in spite of her protests, we still had to wash up the dishes after. At least takeout left few dishes.

One of the things I liked about Klaus was his flexibility. For months, we'd both been in love with Total Power Exchange and being Master and slave but keeping up that sort of relationship was taxing. Some days, on weekends mostly, he told me what to do down to the very smallest details. Sometimes he helped me around the house, like any man, just because he wanted to. And some days he was in uber-sadist mode and we ignored the house and the outside world while he kept me in and out of pain for hours.

Tonight I washed and he dried the dishes, and Steph sat on the floor in one of my white lace dresses. No panties, as was I, and with wrists cuffed, and she looked like she thought this was as odd as a scene drawn from Alice in Wonderland. When Klaus playfully spanked me a few times with a wooden spoon from the drawer, her expression turned thoughtful.

I let the water out of the sink and turned to her, leaning back into the counter. "We're not always serious, Steph, you know." I shrugged and screwed up my mouth, trying to find the right way to put this. "We're just normal sometimes…"

"Yeah?" Eyebrows quirked into a *V*, she held out her bound hands. "Like this is normal?"

She had a point there.

Klaus had hung up the dishcloth and now he went to her, pulling her to her feet with his hand beneath her arm. "Up. We're all going into the living room where I'm going to tell you both the latest news."

After tossing the last dried spoon into the drawer, I traipsed after them, checking the clock as I went past. I rarely wore a wristwatch at home. Ten thirty already?

Steph was again on the floor. Odd, to me, was me *not* being there, on the floor. I was almost more jealous of that than of Klaus fucking her. I didn't call what he'd done making love.

Despite her almost knifing me, if anyone was connected in an affectionate way, it was Steph and myself. The way she'd kissed my leg, and the look in her eyes after that—I didn't know why exactly, considering the completely off-the-wall circumstances, but we'd connected. And if I searched inside, I knew I wanted it to last.

I had a yearning to explore where she and I lay—where our psyches touched. Between one human being and another there might be a whole different world from what had come before. Philosophical crap perhaps? Or could this go as deep as what Klaus and I had?

I settled next to Klaus on the sofa, snuggling in when he put his arm around me.

From the way Steph looked at both him and me, if anyone were to be jealous, it would be her. I made a note to keep an eye on that.

"The news. They've found the bodies."

Alarmed, I turned to him.

"It's okay. So far there's no hint of anything else. Only that they have homicide detectives investigating." With his fingers, he smoothed the top of the shoulder strap on my dress. "Kat rang me though. She's curious, but I think I distracted her. On Saturday night, before I came to get you, I mentioned Leon's house to her. I didn't tell her you'd gone to a party there though. I said we'd been thinking of taking a look at the house. So that's your story if she asks you. Okay?"

"Okay." It was curious that he'd decided to let Steph know all this. I'd wondered if he would keep her in the dark.

Steph cleared her throat and when no one interrupted, she continued. "What about me. Have they said anything?"

"No. Not yet. Or nothing in the reports I've heard. I expect they will though." He sat forward, putting his palms together between his thighs. "Stephanie, I want to run through what I expect you to do from now on."

Both Steph and I nodded. She, wide-eyed. Me, wondering where this was going, as he'd not talked to me about this either.

"I don't want to keep you in the room forever. It's not healthy for you."

Bottom lip caught in her teeth, Steph blinked at him.

Oh, good one Klaus—showing you care. It wasn't pretend. The man would be caring about her. For a sadistic Dom, he had his soft side. I'd experienced it, as had Baxter our cat, and I'm sure others, even if he was sneaky in his kindness. I'd nearly lost Klaus after the accident at the play party because of that softness in his character. He could blame himself for fate and crap like no one else. Thing is, if he didn't, he wouldn't be my Dom. This was Him, front and center. Taking charge or taking blame, this was Klaus.

I hugged him, briefly, from the side. After patting my arm, he went on.

"So Jodie is going to make sure you both exercise. You—" he looked back at me. "Are going to go jogging some mornings, like you should, but before I go to work."

"Sure. I can do that." Jogging around on the island was like a scenic tour. I rarely zoned out and forgot to look at the ocean or at my surroundings. Just a single kookaburra laughing in a gum tree, or the soft washing sound of waves rolling in and crumpling onshore would draw me back to the real.

"Good. And you're in charge of sorting out all the household work. But the hard part is this: I want you to earn money from home, if at all possible. Have you considered that?"

"Yes." I'd anticipated. In fact I'd been wracking my brains—I hated being idle and I figured it was best to occupy Steph too. "I've done online research for other writers before—for magazine articles, for authors, for producers, and I'm fairly sure I can drum up some work again. Steph can help me. You got that, Steph? I know you can write and research. I remember that, even if you and I spent half our time partying at uni. Okay?"

"You want me to help you earn money?"

"Yes."

Klaus added in support. "Do you think we can afford to feed you, get you medications, or clothe you without you contributing?"

"Clothe me? What the fuck!"

For some reason that had angered her more than I'd seen for ages. What would Klaus do? I could almost hear his eyes narrowing, but Steph carried on, straight over the cliff.

"Shit, yes I do think that! You want me to *contribute*? I'm not going to let you do all of this to me and then expect—"

Klaus sprang to his feet, picked her up, and sat back on the sofa with her draped over his lap and her head up my end. "Punishment. No swearing."

I shifted away to give him more room.

"Fuck, fuck, fuck! You can't...you...let me go!" she sputtered then craned her neck back to plead with me. "Jodie?"

"I'm sorry. You can't do what you just did and expect *nothing* to happen."

"Fuck."

Without warning, Klaus flipped up the bottom of her dress, anchored the hem at her waist with one hand then swatted her ass with the other.

"Uh!" Steph put her head down, hiding her face in the sofa. "No," she whispered. "No, you can't. Don't. Please?"

"I can. How many swear words was that? Five?"

"No! Was not. Three?"

"Hmm. Our toy is not good at counting, is she?" Though he angled an eyebrow at me, he went back to smoothing his palm in circles on her butt.

I nudged him gently. "Stop admiring your handprint."

"Finally jealous, Jodie?"

"No. I can understand the attraction. That ass deserves to be spanked. Really it does. May I?" I waved a hand toward her offending rear end.

"Jodie," she whined. "You wouldn't?" Then she wriggled on his lap, but not enough to be an escape attempt.

I wondered if this was firing her up. It damn well was me.

"Go for it," Klaus leaned back, giving me space. "Ten more should do. Especially since I don't expect you to be able to spank harder than a mouse."

"Ten! I never said that many. Oh crap," she muttered. "Shit, shit. Fuck. There. I made my quota."

"Bad toy!" I chuckled then half-stood, propped one hand on her back, and reached across him. I delivered ten spanks as hard as I could—determined not to be *too* outdone by my Dom. She yelped on the last few and I sat back smiling at Klaus before checking the results. "See? I did good. Her bottom is going a nice pink."

"Owie," Steph muttered. "F—" She sighed and relaxed, giving in.

"Now." Klaus lightly patted her bottom as he spoke. "You agree you will be helping Jodie earn money?"

Her swallow was small. "What choice do I have?"

"None."

"Shi..." Her silence still, somehow, seemed full of swearing. "Yes."

"Good girl," I murmured then slipped off the sofa onto my knees, turned her face toward me, and studied her features, while she looked back at me with those world-sinking brown eyes of hers. I kissed her.

Those soft lips entranced me, like always, and I shut my eyes to feel them give beneath mine…the warm intrusion of her tongue tip into my mouth then of mine into hers. I moved my head to get better access, pleased at her small noises of pleasure. We dueled like that a while before Klaus interrupted.

"If you two do that much longer I'll be forced to tie you both up and fuck you again, and I really need to get some sleep tonight. Stop."

"Aww." Dubious, I eyed him then gave Steph a last petite kiss. "Are you sure we can't tempt you?"

He grabbed my hair until I winced, then he made me knee-walk my way to him. With Steph beneath and between us, squirming a little, he kissed me. The difference between his hard, dominant nature and her softer one was so abrupt I moaned into his mouth, not sure what the hell I was doing except that I wanted someone's hand, mouth, or whatever, on me. I tried to pull his hand between my legs but got nowhere.

"Klaus," I protested, pouting. "Please?"

"No." He nipped the end of my nose. "I'm sorry, but it's bedtime for us all."

"Fuck." I pouted.

"Oh?" Fast and powerful he yanked me forward across Steph and spanked me twice.

The sting made me jump. I struggled upright, reaching back to soothe the hurt.

"Say sorry, girl."

"Sorry, Sir." But I smiled, unable to hide my glee at being punished. He knew I liked it and reserved nastier punishments for our real debates when I went way overboard. Which was good, as I, in a way, liked and needed that too.

A hardness came over him then—as happened when the need to hurt me badly struck him—and I froze like a dove pinioned by a hawk, waiting, dreading. "I think I have been too lenient. What do you think?" His eyes had a gray aspect, his mouth was straight as a knife, and he held Steph down on his lap as if she were no more than some inanimate object. A second later, he shook himself and the need passed. His face cleared. "Let's get to bed. You can both sleep naked."

I breathed and let a shiver run through me. "Naked?"

He smiled. "Sounds good to me."

"Me too."

Some nights I wore PJs, some a t-shirt and panties, but tonight was skin to skin as Klaus was naked also. To my delight, he brought Steph to our bed, and made her lie between us.

I wanted her untied so that, perhaps, I could coax her to touch me of her own volition, but I guess he didn't trust her yet. At least her hands were to her front. Like that, they almost framed her breasts, cupping them when she was on her side.

"Are you tired?" I asked her quietly, and drew a finger down her jaw. Since her eyelids were drifting half-shut it seemed likely.

"Yes."

"Poor baby."

Her lips twitched and she frowned but barely opened her eyes more.

"Don't like getting called baby?" I smiled.

She grunted so quietly I almost missed it. Cute.

"Do you, Jodie? Do you like being called baby?" Klaus wrapped his arms about her and pulled her to him, taking a breath with his nose against her neck. "Women smell wonderful."

"Sometimes I like it." Funny—seeing him cuddle with another woman. She'd tensed for a moment but soon relaxed.

Again I searched, but there was no jealousy in me. Why? I couldn't figure myself out. I *liked* seeing them together.

I guess we'd tired her out. Sex and pain did that to me too. She'd had a lot happen in one day. I wondered what she thought of this all, but here and now was a bad time to ask. How much did she hate him…me? I didn't see her as a threat. I didn't see what we were doing as wrong, or not any more. Perhaps when Klaus wasn't around I could get her to talk honestly? Tomorrow then.

I watched as he stroked her hair and simply held her. When she fell asleep and breathed in the slow, steady way of the dreaming, Klaus got up, took her into his arms, and placed her carefully at the end of the bed then covered her with a light blanket. Though she stirred, she went back to sleep, mostly curled up below my feet. It was a king-size bed, but his feet reached the bottom. We had a carved timber frame and it would stop her rolling from the bed in the night.

"Won't she be cramped, sleeping cuffed?" I whispered.

"Maybe. Can't be helped. I can't set her loose, but I want her sleeping with us." He took my hand and kissed it.

I focused on his face, searching for clues. "Are you happy, Klaus?"

"Happy?" He frowned slightly, the crease on his forehead joining the few permanent ones that marked his almost forty years of life. "I'm happy whenever I have you near me." A smile curved one corner of his lips. "Don't you know that yet? You're my everything, Jodie. If you are happy, I am. Whatever hurts you hurts me also. And you are happy, aren't you?" Cupping my face, he rubbed his thumb across my cheek. "This woman makes you happy, despite the reasons she is here."

A statement, not a question. True. I nodded. Wonderful, strange, yet true. "I don't really…" I thought. "I don't want to really hurt her. If you understand?"

"As in spanking not being included in that hurt space?"

I waggled my head against the pillow, flummoxed by my own reasoning. "I guess."

"I understand completely. Jodie, there's a few things I want to say between us."

"Yes?" Oh boy, what was this?

"One." He toyed with my lip. "I am a little worried about Kat, but I will handle that."

"She is very persistent. I've always felt flattered by her attention but, wow, persistent."

"I know. As I said, I can handle her. She's a friend and that makes it simpler. Two. Just in case, I'm getting us fake passports and working out a way out via Papua New Guinea."

*Gulp.* I nodded. "Okay." I recalled something. "All the gear you took—the camera, the vacuum cleaner and all. Disposed of?"

"Mostly. Not the camera." His frown returned. "I should check that. It's just…"

Ah, my Klaus's soft side returneth. "You don't want to see what was done to me?"

"No. I don't."

I shrugged. "I trust her."

"I know. I'm still not sure I do."

"Mmm. You'll learn to. Give her a chance."

I fell asleep wondering which of us was correct. Me, I hoped. Klaus wouldn't be happy if Steph ever proved him wrong, but then neither would I.

The next morning was the first time I'd ever awoken and found a woman curled at my feet at the bottom of my bed. Having glimpsed a hint of her black, tousled hair, I sat up and blinked away the bleariness of sleep.

"Oh my," I breathed. The window light from above my head filtered through the drifting lace curtains, dappling the skin of her face and breasts with moving gleams—pretty as sunlight shining through the leaves of a forest canopy.

Quietly, I folded back the sheet and crawled to her. Careful not to wake either her or Klaus, I sat on my heels just looking. She'd discovered a way to sleep with her hands folded together under her head. The mildness of the day was to my advantage as she'd thrown off the covering. Though, I supposed, unwrapping her would be almost as wonderful a present as finding her like this. With little more sound than the slide of knees across quilt, I went closer and leaned over her, aware of the rounded plumpness of my breasts only an inch from hers.

Her eyes opened and a heartbeat of time later, she smiled tentatively. A gift of immeasurable value. A smile.

"Good morning," I smiled also, letting it show in my eyes. Then I pushed on her shoulder until she shifted onto her back. I swallowed as I surveyed the voluptuous length of her body, all mounds and curves that fairly begged me to touch, to kiss, to devour.

"Stay there." I assessed her quietness and the way she seemed content to merely wait. My smile spread. "Stay, little toy. I want to taste you."

Though for a moment challenge reared in her eyes, she said nothing. Her breathing grew uncertain. Under my hand, her bare skin shivered. Without taking my gaze from hers, I pressed my mouth to her mouth, light as a teardrop, sliding my lips along hers, inhaling her essence, slowly becoming more eager as she stirred and kissed me back.

The journey down her body beckoned. I paused, speaking into her mouth and kissing her between words. "I want to taste you. I want. You."

Steph shuddered, straining upward and opening her mouth wide to encompass mine.

I sat back and pushed her down then put my fingers around her jaw. "No. You're not to move. I'm going to kiss my way down to your thighs. Be good and I'll kiss you there too."

"Jodie? I can't—"

"Shh. You'll wake Klaus."

The plea in my spoken name had made me grin evilly, as did the little writhe of her hips. But I bent and kissed her jaw then the hollow of her neck. I left tiny nips and licks there and on the upper curves of her breasts, plus at least one mark from my teeth on her nipple that made her whimper and try to grab my hair with her tied hands.

I pressed her back again and resumed my gentle torture. I tasted her a hundred times on my way down, circled her navel with my tongue and spiraled around and around that tiny dip in her belly. By then her breathing was jagged and punctuated with gasps. By teasing her endlessly, by nipping her thighs and licking closer and closer to where she truly wanted me to go—two inches, an inch, a half-inch from her very visibly erect clitoris—I had her moaning and attempting to shove her pussy at my mouth.

"Bad girl," I whispered, and I repositioned my body atop hers, straddling her face with my legs. She couldn't pull me down to her, but I slowly lowered myself until her tongue flicked on me. "Oh fuck." I shut my eyes.

Her giggle brought me back despite the mounting pressure in my groin as she studiously sucked on my clitoris. I looked down at her mons and had my tongue out, about to tap upon her nub when Klaus sat up, leaning on his elbow.

The sheet slid from his body. "Up early and being naughty, are we?"

"No." I gasped and wriggled. "Yes." Damn, Steph was still licking at me. My hips undulated of their own accord.

"Wait." He slipped out of bed, retrieved a condom from the bedside drawer, and came over to me to where I was poised above our girl's pussy. He was already unrolling the condom down his cock. "Keep teasing Jodie, little miss toy."

She grunted and, I swear, sucked my clit entirely into her mouth.

"Uh." I ducked my head at the swell of pleasure. The little bitch was obeying him. But she lifted her hips from the bed in a silent call to me to do the same.

"Jodie, make her come while I fuck her." While Klaus lifted her bottom up with his palms beneath, offering her to my mouth, he probed with his cock for her entrance.

I shifted sideways so there was room for him and had a grand view of the proceedings as the head of his phallus disappeared an inch inside and her cunt spasmed. Magic. I stared. Stage shows had nothing on this. The slow thrust in then the pistoning out and in again mesmerized me. The wetness of her on his cock as he drew it out, the tightening of her thigh and stomach muscles as he worked at her over and over. Oh my god.

I bent, still watching. His cock in her pussy, my tongue and teeth and lips on her clit. Her groans and whimpers built, dragged from her. Mine did also as she'd found me again with her hand. I panted and had to clamp down on the hot coiling lust she evoked with all she did to me. I could hold out. Yet I moaned as I played with her nub, stroking my tongue across and biting her so she squealed.

"What about here?" Klaus paused and slid his hand closer, below her slit. From her squeak and attempt to shift away, I figured out where he probed.

"Not there!" She tensed.

Smiling, I swirled across her once with the flat of my tongue to keep her still.

"Hmm. You're pretty open. Maybe next time, toy." He gave a slow, deliberate thrust. "Fuck, you're tight in here as it is."

Oh my. If he took her there, I'd be watching avidly.

"Mmm, Jodie. Please. Please," she breathed. She was close—her thighs came in like a vice, trying to grip Klaus.

"Fuck. Fuck. Slow down," I pleaded to her, squirming. "Not there. Not…not." I squeezed my legs together on her fingers.

Klaus chuckled and thrust so far in she screamed and I managed to remember my job and gave her a series of hard tongue swipes and a rhythm of sucks guaranteed to eventually—

She screamed and came under me, bucking, while he speared into her arching body a few more times.

Once she'd relaxed a little I put my head up.

"Me too?" I begged Klaus, squirming.

Without further encouragement, he withdrew from her. Her moisture leaked and dampened the sheet at the join of her legs. Hoping to provoke another climax, I straddled her again and kept licking, with the lightest touch, only to be interrupted by Klaus rudely grabbing my butt and thrusting into me.

Damn.

Bare cock. So much nicer than a condom.

For a moment I forgot her, absorbed in the multiple sensations—her wet lips and searching slippery tongue at the very core of my pleasure, his cock hammering into me so high, fast, and deep.

No. Not yet. Not…

My tongue stuck to the roof of my mouth, my neck arched, my eyes saw nothing, and an orgasm tore through me like a tsunami, bearing away every speck of consciousness except the last drive of his cock into me and his last shudder as he came.

Light sweat coated my skin, cooling already.

I gulped in air and rolled off her, weak and spent. After disposing of the condom he'd worn to fuck Steph, Klaus crawled up onto the bed then dragged Steph around the right way up. With an exaggerated sigh, he collapsed between us on his back. I chuckled at his melodrama. He kissed my nose, then turned his head and kissed hers, before he drew us together.

I peered across his chest at Steph. Though she looked as messed up as me—red of lip and flushed, with hair like an aroused medusa—she was also staring at Klaus as if she'd found a small but amazing creature in her house and didn't know whether to rehome it outside or squash it. Then she spotted me and looked aside.

Had I read more into that than was there? Minds are funny things and mine was a little blown right then. I sighed and hugged Klaus some more. This would sort itself out.

# Chapter 14

## *Klaus*

Before I went out the front door to head off for work I double-checked how Jodie would handle Steph. Jodie's safety was my main concern. Nothing would ever be perfect—that was impossible—but I could make it as close to perfect as I could.

I held Jodie's chin and moved her head slightly to and fro. "Don't remove the cuffs. Okay?"

"Yes, Sir."

"When you get her from the room, make her click the lock on the link of her cuffs to join them."

"Yes."

"And no orgasms while I'm gone today." I smirked. That one might make her squeak.

But after a pause: "Yes." She twitched her eyebrows up as if in pain. "That's going to be difficult."

I chuckled. "I'm sure it will, knowing you. You are both to be waiting here kneeling when I get home. Actually, be in my favorite position. Over the hall table. I want to see two pretty, naked asses. You can wear a dress, though."

"We might need more clothes soon. Since I'm sharing with her now."

"Yes. You should go shopping this week, as long as you aren't away too long. Hook the fire and burglar alarms to the app on your phone. Make sure they're silent. We can't risk the neighbors or the police coming here because the cat set them off." When she nodded I thought of my last request. "Last of all, I want her wearing the new diamante butt plug every day when I get home."

"You want our toy's butt to sparkle? That plug was going to be mine, Sir." Despite her small dissent, there was mischief in her eyes.

"I'll order another. As well as more cuffs. Hers seem to be getting wet from showers an awful lot." I bent and kissed her well. "You taste so good. Have fun putting the plug in."

She grinned. "You have me figured out already."

"I do, yes. You have permission to get her close to coming. If she goes over and it's her fault, spank her for me."

"I will." Jodie inhaled deep, her grin even more intense.

"But…no emails mentioning her in any way, ever. If you ever have some emergency, phone me and mention the word…" What was an innocuous thing to say? "Say you've seen another stray cat in the yard."

"Stray cat. I'll remember."

It was only a five-minute drive to my office. I parked my jeep in my usual spot, but before I went in, I crossed Nelly Bay Road to the beach opposite, took off my shoes and socks and ventured down to the sand where it merged with the grass under the palm trees. So peaceful. Already a mother had her toddler exploring the dunes and the shallow frothing water. The screams here were ones of pure delight. The screams at our home were as likely to be from pain as from pleasure.

I took a deep, deep breath and let the gentleness of my surrounds calm me.

Where was I going with this? Did I really know? I hadn't faced my fears or my hopes properly yet. Everything had been too messed up. Too hurried. And so many surprises.

Jodie had turned into such a Domme with Steph.

I liked that. Kink was more fun when things were changing. But this wasn't BDSM any more, was it? If it wasn't completely consensual it wasn't truly BDSM. I could make Steph enjoy it. I'd proved that. But the little looks she gave me, the ones I'd caught anyway, were half-fear, half-curiosity. How to convert her to full on acceptance? Because that was my aim, wasn't it? Trust her, get her to trust me then let her go.

A seagull landed a few yards in front of me and gave me a once-over with one yellow eye before pattering off across the sand toward a dead fish. Even the seagulls suspected me of something bad today.

And yet, this was necessary for Jodie and I to stay here, free and able to enjoy our life. History had precedents. Grabbing Steph and making her our toy wasn't exactly normal *now*, but go back to earlier societies and it would be. Society and its perception of what was wrong and what was right changed depending on what was best for it, for the people of the time.

If a Viking had someone take his woman and make her drunk so as to fuck her, like Leon had, like Stephanie had condoned, he would consider it his right to take revenge. People would die under his axe and that would be the correct justice.

Laws were made so the biggest group of people came out on top. Looked at that way, I was doing what was right for *my* people—for Jodie and me. Was that enough though? Was I happy, as Jodie had asked me? Fucked if I knew. Happiness came and happiness went. Life handed you shit and you either turned belly-up or you made something out of it that was far better than shit stew.

When I'd had our little captive this morning, I'd wanted to fuck her ass. I sucked in a hard breath, held it, thought. Yeah, I still did. My cock twitched at the idea even. If this wasn't making the best of a bad situation, I didn't know what was. Something about having Steph under my utter control pushed all my dials into overload. Very like when Jodie and I had tried out capture fantasy, only perhaps a shade darker.

I stood and brushed sand off the back of my pants then trudged up through the trees. From BDSM I'd learnt control, hadn't I? This wasn't just my baser desires taking me over, it was me doing what would give us the best outcome. I paused and shut my eyes. Getting to make a woman crawl before me, kiss my cock, and suck it into her mouth on command…sticking it into her little asshole and fucking her there and then…that was all just collateral damage slash side benefit. Wasn't it?

I coughed to clear the obstruction my throat had acquired. My dick was awkwardly positioned and painfully erect. Figured. Maybe I should hold back and see where I could go with Steph without letting my dick have its way?

I crossed the road, barefoot, shoes in hand, feeling the warmth of the sun in the asphalt on the road. Maybe. Hold back, not touch our little slave, for a while. My dick was going to be unhappy.

That night I arrived home, opened the door, and there were both Steph and Jodie in position as requested by me. My subconscious had somehow forgotten to remind me to cancel this event. I blinked, walked forward, and did my obligatory inspection, running my hands over both of them, over the sumptuous rising mounds of their bottoms. The temptation was too much.

When I played and pulled the butt plug out by a half inch then let it pop back in, Steph whimpered.

"Use the next size up in two days."

Jodie turned her head. "Yes, Sir."

I had a last good look at the diamantes winking on the end of the plug then at the glistening line of her cleft drawn between her legs where her swollen labia met. Getting Jodie to wait like this always got her aroused and wet. Was this the sign of a submissive? I put my hand on her, draped one finger right down the middle on her moisture then let the length of my finger slip between her lips. Steph made a small noise. The muscles of her cunt moved in—the automatic response of a woman waiting for a man to fuck her.

God damn. I wanted to unzip myself and put my cock in her. But I took my hand away and resisted teasing her some more. Restraint was my own order to myself.

My fingers shone with her wetness. *Be good, man.*

I stepped back.

"Nothing for you tonight either, gorgeous." I pulled Jodie to her feet and kissed the top of her head. Nothing spoke of control more than wanting something and denying yourself.

Even if I wasn't going to do anything to Steph, it would reinforce my authority to have them perform this welcome, so I left my order in place. Each day I'd just steel myself to be greeted this way. I smiled inside. Not exactly a chore. But I needed to get everything in my head lined up, one, two, three. No more going charging off like a maddened rhinoceros. I'd deal with the camera footage too, on the weekend, when I could be thorough.

On Wednesday, the newspapers finally reported that a Miss Stephanie Parker was missing and presumed involved in the deaths at the Edante mansion. Police were again hoping for public help and would anyone with information please contact them. A relative of the missing woman, Thom Parker, was flying in from Switzerland.

I sat back in my office chair when I read that on the PC screen. Damn. She had family. Though it was to be expected, somehow this made her more of a person. More someone who should have my sympathy than someone I needed to manipulate until they did what I wanted them to.

Or someone I just fucked because I wanted to? I rubbed my temples where the hint of a headache was thumping in. I needed a distraction. Extreme exercise was the best solution. The adrenalin would wash away the crap in my head and let me think clearly.

So I volunteered Chris for another session—one of the great benefits of being the boss. Half an hour to fight. Twenty to dress and recover, tops. We skipped a proper lunch and worked through it most days anyway. This would get the cobwebs blown from both our stodgy accountants' brains.

We retrieved our gear and made our way up to the park.

"Make this three days a week? Regular?" I faced Chris after a few obligatory stretches.

"Sure." He grinned. "That's if your old bones can take it."

"Fuck you, you little upstart." I smiled back.

Not that Chris was little. He topped me by an inch even if our musculature and fitness were similar. The man was more dedicated to his fighting than me though. Three disciplines? And he'd tried freestyle bouts for a while too. Those were nasty. You could get your spine kicked out of you, let alone your teeth.

"See if you can really show me what you can do today. Show me your worst."

"My worst? You don't want that, man."

"Okay, enough to impress me then. I feel the need. Work is bugging me at the moment. Just remember I need to be able to type after."

"Okay." He nodded and settled into the lithe ready stance of a man looking for a fight to begin and ready to take advantage of whatever flaws showed in an opponent. "Let's do this."

We approached each other. My muscles, my awareness were hyped, prepared.

Prepared for anything except the raw violence he unleashed.

Within seconds, after a flurry of mock hits, of blows that never followed through, of dancing, we got into it and exchanged real hits. One of his fists thumped through my defense into my side, a second glanced off my jaw and then I was taken down to the ground and wrapped in a headlock with his fist drawn back and quivering. He glared down at me.

"One hit and your throat would be crushed and you'd be dead before anyone could do a thing." The feral gleam in his gaze almost caressed me. "I'd do it too. If I had to."

I'd never seen such utter honesty in such a moment before. If you could judge lethality in a man's words and actions, Chris was a man who could kill.

Then he released me.

We scrambled to our feet and slapped each other's hands. "That one's yours," I said wryly. From the sting and liquid cooling on my chin I was bleeding. I wiped at it, and yes, blood marked the back of my hand. "Damn. That's going to impress the clients."

As if a few seconds before he'd not been growling death threats, Chris nodded, chuckling. "You've got street fighting cred now."

"And accountants need that? I guess I'm behind the times. Let's go back to lessons. I'll take you on again in a month."

The rest of the training went quickly, though I could feel my lip swelling.

At the office afterward, we changed and showered then Chris rummaged in the staff freezer for our ice pack. "Bit late to do the most good. You might get a bruise from that."

"I'll live." I wrapped a towel over the pack and applied it to my throbbing face. The small mirror on the wall showed some bruising all right. "Lucky you didn't break my jaw."

"No. I'm accurate. I wouldn't have." He perched his butt on the kitchen counter next to the sink. "Are you coming to the next play party with Jodie? Next weekend?"

I grimaced. Even if we just watched, somehow talking BDSM with people who followed the rules of safe, sane, and consensual did not seem wise. Not with what I had happening back at my house.

"No. Jodie and I have decided to stay away from get-togethers for the time being."

"Yeah? Kat was only asking about you two today."

I cocked an eyebrow. "She was? That's Kat. For her, giving up is not an option. Maybe it's best for her too if we stay away?"

"Maybe. I've got a question for you about kink if it's not too off base." I nodded and he continued. "I've heard what you said about you and Jodie acting out that capture fantasy for months and, you know, I wish I had a lady who wanted to try that out. Any hints?"

Where was this going? "Normally you'd have to ease into a D/s relationship first. We already knew each other, but Jodie is a bit unique. Her idea was, let's say, startling to me." I smiled.

"Startling? Yeah, for sure."

"Keep looking. You need someone who's more than a casual partner at a play party, though."

"Yes. I was just curious. You're a lucky man. Sounds like a really intense experience."

The dark steadiness in his gaze said more than merely curious to me. Though I couldn't pin it down, it resembled whatever had shone from them in that crystalline moment when he'd held me down and declared death had arrived. I guess Chris was another accountant with hidden depths.

"Yes, it was intense. More than you can imagine."

"I can imagine a lot, Klaus." He tapped his head. "I like using my head to think through situations well before they happen. That helps with work too. I believe it makes me a better accountant. Anyway, keep that pack on your face for ten minutes. I'll tell Marjorie to hold the fort while I go buy you some analgesics."

The rest of the week went past slowly. Painfully slowly. Going celibate was not something I did often. Thank god.

I told Steph about her stepbrother arriving on the day he got off the plane and she looked both sad and regretful. Tough. I couldn't afford to let it bother me.

But it did. The more I thought about it, the more it did. This was a real person we had kidnapped. A real woman with friends out there and a family. With hopes for her future.

So I ignored her as best I could while keeping her in our bed each night and supervising how Jodie handled her. If anything, I was growing more distant from Stephanie emotionally. Not good. Also not good was Jodie's puzzlement that I wouldn't make love to her, or allow her and Steph to.

Jodie domming Steph was fascinating, but only if I was in the equation. Messy perhaps? Confusing? I had to sort my head out. The weekend loomed. I needed time to think and Saturday would be it. Crunch time. Get the data sorted and set in place a true plan. Before had been a rush job. Facts, facts, and more facts. None of this random jerk-of-the-knee crap.

I set out on Friday night what I'd go through and at eight o'clock, Saturday morning, I began work in the study. I let Jodie go out for a jog while Steph was locked up downstairs in the room.

First, the news reports. The most up to date I could find would never tell me precisely what the police were doing, but it was the best I could do.

Some reporter had leaked laboratory reports on the post mortems. Leon's new drug was GHB. It had been detected in both his body and Melissa's. Well then. I sat back in my chair. Nothing new there. What a loser. I did some research into it and found that some people used it recreationally to get a high, as well as it being a date rape drug.

The cops were livid about the info leak. To be expected. I moved on. Nothing else was amazing or new on that front, except a picture of Stephanie. It was being displayed on most news sites. She was pretty, even innocent looking. The articles were discussing what she might have done. Most thought she'd murdered them somehow then run away.

Of us, there was no mention, of course. If there was suspicion we'd have cops hammering on our door.

I ran through what I'd found out about passports and escaping the country illegally. A friend of a friend had done some digging. It was doable. No matter what, I would set that in motion. Ecuador seemed a possible destination to end up. But it was a dangerous place—a last resort.

Main option. Us. Staying here. Not running. I tapped my fingers on my desk, thinking. We still couldn't just let her loose. And really, if we did, it would have to be somewhere else. Maybe even outside the country. Her picture was out there now. I'd need to set her up somewhere else. Doable. Just expensive. And no way was I going to hand over money without being sure of her loyalty.

Then there was the question of her smartness. That was something I had to doubt considering her history. She'd wandered about from job to job like a lobotomized ant. Being loyal to us wouldn't do us much good if she bloopered and said something stupid that gave away who she was. We'd be taking such a chance with our lives that my heart was in my mouth just thinking about doing that—setting her loose.

I wondered, was there anywhere overseas we could place her that would keep her happily and yet never let her go? I propped elbow on desk and leaned on my palm. A young Caucasian woman, given to someone overseas? Slave meat for sure. She'd be a whore servicing a hundred men a day after she arrived. A stupid idea...but still, it wouldn't hurt to keep it in mind. There might be somewhere safe. I wrote it down on my *possibles* list.

Right.

Which left me only one last bit of hard evidence to cover. I had to be thorough. The camera footage. I connected the camera and started it going. There was only half an hour or so with Jodie in it. The rest was Leon and Melissa having sex, and Melissa dying while he slept. Fuck. When it was done, I swore a while and sat trying to get that out of my head. That was goddamn-awful. It hadn't been fast. You didn't strangle fast. But the other footage, of Jodie and Steph...I stared out the window at the cloud-swept sky. I needed to do something about that.

She'd fucked us over royally. Not strictly a lie, perhaps, but she'd evaded the truth and I'd not an inkling of that until now. I'd been clueless. Not good.

She'd just torn our trust to shreds. No use repeating what we'd done before. I needed to try something new, maybe something a tad more startling. More vicious. My balls tightened.

Jodie returned from her jog and I made her sit on the lounge, all sweaty in her shorts and t-shirt, then I went down to the room to retrieve our toy.

# Chapter 15

## Steph

I looked about the room. Staying down here had been rare during the week. Jodie and I got along fine; it was only Klaus who scared me. Jodie was possessive and ever so kinky, but I knew her, and in some odd way, I trusted her. Her man however, every so often his eyes filled up with *mean* and he reminded me of a wild animal about to bite. I'd figured out that it happened when he wanted to cause someone pain. Thank God that was Jodie, nine times out of ten. She liked it. They suited each other to a *t*. Me, I doubted I'd ever be comfortable around Klaus. Not after what I'd seen him do to her. Not after what he'd done to me when he lost his temper in the bedroom.

How did you ever trust a man who liked hurting women?

I sucked in a breath and looked about again. Door. Blinking camera. Window.

I was dreaming if I thought I could be safe here with him. Jodie caved if he crooked his little finger. But, I had ideas. From the moment they'd mentioned doing research for others my brain cells had swarmed around in my head muttering an idea to me.

I climbed to my feet and went to the small head-height window. Darkest tint ever. Thick glass with a security screen screwed onto the inside. A louvered metal shutter on the outside that slanted upward from the outside and from the glimpses of plants this window must be just above ground level. I hadn't a hope of getting out through that unless I smuggled in a fucking crowbar or a rocket launcher. As if.

But if someone went past and if I scratched or tapped on the screen, I could make a loud noise, and then…then I needed a way to show there was *me* trapped inside this room. Even if they had their head down this low all they'd see would be the ceiling in here, and a blurry view of it too. How could I show I was here?

My first idea resurfaced. I couldn't fire off an email. The PC I had to use for research only received copies via USB of articles that Jodie found on websites. No internet connection. My job was to read through tons of those and distill out the info and links so that another person could use it in their book or whatever. But I also had access to flash drives so Jodie could take the data back to her internet-linked PC.

If I could put the story of my kidnapping on a document and transfer it to a flash drive, I then had something easily hidden. Get that into a stranger's hands and someone else would know where I was, as long as they read it.

Flash drives were so craptastically tiny they often got lost at the back of drawers. I'd already stolen one and hidden it near the PC I used. I'd get another if I could. It might be safer to store it in here on the window shelf. There was only one dim light at night. I could do it then. Perhaps I could get the window open? What were the chances someone would find the flash drive if I pushed it through a gap to the outside? One in a trillion?

But surely Jodie and Klaus had visitors? They had to. Had to. And what visitors would read a random flash drive? None. I'd need to label it with something like, *please read this as its got stuff on it about a kidnapped woman*. And that would be *so* well received if Klaus or Jodie found it.

Things were settling into place here. With Jodie being, in a way, a barrier between me and Klaus, I could just take my time and eventually, they'd either let me go, or I'd escape, or I'd let *someone* know that I was here.

I went back to the mattress, sat, and chewed off a few fingernails.

It was nice having a plan, made me less a victim, and more like me instead of their…toy. Though sometimes being that made me feel, I swallowed and stared into space, strangely good.

Sex had that effect though, didn't it? Orgasms did. Especially, maybe, ones like these. Klaus fucking me while Jodie went down on me… *Shiver.*

I needed to get that in the real world. Earth-shaking orgasms. Only minus the abduction, caning and general all-round sadism. Minus the fire in Klaus's eyes that made me want to hug the ground or hide in a corner where he couldn't find me, ever.

Not that I had much experience with good sex. Most of my boyfriends, even the ones who said they loved me, had turned out to be shitheads looking for a lay and not a relationship. Either I had poor taste, or my shithead detector needed fixing, or both.

The door made the clicking sound that meant it was being unlocked. It swung open and Klaus entered. No matter how many kindnesses he did me, no matter how normal he seemed, I could never seem to forget how, in Leon's garage, he'd casually stepped up and assaulted me then tied me up like it was something he did every day while out for a stroll.

Wariness and a smidge of fear surfaced whenever he arrived. I was used to being on edge.

My eyes seemed glued open.

This time, something about his silent step, from door to me, hypnotized me and conjured up some nameless dread. No sound except the brush of the cloth of his pants as he came closer and his soft breathing. No words. I shuffled backward on the mattress, just a few inches, afraid to move too fast in case it attracted retaliation. The black leather leash swung from his hand.

"Come." He opened the clasp at the end then beckoned.

There was nowhere to go. He seemed calm. Whereas I was frantic, cowering in my mind, as if a monster waited before me, the brittle bones of victims snapping under his feet, and I was his next meal.

Christ. I had to stop watching horror movies. Sleeping at the bottom of their bed hadn't been the best for getting a great night's rest.

I crawled forward and let him leash me and lead me upstairs with my hands clipped together at my front. Nothing unusual in any of this. Standard procedure 101 for my kidnappers. In the living room, Jodie waited in a cute pair of black running shorts and clingy blue t-shirt. When he made me sit in front of her in the spot usually occupied by the square coffee table, she smiled.

In her company my heart rate descended from that blackthinglurkingunderthestairs level to watchingchickflicks-with-my-girlfriend level.

Everything was brilliant. Until he started the recording and I found myself watching a home video featuring myself and Leon and Jodie. I hadn't known ears could actually ring but they did as the room grew hollow and distant and the TV screen seemed both a million miles away in another universe and yet also right there, in my head, in my past, when I did something to Jodie while she was unconscious. It sickened me to know that she too was watching.

Behind me, they spoke.

"This is from the camera in Leon's bedroom. You don't have to watch if you don't want to."

"What's on it?"

"Bad things. But if you watch, remember, this is done. Over with. The past."

"Okay. It won't bother me."

I thought I'd lost this, forgotten it, buried it, but that bastard Klaus had dug it up like an undertaker resurrecting a corpse. There was Leon urging me on, and Jodie, half asleep it seemed, and I knew what I was going to do next. I hated myself in that moment. I looked so bright and happy but I knew how stupid with drugs I'd been inside my head. How stupid, full stop.

What had I told them I'd done? Helped hold her down? I should have said it all, even if they didn't ask me. I couldn't turn around and look at her. Because maybe if I didn't this would be all imaginary and she wouldn't be there.

"What?" I heard, and it was her voice, incredulous and already angry.

Oh no. Please no. Why was he letting her see? I bit my lip, staring down at my toes.

Fingers clawed into my hair, dragging my head back at an angle, and Klaus said in a harsh whisper, "I hope you're watching this. Because this is the start of your lesson."

# Chapter 16

## Jodie

She'd told us she'd helped Leon hold me down. I was sure that was all. Yet there she was on-screen, giggling, biting me, tonguing, and going down on me. I was completely out of it and unaware. So odd seeing myself like that. I wasn't sure what I felt. Numb...betrayed...sick.

Klaus paused the playback then clicked off the TV. He sat back and hugged me to his side, kissed above my ear, and smoothed my hair.

This was where it all began. With their drug-taking and the deaths and their little orgy, none of which I'd willingly taken part in. So stupid. So awful. I didn't really know either Leon or Melissa, but they'd died. They'd fucking *died*. I rocked the base of my palm against my forehead. How could you ever understand that? I could recall her laughter, her smile. The sunshine at the jetty...

She must have known what they were going to do. Melissa must have known.

How could Steph have participated in that?

"You okay?"

I nodded, glancing down at Steph who seemed to have discovered something fascinating on the floor. She didn't want to face me. Well, right now, I didn't want to face her.

"It's not that bad…" I started. It was and it wasn't. Why was I so knotted up? If this had been a stranger it would have been simpler to brush off. But Steph had become my lover during these past few days. We had that rapport Klaus aimed for, only it had come naturally. I'd not have hurt her emotionally for a million dollars.

"Why didn't you tell me? Steph?"

She shook her head. "I'm sorry. I was scared and it seemed easier at the time. People had *died*. We were all upset. Would you have told me? If that was you?" She peeked back at me then looked away again.

"I'd never have done that to you." Anger flared. "Not while you were damn unconscious!"

"It was the drug," she said quietly. "I swear."

She hadn't looked drugged. Did people take it just to get high? Why wasn't she knocked out like I was? I shook my head. "I don't know if I believe you."

"You've done worse to me while Klaus held me down." Her clogged voice told me she struggled not to cry and I also found myself tearing up.

Damn her. "And you didn't enjoy that? You didn't sit there in his lap moaning and carrying on? You didn't want what I did, deep down inside you? If you'd screamed, I would have stopped. And that, girl, is the dead set truth. Which is more than you gave me."

Klaus rested his hand on my thigh, squeezed. "Stay there. I'll be back. I'll put her in the room."

"Okay." I rested my forehead in my palm. "Okay." I needed time to think. I'd lost track of where Steph and I connected. If we did at all anymore, it was so in danger of snapping. I half wanted to slap her. "You do that."

She went quietly.

When he came back upstairs, he kissed me and made me lie down on the couch with him then he caressed my side and breathed with me in the way he knew calmed me. His warm body against mine was as good as being in a boat rocking on a warm sea.

"You're too good to me," I murmured.

"Hmm. You deserve it."

"What are we going to do? I think I was growing to love her, almost? Was I stupid?" I frowned.

"No. Never. Never stupid." He stroked me some more, and his fingers rested on my hip, tightening as he went on. "I'm going to punish her. You said she couldn't lie but now I don't know. Even if you get close again, love alone isn't enough. Jodie, before I can trust her, I need her bonded to me.

"I'm going to punish her, and you are not going near her again until I say so."

Oh my. I rolled over and turned to him, finding him studying me with those gray-green eyes. After a moment, I dared to ask a question. "You will be careful?" I realized I feared for Stephanie, because she wasn't me. "I mean…what she did to me, it really *hurt*, but I do still care for her."

"I guessed you would. And I will be." He kissed me. "However, I need to break her to my will. I'm done with pussy-footing around."

His face held that feral hardness. When it occurred while he was beating me, my breath caught in my throat. All stiff lines, all ungiving. Yes, he'd bleed if you cut him but he'd cut you back, deeper, and watch every drop of blood as it dripped to the floor.

"You understand?" Gently he cleared some strands of hair from my face, drawing his fingers down my jawline.

"Break is a violent word."

"It is. I'll only do what I have to, you know that. I'm an accountant. I measure everything, including the pain I give. I will do whatever I have to." In his eyes, and in the quiet pause he gave me, dwelled a question.

*Whatever?* But he was actually asking me, even if the alternative was unclear. I inhaled and held it a moment, thinking, then exhaled. The room focused in, sharp. "Okay. Just remember to let me in too, after. Because, fuck her, I care." With my forefinger, I touched his lips. "I know you, Sir. Be good."

There was a restrained satisfaction in his returning smile.

"Is she…is she your new playground?" I watched his face for shifts of mood but he gave me nothing. "Sir?"

"Yes, she is, and when I say, you're going to help me play."

His *whatever* could mean so many things. Funny. This excited me. I knew the journey she was about to make because I'd been there. Klaus could be one evil bastard.

"Good." I nodded. "I like that idea."

Though I wasn't sure why.

# Chapter 17

## Klaus

The couch bowed under me as I shifted. I kissed Jodie on the shoulder and sat up on my elbow. She'd been drowsing beside me. Which was good. "I'm going down to her now. Okay?"

"Okay." She looked up at me, sleepiness in her gaze.

"I'm going to take all her meals to her for a few days at least. So until I say, you're not to make contact with her, unless it's an emergency. Clear?"

Those little front teeth of hers met on her lip.

"Worried?"

"A little. But you said you'd take care, so I won't from now on."

"Good." I kissed her on the lips this time. "See you later."

As I slid out from behind her, I was already thinking about what I was going to do downstairs. This appealed to me so much it almost disturbed me. The fires of sadism and dominance that I'd thought were mine to control were now blazing high.

I knew how I'd left her—in the hogtie straps with her hands attached to her ankles and to each other by straps and cuffs. "I'll be back soon," I'd told the girl. "You'll be seeing only me. I'm banning Jodie from seeing you for a while until you and I have an understanding."

Oh yes, I knew what that would do to her head. I knew that I scared her and that she'd come to think Jodie would protect her. Now she'd be down there, shivering, wondering what I intended to do to her. Fuck, I liked that.

One of the rules of BDSM said never ever leave someone alone in bondage. The chances were small that anything would happen to her like a panic attack or a snake arriving to bite her. Small, infinitesimal even perhaps, but not zero. I liked that too. I liked this departure from safe and sane and average.

I'd never suspected this could be a part of me, but I couldn't deny it any longer. Illegal, unsafe, immoral, whatever the fuck it was, it was me.

As I went down the stairs, with my bare feet thumping on the timber, I already had an erection hard enough to make me want to jerk off.

I figured she'd be noticing that a lot in the next few days. I felt like footballer about to boot one between the posts, like an astronaut about to land on the moon, like a man with a woman in my basement who had no escape, no way to stop me doing whatever I wanted to.

With Jodie, I'd always, *always*, known I had limits, sensible ones. Even when I'd doubted myself, I think I'd known. The only time I really lost it was when I was overcome by a new situation, by the prospect of Kat putting that needle through her nipple and of seeing blood. Blood made me a bit nuts.

I stopped outside the locked door to the room and adjusted myself, gripped my cock through my pants for a minute. *Behave, you bastard.*

This time, it was so purposeful. I wasn't overcome by anything, but I knew that although I would and could restrain myself, I would also go much further than my toy in there expected or wanted. And, no matter what she said or did, I wasn't stopping. That was the difference. Big, huge, fucking difference.

My heart was racing.

"Zen, man. Zone in. Get your shit together." I reassembled that iron control, unlocked the door, and stepped in.

There she was. Hogtied, on her side, on the mattress. Naked, of course. A woman who was all mine to play with. I'd discussed it with

Jodie. That had been my last hurdle. Because she and I had limits. With Steph, the limits were mine to decide.

I walked to her and kneeled in front of her, placed my hand on her shoulder. Her bones underneath were so small compared to a man's.

"Scared, Stephanie?"

After blinking slowly at me, she nodded the tiniest amount.

"Good."

Then, despite her whimpers, I slowly ran my hands over every inch of her body—through her silky black hair, down her front to her breasts, around them, down over her belly, and between her legs, where I was amused to find her wet, but then women's bodies often automatically responded to tactile stimulation that way, whether they wanted to or not.

"You're mine now," I told her matter-of-factly, as I appraised her legs and ankles. I rolled her onto her stomach and undid the hogtie clips. She was still bound but only wrist to wrist and ankle to ankle. I massaged from her thighs to her buttocks. I squeezed her ass and felt my way up her back, scraping my calloused hands against her tender skin and hearing her gasps. I caressed the indentation of her spine, marveling. Even women's backs were amazing.

"I'm *not* yours." Her answer was quiet and tremulous.

Such bravery in the face of overwhelming superiority.

I stopped with my palm pressing her upper back down onto the mattress. Enough pressure that she could feel my strength, enough so that she tensed then, since I didn't relent, she gave in, her head lowering, her body quivering. Was she a true submissive? I was fairly certain she was.

"You're pretty, beautiful even. Desirable. Fuckable. I scare you because I like pain more than you can comprehend. I'm not going to kill you. I'm not going to carve off your flesh and eat it. But, little toy, I am going to hurt you more than you think you can take."

She froze in the middle of inhaling. I smiled and grasped a big handful of those dark locks just above her nape. I levered her head back until she was arched and her breasts were no longer concealed beneath her. So I took one in the grip of my other hand. "Mine," I whispered. "You're mine whether you fucking want to be or not."

I squeezed both her breast and the fistful of hair, and I leaned down to look into her fear-darkened eyes.

"You need to learn not to be afraid of pain," I murmured. "And you know why?"

She swallowed and I felt her endeavor to shake her head. Long strands of her hair fell across her face.

"If you lose that fear of pain, you will lose some of your fear of me. Not all, some. I'm not your nemesis, girl, I'm just going to be your master."

Steph was a person, not a thing, and I'd not forget that. Yet, in an amused way, I regarded this as the inspection a horse buyer might make after a purchase, to not only recheck the mount but also to get the mount used to the new owner. Smell, touch, sight, and now, last of all, taste.

I released her breast, put one finger into her mouth, only to find her teeth together. "Open."

When she didn't move, I smiled. "Open, girl. Open or I start my experimenting early. You will not like that."

She opened and I slid my forefinger in and played with her tongue, the edge of her teeth, the roof of her mouth.

"Taste that. It's you, your cunt juices and the taste of my skin. From now on, whenever I say to, you open your mouth, you spread your legs, or you present your breasts to me by cupping them and holding them up. If you disobey, I will punish you. If you're too slow, I will punish you. If there is a smidgeon of a possibility that you did something wrong, I will punish you."

And that last, was so very wrong, but I loved the idea. Punishment that wasn't quite earned? Bad. But it felt so good merely to threaten her with that.

Then I removed my finger from her mouth and I sucked the tip.

"That's the first time I've tasted you, pretty thing. Now we're even. And now…" I bent and picked her up, laying her over my shoulder and standing. "I will explain some more." I hefted her into a better spot. "Everything else that I missed explaining. Which is a lot." I moved over to the spanking bench and put her on it stomach down. Though her upper body lay on the padding, she was bent at the waist and her feet touched the floor. I unclipped her ankles from each other and used the bench straps to fasten her ankles to each leg of the bench—leaving her thighs spread apart just enough for access.

I eyed her. Access meaning I could see all of her sex—finger her, fuck her, whatever I wished.

I could. But I wasn't doing this just for instant gratification. Delayed gratification then? I was going to fuck her eventually. I'd vowed to Jodie that she was the only woman for me, until she had fallen in love, or lust, with this one. That had made Steph a special exemption. And what an incredible exemption she was. Jodie had good taste.

"What are you doing?"

"At last, you speak? I'm making sure you can't move too much."

"Why."

"You'll see."

I undid the wrist clips then went to draw her hands down to fasten them at the front. She yanked away from me then but I caught her wrists, held them at her back.

"Stop struggling." When she kept it up, I transferred both wrists to my left hand and smacked her sharply twice on the ass, far harder than I'd done before. "Stop!"

She yelped but stopped and I couldn't help smiling. "Thank you. Now you have a nice handprint coming up on your butt." I had a thing about marks. I bent and kissed her there, right over the blush of the mark, breathed in, and bit her hard.

Steph squealed indignantly but I ignored it and managed to fasten first one wrist, and then the other, to the front legs of the bench. "Oh, I'm going to have fun with you, baby." I stepped back and folded my arms, waiting for her to turn her head. Even now she managed to glare at me.

"Jodie would never agree to this!"

"*Tsk. Tsk.* She has. She knows me, and knows what I mean to do to you. This is how it is, toy. You may think this is some random punishment, but it's not. You betrayed us, but in particular, you betrayed Jodie. Right now, you don't deserve to be near her. And you won't be, not until I think that you are worthy. Understand? I am the judge of your behavior. Answer me."

She licked her lips. "Okay. I don't have much choice."

"No. You don't. You really, really don't." I surveyed her body, strapped down, waiting for something to be done to it, and clenched my fists. "Except…"

How to say this? But I needed to. I needed to explain to her.

"When I'm done with you, we will let you go. Either we leave you behind and we leave Australia…" I could see her interest perk up. "Or we set you up in another country. I can pay you well, for the rest of your life, or mine anyway, but I have to be able to trust you, absolutely. Right now, I can't."

I took her chin in my hand and made certain she looked in my eyes. "Want to not to have to worry about earning a living, Steph?"

"I…guess?" She shut her eyes. "But this isn't about that. If you hurt me, I won't play along."

"No? You think? If you want to be well off, you first have to pay a price. Let me see your darkest thoughts, your deepest desires. I want the very worst of you as well as the very best. Guess what, little fucktoy?" I swept aside the long drapes of her hair that covered her face and I kissed her hard on her mouth. "You have to prove it. You want it, you show you're mine. And then, you show me you're also Jodie's."

"You're crazy," she whispered. "That won't convince me."

"You haven't figured this at all. It's me that *you* need to convince." I went to the toybox, unlocked it and pulled out something I hadn't yet used. A sheath with a small blue-steel knife.

"What's that? What are you doing? Do *not* come near me with that."

"This is the start of your lesson about fear. A K has three strokes to it. I'm going to cut the backbone of it on your ass today. When I think you're ready, I'm going to ask you if *you* will allow me to cut the next stroke, and then the next. You get Jodie back after the second is carved into you. Notice I said carved? I'm doing that to try to scare you more. Words are like that."

"Fuck. It's working then. Shut up with the carving!" She wrenched at the cuffs then said quietly but urgently. "Let me go!"

"I won't do more than cut a short line, an inch or so long. Remember, it's all in your mind." And in my balls, which were aching at the prospect of doing this on her pretty little ass. What I said was true, and yet also, I craved this.

There was a strap that would sit just above her butt and hold her still even more. So I fastened that on too, cinched it in.

"Do you want me to just let you go in a few days, let the cops deal with you? If you say no to the next cut, that's what will happen. You haven't forgotten that you'd be up on charges have you? Sexual assault as well as charges to do with helping administer a drug to someone for the possible purpose of rape. Don't shake your head, girl. That's what the cops will argue. Accessory to manslaughter too, probably.

At that she stilled. "Noo," she breathed, with a faint whine in her voice.

I bent and stared at her face. "Then be still. Understand your situation. You cannot go back to your old life. No one will see you as innocent because you're not."

She merely blinked, watery eyed.

"This will be quick. Show me you have strength. Be good for me. In a few days, a week, whatever, ask for the next stroke of the letter if I say you're ready." I straightened. "After this, Miss Fucktoy, I'm going to give you pain, and I'm going to make you come harder than you ever have before. I'm going to start you on a path that will let you swallow up pain when you have to."

"Oh shit. No. No." She shook her head vigorously. "No."

"This though. No choice." I unsheathed the knife. With my fingernail, I traced a small line at the side of her ass. "Here. This is where." I held up the small knife for her to see. "It won't go deep. Just enough to draw blood. Now, be silent. If you scream I will gag you. Understand?"

At that she again tried to writhe in the straps but eventually gave up and stared back at me, panting.

"That was an order," I murmured. "Say you understood or I will punish you."

After turning her head so she was face first in the padding, she replied, with a sob, "Yes, I understand."

"Sir. You call me Sir from now on, and when you see her, you call Jodie, Ma'am."

"You are a…" She sighed. But when my hand touched her skin, she shivered. "Yes, Sir."

Triumph reared up, bright and burning. I poised the knife on her, above her ass cheek. "Now."

I'd said it would be fast. I lied. I made it last, all ten or fifteen seconds of it. With the tip, I scored her skin to the length of an inch, over and over, and made it bleed. She screeched then keened a little. The tiny drops welled up like water from a slow spring. Fresh and red on her paleness. Truthfully, I'd exaggerated. This was a bit of a mindfuck. I'd scratched her repeatedly rather than truly cut.

I touched the red line with my finger, exulting, and drawing it across her skin as if it were paint. *It's my kink. That's all.*

I put my fingers either side of the scratch making a clawed cage, and squeezed. So tempting.

After all that, I still took for granted that she would resist, so I reversed what I'd done carefully, securing her wrists and ankles together before I picked her up. Tie her down on top of the mattress or…

I swung, eyed the overhead chain and ring. Yes, that gave me ideas.

With her hands at her back and her feet together also, she might overbalance while I fiddled with ropes. I needed to start getting her accustomed to obeying me. So I put her on her feet beneath the dangling ring, undid her ankles, then took hold of one elbow and the back of her neck. Neck holds made Jodie passive. Even in the animal world they were such a key part of dominance and they worked with women too.

"You've seen me cane Jodie hard." I shook her neck a little. "Answer."

"Yes."

"Take care to obey me then, the cane is my first resort if you disobey. What I do next won't leave you with many bruises, if any. But, if I have to use the cane, you will have severe bruises. Understood?"

"Yes." Her inhalation was shaky.

"Good. Stay here, do not walk away. Do not sit down."

"But…" Her lip trembled. "I'm scared."

Those words triggered something.

Empathy rushed back in. Instead of a victim of my sadistic desires, I saw Stephanie. A person. A human being. I still wanted to do what I intended to, but the need to reassure her tussled with that, and won. And truly, I didn't mind. It was a relief, of sorts, to do this. It made some of my humanity leak back in.

I squeezed her arm. "What I've done so far was punishment. From now on, though there will be pain, you will enjoy it. You will look back and perhaps wonder why you feared so much." Then I bent and kissed her gently until most of the tremors died away, and I rested my cheek on hers. With my mouth beside her ear, I murmured, "Have you ever had a lover who has devoted themselves to you, Stephanie?"

After a moment, her cautious reply came. "No, I guess not."

"I'm going to devote myself to what will come. I'm going to watch you and the signals that betray you." I shifted my hold on her neck, tightening it a little, and feeling the bump of her carotid pulse against the *V* of my fingers and thumb. "Your every move, your every breath, every flinch of your body, every sigh you make, every cry as you climax, every gasp. I'm going to try to know you as deeply as any man can know a woman. You *will* enjoy this."

I wasn't God but I knew I could make this come true.

Since she'd calmed, I gave her hair one last stroke and I reached up and grabbed the ring. Ever so matter of factly, I unlinked her wrists, pulled them up, and attached them to it above her head. As I walked to the wall to haul the rope in tighter, she cleared her throat then asked me a question that she obviously, desperately, wanted an answer to.

"So, you're not going to hurt me?"

Of course, I didn't answer.

I pulled, watching as her arms were drawn upward. When high enough, but with enough slackness left to allow me to move her legs apart, I tied off the rope at the wall ring.

Not replying to her question had fed tension into the room. She watched nervously as I walked to her, crouched behind, and tapped the inside of her leg.

"Spread your legs."

"What? Um." Her swallow was loud. "Well?" But she moved her legs enough that I could link them, a shoulder-width apart, to the rings that popped up from recesses in the floor. "Please answer me... Sir."

I pulled off my shirt and tossed it so it fell near the wall. For this, I wanted my skin against hers.

As I rose, I shaped my hands to the sides of her body, marveling in the softness of her shape, in the beautiful structure of this woman who I got to touch, and finishing with my palms curved beneath her breasts. I fitted my body to hers.

"You're beautiful, Miss Fucktoy. Now I'll answer you. Yes, I'm going to hurt you."

She shuddered. "But...you'll stop if I scream?" She seemed to reconsider. "Or if I scream a lot?"

I replied in a slow and careful tone. "No. I am not going to stop if you scream because that's what *I* enjoy. I like hearing you scream, giving you pain. But I also enjoy seeing a woman getting hot..."

"No, no, don't. Please don't. I don't want to be hurt. I don't—"

"*Shh.*" I kissed her neck while I searched for and found her nipples, then I pinched them lightly between finger and thumb, rolling them, tugging, making them peak. "I love seeing a woman want to come...a woman climaxing." I bit her neck. It was fascinating to see her yelp yet keep her mouth open and push her chest toward my touch.

My cock throbbed at the prospect of what I was describing and at the responses she already showed. "You're such a gorgeous victim. I'm going to do all that to you, Stephanie. Until you're fucking limp and exhausted and you hurt all over, and your throat is sore from screaming, and between your legs is sore from me fucking you. And you're going to thank me afterward."

"Shit. No, I'm not." She breathed raggedly. "I'm really *fucking* not."

Then I squeezed her nipples harder, until she was both squeaking and cursing me over and over.

"Let's find out, who is wrong."

I began my massage. I covered every inch of her from her toes to her neck to her bottom. Pressing my fingers deep into muscles. Concentrating on the erogenous zones when I came near them, pressing in areas of her butt, squashing, swirling my hands across, and moving on. By the time I moved around to her front she was moaning a little. This time I travelled downward, to her breasts, her belly, her mons, her inner thighs, her toes. Then back to her mons again where I ran two fingers deeply up and down her cleft without quite entering her.

Her toes scrunched in, her legs strained alternatively to both crush in on my hand and to back away. Every muscle in her body became involved in either her futile attempts to dodge my touch, or her striving to get closer. Each time I did that sweep of my fingers across her entrance, air huffed in and out of her lips and her eyelids fluttered.

"You're so sensitive. Aroused so easily." I smiled, lingering near her clit with two fingers in a *V* on either side and pressing in enough to let her feel it.

"Fuck you, Sir."

"You will. I promise."

She glared.

"But I'm in no hurry. I can do this all day." My fingers did a dance around, beside, up and down, but not on, her now very engorged clit. "I plan to do all sorts of things to you here. But I'm not putting anything inside you now, except for a butt plug."

So lost was she in the sensations that it took a few seconds before her eyes popped open.

"Yes, I'm going to fuck you there, today."

That she didn't bother to answer was curious. When I returned to her with the lubed plug, I didn't show her the size. I simply went around to the back of her and found the place, and probed. Slowly as I pushed, it entered her anus further and though she protested, it went in more and more. My other hand played with her clitoris. "You're so slippery. I can tell Jodie has gotten you used to this. Your little asshole is letting me push this in so easily."

With a last firm press, the plug slid all the way in. Steph dropped her head and trembled a moment. "Done—" Fuck. I'd almost called her gorgeous. That name was Jodie's. I gave the plug a last teasing tug to make sure it was seated properly, and stepped back. "Now, for some pain."

For an appetizer, I smacked her lightly, her thighs, her bottom, her breasts, then I moved on. I used a flogger with many, stingy, falls, also lightly, but I worked up a sweat, layering her body everywhere it was safe. Pink decorated her in many shades. The marks drew my eye. I pulled out a heavier flogger and worked her over harder, letting my muscles get serious. By the end of that she was hissing, screaming, and swearing at me too much, trying to stamp her feet even, so I gagged her. Only a ball gag, but it looked pretty between her lips.

Though we had a mains rechargeable wand that Jodie adored, I wanted to keep this personal, so every minute or so, I stepped in and played with her sexually. Nipples, clit, her whole mons area even, moving her flesh there with my palm shaped to her. I mixed in the pleasure enough to keep her arousal humming.

Then I stepped up away again and played with pain. Soon much of her was a delicious pink, including her pussy. The flogger when aimed there drew a shudder and a series of moans. I drank, gave her water, and began again. When she climaxed before I wanted her to, I chastised her with words and with a few strokes of the cane across her thighs that made her shriek.

"Lesson learned?" I asked, before I went back to work.

Flogger, play with her cunt, almost finger fuck her, but don't. She started sobbing and moaning to the tune of the flogger as well as to my fondling of her breasts or her clit. At last. Even her breasts seemed more engorged, bigger handfuls. When I sucked on her nipples at the same time as my hand caressed up and down in the liquid between her thighs, her hands formed into fists, and her spine arched so hard I wasn't sure it was safe. I removed the ball gag.

"Would you like my mouth on you down here? My tongue on your pussy?" I asked her, but she only panted at me. Mindless perhaps. Overcome by pleasure? Or did she still half-resent my appropriation of her body? I didn't ask.

"You may come from now on."

Her first orgasm wracked her so thoroughly the full body shudders made the ropes and metal links attaching her creak and clatter from the strain.

"Beautiful," I told her yet again as I admired the shine of sweat on her torso and breasts and the front of her strong thighs. I began the cycle. Pleasure, pain, and I watched her come, over and over.

I no longer needed to search for her clit. It stood out proud like a tiny pink beacon for my instruments—for my hands and whatever else I used, including some milder thuds of the flogger.

I flailed at her some more, stepped up close. Foggy eyed, she pushed her groin toward my hand as I moved it in from inches away. A trained response, already? I smiled.

More pain. Red blossomed from the pink. A little more, a little more time, more violence and I would have her *there*. Could I make her come while in pain? Even if she wasn't a masochist?

The dance of her body even while restrained enthralled me. The play of the leather, the smack of it on her skin, and the way the pain made her react. Even, most of all, the fact that she couldn't escape. Time for pleasure, a voice told me. I kept going even, determined to find my answer. Would she come? Or not?

It wasn't until she began to sag in the ropes that I stopped.

With the back of my forearm, I wiped the sweat from my face then held up her head with a hand under her wet chin. "The drool becomes you." The fire that generated in her eyes shook me.

I'd lost myself there, been carried away. I blinked sweat from my eyes, and lowered the flogger then dropped it to the floor. I made a note to myself—delivering pain to Steph without limits messed up my restraint.

Payback time. I let her drink until I saw her mind return. I went to my knees. Oral was a favorite of mine. Jodie understood that. Though vibes had their place.

"Don't come," I told her, gazing up at her looking down at me, flushed and weary, through the tendrils of her hair. "You know what will happen if you do."

"Bastard," she croaked.

I stared. Ah, a flinch. I squeezed a handful of her abused bottom until she whined.

Then with tongue and sucking and some biting, because teeth were a good way to take off the edge if she was close, I brought her to the edge. When it seemed her O was a single flick of my tongue away, I let her down again. She breathed fast as if about to ignite, her thighs quivering under my palms.

I pulled her thighs toward me and gave her one last probe with my tongue, for the first time pushing into her entrance. With my nose buried, I strained forward, going deep. The whine from her reminded me to give the butt plug some little tugs and shoves. I fucked her with my tongue some more before rising to my feet.

I wiped my mouth, and again let her drink some water—myself also. Then I turned on my heel, dragged in a chair from outside, and I sat down to look. At her. At the most delightful subject of my attention apart from Jodie, ever.

I was so fucked in the head. I loved this. And I wondered who I was. I'd thought I was a pillar of society. But now, I knew I was a thousand miles from that. And I wasn't sure I cared anymore. My empathy waxed and waned with the tides of my sadistic desires.

Like a little conquered animal she peered out at me now and then, through the swaying cage of her hair—for it hung across her face and stuck to her sweaty shoulders. Most of her skin was a warm palette of pink and red blotches and stripes. Her arousal shone on her inner thighs and she hadn't consented to any of this. And I knew exactly what I wanted to do next to her. And why I shouldn't. I'd finally cracked apart some of my own reasons, and it shocked me.

I'd been lying to myself. I did *not* have to do this. The extra intensity of having an unwilling captive who I could make enjoy this, it sucked me in, relentlessly. I thought I'd fallen when I'd first discovered the intimate choreography of sadomasochism and dominance with Jodie. Wrong. That was a spit of rain, the tug of the wind. This…I drew in a ragged breath while I stared at her hanging in the ropes…this was the hurricane.

A sensible man would not go this route. If anything forcing sex and pain on her might trigger the opposite reaction to what I wanted. And, instead of merely involuntary manslaughter, I would now be up for far more serious charges if ever brought to court. She might hate us so utterly we had no hope of success. Yet Jodie had agreed to all this. It begged the question—did she have the same kink as I?

With head in hands I sat just looking at her and thinking. Finally I stood, shoving back the chair, I strode to her, though I stopped on the way to get a condom and a sachet of lube from the pile of my clothes. She watched warily, but I freed her then. I released all the cuffs and I carried her to the wall.

I needed to know where I was with her. Had I gone too far?

"Put your hands to the wall," I grated out. "Lean in but keep your ass out where I can fuck you easily."

Would she do this? Yes, she did. Greedily, triumph burning in my veins, I inhaled through my teeth.

I ripped the packet, rolled on the condom. Then after carefully extracting the plug, I lubed up my cock and her ass.

"What are you doing?" she whispered.

I pulled her head around. "What do you think?" She knew, of course. All she did was blink at me. "I'll be gentle. I know you're not used to this." I released her and pressed my cock to her there; feeling the tiny circle of muscle widen, I pushed some more. Her heat slowly swallowed me, squeezing my head, tight.

Mouth opening wide, I took some hard breaths.

The test, remember? I had to stop, didn't I? I touched her clit, slowly bringing her into the headspace of an orgasm, getting the rhythm going while I barely rocked in and out of her by a fraction. And she let me in, a little more each time. Her fingers on the wall clenched in like claws, her back bowed toward me.

Then I stopped moving, everything, though every muscle, every screaming atom of me, wanted to spear into her all the way to my balls.

"Stephanie. You have to choose. Now. I've changed my mind. I'm not deciding in a few days, not on the basis of whether I scratch my letter on your ass, not on anything but what I ask you next. I want you to think." I sank my teeth into the natural place for a man's teeth—the angle on a woman's neck where it curved into shoulder. I hung on until she groaned and whimpered and her anus contracted strongly on my cock.

The rest of my words I rasped out with my lips brushing the lobe of her ear. I breathed my words into her, and I prayed.

"Your choice. If you want me to fuck you here, in your ass, if you want to be our little fucktoy, to be taken whenever we want you, however I want to, until the day we free you…if you want that, stay here, with me. If not, walk away, now."

Then I waited, partly inside her, blood thumping so urgently through me I was in danger of erupting any second. I wanted to fuck her hard against the wall, but I also needed her answer.

She didn't move or speak. Afraid to? Or not sure? If that…damn…yeah that was so significant.

I wrapped my forearms around her below her breasts, squashing them in, making her feel how easily I could subdue her, if I wanted to.

"Ours, or not? Are you my naughty little fucktoy, or not? Slide back onto my cock, and you're mine, girl. Or walk. Which?"

"I…" She heaved in more air, and her throat moved in a swallow. A bead of sweat dribbled down the side of her face into the strands of hair sticking to her cheek.

*Yeah. I've done this because I wanted to. I wanted to take her and hurt her and I really don't know if I can let her go. But if she says no, I'll try. I will fucking try.*

As I held her to me, I could feel her heart thudding and hear the harsh in and out of her breath. I could smell her sweat, feel her pain, and with my cock impaling her, I couldn't stop wanting her.

"Decide." I shifted my hips forward a minute amount and smiled at her gasp of pleasure.

# Chapter 18

## Stephanie

The most poorly timed question *ever*. I could barely think with him inside me like that. The ache to come was overwhelming. The need to have him finish fucking me there, to have him come inside me in that dirtiest of places, it trampled on all rational thought. I groaned as he moved the tiniest amount, exquisitely aware of how my body gripped him, of his cock tunneling in.

"Fuck," I whispered. My legs shook, my arms shook and would not be holding me away from the wall if his arms weren't barred across my front. As it was I had my sticky forehead leaning on the hard cold surface as well as my poor flogged, bitten and abused nipples.

I was a mess of sweat and a weary woman. From the juices dripping from me and slicking my thighs, I must look like a whore done over by a football team.

But it was just him.

*Stupid. Walk away. He's said it. I can walk. Surely this is the bad alternative?*

"Well, Steph. Walk? Or stay." Then, contrary to his words, he began going in and out more and more to the timing of his speech. "Walk or stay?

"Stop." I gasped.

"In. Out," he murmured, and I felt him chuckle. "Can't decide?"

"Bastard. Bastard. Bastard." And then maybe, just maybe, I pushed back, the most minute amount. I felt the pulse of his cock. Felt the imminent burn. Felt the weight of his hard muscles pressing on me, pinning me, keeping me his.

Would he even let me go? It seemed not. The way he held me like I was the most precious thing ever, and wanted, threw me in the deep end. I was drowning, and didn't have the faintest idea how to rescue myself.

"You moved, didn't you."

Rhetorical fucking question. I tried to shake my head but he kissed my hair.

"Bad girl. I'm done waiting. Clearly you're staying." And at the last word he thrust deeper, further, all the way, parting me easily. "I'm fucking this little almost pristine ass, all the way…in."

A last thrust and I was shoved to the wall, my breasts flattened. I had to turn my face sideways to get air.

Klaus withdrew almost to the tip then shoved back into me. Pleasure flared with a tinge of burning pain when I was stretched just a bit too far.

"Unnh." My tongue seemed stuck to the roof of my mouth. He plowed in and out of me like a piston, stroking my clit with his free hand, making me *want* his next drive inward, making me throb and moan quietly as another climax built then spilled through me, roaring in my ears, tumbling my thoughts, fast and hot as a fire.

My eyes rolled back. I let him take me as he willed after that. I curled up my hands, letting them slide on the wall as the force he used thumped me into it, over and over. Too exhausted to fight, or to move, or do more than be his fucktoy. He was right. I'd never had a lover like this. When he came, I smiled a small smile, but I knew he couldn't see it.

He was done, and panting in my ear, the bristles of his poorly shaven face scraping my neck and cheek. More hurts. My whole body throbbed in unison with my blood. When he released me, withdrawing slickly, I sagged then slid a small distance down the wall until he caught me. He let me down the rest of the way carefully.

"I'll be back. I have to go clean up."

True to his word, he was back soon. Huddled there, I hadn't counted seconds. Besides, everything was a warm buzz. He carried me to the mattress then lay down behind me, cuddling in. That woke me. Klaus cuddling? Spooning?

"What the—" I slurred.

"Rest. I'm staying for a while. You can shower and I'll get you food and check the damage I did, after you rest."

"S'okay." I muttered, eyelids closing, brain shutting down fast. Black rolled in and smothered me in sleep.

When I awoke, I found that Klaus had turned me onto my stomach. I half-rolled to look over my shoulder and found him staring.

"Marks," he explained, tracing a finger so lightly over my butt that it tickled and made me shiver. "I like them."

"Oh." I shrugged.

"Okay, shower time." He put out his hand and helped me up. At some time, he'd pulled his pants back on.

The gentlemanly behavior had me puzzled, but the look he raked over my front made me cover my breasts.

"No. Hands down. I've seen all of you already, anyway." Though said softly, I knew there'd be consequences if I disobeyed.

There wasn't much point in hiding, so I lowered my hands.

"Good. Just so you don't forget, they're mine, girl." He nodded. "Put your hands under them. Hold them up for me."

Hell no. This was so foreign, so odd. Nudged by a sudden shyness, I ducked my head. I should look up. Chicken. This was totally the wrong cue to give him. I may as well roll over and whine.

"You're going to do it, Steph. Get used to this. You had two choices and you chose this one, staying and being mine, and when I allow it, being Jodie's also." With his fingers underneath, he made me raise my chin. "Look at me."

Slowly I did, uncomfortable meeting his eyes, and aware of my femaleness, of my nakedness, for the first time in ages. I'd forgotten, hanging there, tied up, I'd just been *me* for what seemed hours. The things he'd done to me...

"Shy, suddenly?" He cocked an eyebrow. "I like that. Hold your breasts up for me, unless you want me to crop them."

*Shit.*

And so, though my face heated as I did it, I cupped my breasts, and raised them a little. The tiny quirk of his lips and the blatant way he studied me, brought heat back to my groin. I was naked, and my clit was swelling.

"How does it make you feel, doing this for me? Before you answer, I have to say you have great tits. I like them heavy and yours are perfect."

I curled my toes and tried to stay calm, or calmer. Sex was a constant preoccupation around Klaus. The man had me programmed like a push-button doll. I fumbled for something to say.

"Do you feel aroused?" When I still didn't answer he covered my palms with his own. Every place on the skin of my breasts where his fingers slipped between my own, where his skin touched mine, I knew.

*Answer him.* "I feel...that, yes." True, of course. Nothing like a man making me hold up a part of me that's a major sexual part to get me hot and bothered. Obvious. Both of us holding my breasts at once. I resisted squirming.

"I thought so." His eyes spoke of mischief. He bent at the waist and kissed and lightly sucked on each nipple.

"Oh God," I whispered, melting at the flood of warmth tingling through me.

Smiling, he straightened, putting his hand on my shoulder. "Let's go have that shower. Then I'll massage some ointment into you. I'll keep my hands off you until then."

"Huh."

On the way past the tiny bathroom mirror, I caught sight of my back and ass and I stopped to check. *Ow.* Twisting my body had reminded me of the stiffness in my muscles. Like him, I had a curiosity about the marks. A little scared, a lot curious. But it wasn't the bruises that grabbed me, it was where he'd begun to do the *K*. Because there was a full letter *K* there, red and drawn in thin blood.

Only he could have done that. I wasn't sure why, since he'd done so much that freaked me out, but seeing that had sent a streak of cold down my back – resonating like a violin playing in the darkness in a B-grade horror movie.

He'd said Jodie knew what he was doing and I guess I accepted that. She wasn't someone who would lie down and let him do this if she disagreed...I thought. I could be wrong. Hell, I didn't really understand their relationship. I would never have thought she'd help someone kidnap me, but then, we were all in outer space with this. It was way beyond normal.

I didn't know anything for sure, except that I wanted her to be my girlfriend, and I'd done something she regarded as so awful that she'd, probably, consented to *Him* doing this to me. Drawing letters in blood, fucking me in this room down here after beating me. I was lost. I'd betrayed her. Maybe this was karma, my penance for being a fool.

I wish I could take back what I'd done to her.

I shook off my unease and my stupid guilt. Least a shower was ordinary. Except that he joined me.

Having a naked man built like Klaus sharing my shower...I'd probably have paid someone a fortune for this...before, if I'd had the courage.

I barely resisted reaching out and caressing his biceps. I didn't know too many guys whose muscles shone when wet because they were so ripped. He was handsome too. The short sandy-blond hair reminded me of surfers who spent days in the sun. His shoulders were bulked out just enough to look biteable, his thighs were heavy and with enough hair to say all man, his dick was on its way up...god. I was staring like a lovestruck fan.

I think he guessed.

Despite his declaration about no hands, he took stock for a few seconds then grumbled, muttered *fuck*, shoved me backward, and kissed me thoroughly. His favorite seemed pinning me to the wall while he fondled me. I breathed through it, attempting to recover some brain cells.

"What if..." I began to ask him. My wrists remained fastened to the white tiles above my head, gripped by his hand. My lips seemed swollen. But I was feeling feisty again.

Though he held me, I could see the power I possessed. I might have the man in the palm of my hand if I played my sexual cards right. "What if I said now, that I want to walk?"

He smirked down at me. "Too late. I wouldn't let you."

What the fuck? This was scary.

"But, you have to! You said—"

"That you had a choice? That was then. This is now. You can't go until I free you, little fucktoy."

"That's not an endearment!" I spat.

He gripped my throat. "It will be. One day. Speak to me again like that and I'll put you over my knee, sore ass or not."

I sucked in my bottom lip, reconsidering my rebellion.

"Apologize, properly."

"I'm, I'm sorry." I shut my eyes. "Sir."

"Look at me."

I did, and found myself mesmerized by the gray of his eyes. "I'm sorry, Sir."

"Good fucktoy."

Damn him. I shook. From fear, outrage, the aftereffects of being so amped up for so long? Who knew?

Finally, I stopped shaking. "I need to know something."

"What?"

"Why are you doing this?" Before he could answer I rattled out the thoughts I'd just assembled. "You don't need to. You don't need to beat me or tie me up, or..." My voice lowered. "Or have sex with me. You should have just sat down and said, let's be friends. Maybe that would have worked." I blinked away a stupid tear.

"Oh? But then I wouldn't have so much fun, and I'd not be so certain about you. I'm not sure simply friends is enough to tell if someone will betray us to the cops. But a fucktoy…believe it or not, that's a firm bond, once you know your place." He stroked my belly. "I love women's belly buttons.

"There's the truth and truth is a good place to start a relationship. That goes both ways. Remember that I expect you to be truthful also." Gently, he ran his finger through the water trickling down me.

"I did it this way because I wanted to. I like making you suffer. I like making you scream from orgasms as well as pain. I like fucking you." His eyes turned mean and implacable—a stone god, preaching to his subject. "I like you at my feet and under my hand."

*Christ.*

"But you're going to let me go, afterward." I said it firmly, made that not a question.

The pause worried me.

While he swirled his finger round and round in my navel, he let his gaze take in my body from my face to my pussy. His hand above, pinning my wrists, was hard. "I don't know. You wanted the truth? That's it."

This revelation floored me. "You can't…you can't do that."

"Maybe not, but I like to dream of possible. See, that's how much I like you and I like this." His grip tightened, hurting. "I like having you. Owning you."

"You have Jodie." I strained against his grip, pushing outward and getting precisely nowhere. "You said truth was important! You said you'd let me go."

"I would have, then. Seems I have this little quirk. Just that once, I needed to see that you liked this situation enough to not walk away. But now I know what's deep down inside *there*, Steph." With the forefinger of his free hand, he pressed on the center of my forehead.

"I know, and that's enough. Protesting now..." He shrugged. "It adds to the spice."

"It does?" I said weakly.

"Yes, sweetheart, it does."

Then he freed me. I stood there underneath the warm running water, rubbing my wrists, and wondering what in hell I'd gotten myself into.

Criminal charges? The differences were astounding. Who wouldn't rather be charged with whatever the fuck it was that I'd done, maybe sent to jail a while, compared to this madness? I shut my eyes, ignoring him for once, while I rallied my bedraggled mind.

"Turn around, girl," he said quietly, and with his hands on my hips he encouraged me. "I'll soap you up."

He ran his hands and the soap over me, everywhere. Though it stung in a few spots, like where the K was cut, and my thighs, back, and arms ached from bruises and sore muscles, I became aroused again. I couldn't help it. I shut my eyes and let him play with my body, remembering Jodie doing the same.

I moaned when he spread my legs and roughly soaped my pussy. My traitorous mind whispered to me, *who wouldn't rather have this than be in jail?*

*****

Over the next week, he trained me...I guess I had to use that word. *Trained.* I associated that with dogs and pets, but it was the best word to describe what he did. I knew what he was doing and why and even knew why all the praise and the pain and the possessive ways he touched me should be ignored as the underhanded actions that they were. Negative reinforcement. Positive reinforcement. I was a self-aware Pavlov's dog.

It was clear as glass to me. I understood all the whys and yet I still began crave his approval and his touch, to dread earning a punishment. I wasn't dumb. I'd passed most of my exams at university. I just couldn't be bothered devoting myself to finishing something in which I'd lost interest.

Maybe that was why this worked so well? Dead simple. No choice of subjects. No distractions from the path. I did this, or else. Instead of the crazy clutter of life, I knew my purpose. The only thing I lacked and could not have was diversity. I wanted out to see the world. To feel the sun on my face. I wanted to be able to race down a riverbank and plunge into the water. I wanted more than life in a room.

One day, he let me out.

The door clicked as it unlocked. Quickly, I knelt. That was my first task when he entered a room. I'd put on the little red dress with the overlaid red lace and no underwear that morning. The hem came to slightly above the crease of my ass. A deliberate length, of course. No matter how I tugged on it, the very edge of the lips of my pussy were visible, even more so when I knelt with my forearms flat on the floor. I'd checked in the mirror by bending over and looking back at my reflection. It had both annoyed me when I'd first tried one of these dresses on, and made me imagine him looking, and touching…

Which is what he did this morning after circling behind me and standing there a while.

"Good girl." I heard the scuffle of his shoes, and the soft noise of cloth on cloth as he crouched. Then his voice, closer, a few feet back. I kept my forehead down. I'd felt the cane enough to know I'd rather display myself and be admired, than be punished.

I was already anticipating what he might do, already wet, and so his finger entering me only made me choke momentarily then moan. I wiggled and his finger slid deeper then in and out a few times.

"You realize how wet you get for me now?"

He waited. Expecting an answer? As if I'd admit that out loud. I would *not* say that.

I grunted, tensing in case he decided that was an insult, but he only laughed.

"Poor thing. You'd go down on Jodie when she's unconscious…"

Oh fuck, I tensed more.

"But you won't say how aroused thinking about me touching you makes you? I know that's what it is." Propping one hand on the floor, he leaned over my back. So close. The heat of his body warmed mine. "I find that amusing. A week ago, I can guarantee you'd not have reacted like this. I can see your moisture down there. That's how excited you are. Answer. Why do you think that's changed? Hmm?"

He jammed his finger up as far as it would go then shook me side to side using it, like I was a popsicle on a stick. "Why?"

Saying this out loud bothered me. Even more so when he was forcing a digit into me, and finger fucking me. I said my answer softly. Maybe hoping he wouldn't hear? I had no idea except this mortified me. "Because you're always touching me when I'm kneeling like this, Sir."

"That's it? Tell me more. What else do I do?"

*Crap.* "You put your fingers inside me."

"And I make you come."

"Yes, Sir," I whispered.

After his finger left me, I felt metal tinkle, and he clicked a chain to my collar. A few times he'd used the collar to tie me to something, but this was the first time for a while that he'd attached a leash.

"Rise," he ordered and I obeyed. "We're going outside. The back yard. Our one neighbor is down a drop off to the left. Do not talk too loudly or I will be forced to gag you. Your wrists will stay cuffed and linked." He attended to that. "But you can walk with your legs unlinked. I trust you that much."

I'd never visited their house before and only had a vague idea as to where it was. The beach must be near—I'd heard gulls crying and smelled the sea. From the kitchen window I'd even seen the waves rolling in. Trepidation made every movement like walking on fractured glass. We had to go up to the next floor then down an external flight of steps. This was an old house, refurbished, but pretty.

I smiled as I descended the steps, despite the peculiar circumstances. The sky was a blinding blue, the breeze magnificent and salty as it cooled my face. The house was rendered brick and timber shutters and Mediterranean in colors—azure blue trims and terracotta against expanses of white. I absorbed all this like the proverbial sponge.

"You look so happy." Klaus observed me as I stood on the lawn at the bottom of the steps. Bare foot. I wriggled my toes, smelled the grass. Smelled *everything*. I'd barely moved two steps before being struck dumb by my surroundings.

"It's been…" I blinked, swallowed. "Two weeks?" I wasn't sure of the time. "Without the sun." With hardly anyone to talk to, as Klaus was at work during the day. I'd had snacks for lunch and not seen Jodie at all, only heard her moving about upstairs.

"I figured you needed to get outside." He tugged on the chain leash. "Come. The beach is that way, below a big steep cliff. No one can see us up here though."

As we approached the edge, the salt-gray grass dropped away in a small slope, petering out to bare earth and crumbled rock before the ground fell away. With my wrists linked, I was afraid to get too close, but I went up on tiptoes, in a vain attempt to see the beach. I couldn't but it didn't matter. I smiled again and squinted out across the expanse of the sea, which slowly, massively, rolled landward with lines of lacy froth decorating the tops of the waves.

"You may sit."

"I love it," I whispered, sinking down onto my knees then shifting so I could sit with my legs to one side. As I'd lowered myself, Klaus had put a hand to my elbow, as if afraid I would topple. I frowned at him, puzzled, but he'd sat down to my left and was looking out to sea. My dress had ridden up so I tried to tuck it down to no avail. If anyone out there on the distant yachts or speedboats had binoculars they'd get an eyeful.

I didn't often get a chance to study him, my cruel yet also loving captor. I knew he was loving, as I'd seen how he treated Jodie, when he wasn't beating her. He even, I had to admit, was caring toward me at times, like that hand on my elbow. Love and beatings. But she wanted pain. What a mad concept.

The wind hummed in my ear and whipped my hair about my face. His features were sharp enough, square enough, to look beautifully masculine, yet regal in a way. Kingly? I smirked at that notion. Maybe he'd put crack in my bowl of cereal this morning?

Blond stubble marked his chin. I remembered the roughness of that from the last time he'd made love to—no, wrong word—fucked me.

Where was Jodie? I'd like to ask her to her face what she thought of her man keeping me to himself in their basement. I'd like to say sorry to her, again, maybe this time she would understand. Sadness leaked in, in spite of the cheerful surroundings.

"Where's Jodie?" When he swung his face to me and frowned, I added, "Sir."

"She's coming."

She was? My heart beat faster. I toyed with what to say, wanting to be nonchalant before him, but desperate won out. "Does she forgive me?"

"You'll have to ask her that." I guess I looked worried because he added, "She will. I know she will."

"Thank you." I swept my wind-teased hair from my eyes and pretended I was unaffected. I must be mad, pleading for forgiveness after what he'd done.

My eyes ached from restrained tears. *Thank god, she's forgiven me.*

I tripped into an assumption. "Does this mean you trust me?" I sat up a little. *Does this mean you're letting me go?*

The way the skin around his eyes crinkled when he smiled was actually cute, and I smiled back. So easy to see him as normal when he was like this.

"You'd like that?"

I nodded. A stupid question.

"What would you do if I released you today?"

I opened my mouth to answer, shut it. What would I do?

He was going to send me outside Australia, or so he'd said. I didn't want that. But then I didn't want to be arrested either, and…I held my breath, thinking…and I didn't want to send Jodie to jail. I stared at him, seeing that he was waiting for whatever I came up with. Like he knew my confusion. What had happened in this house, by his hand, mostly, was something I would never forget. He still scared me but, damn him, in some twilight zone way, he attracted me too. He always had. I'd survived his worst, hadn't I?

And strangely, most terrifying and telling fact of them all, I'd experienced the depth of his desire for me. He loved Jodie, and yet desired me also. Not love, no, I really doubted that, but it was more than I'd ever had from any man. Crystal clear, hot as the center of the sun, desire.

Klaus didn't mess around with misdirection or lies. What he said, he meant.

What would I do if he released me, right now?

I shook my head, unwilling to commit, or to say something dumb. Which was likely, knowing me.

A cream-colored cat strolled up and stepped onto his lap, begging for a pat by rubbing its head on his hand. To my amusement, Klaus obliged, giving it a full body pat that made the cat stretch and purr even more while treadling its paws on his leg.

I knew so little about what happened in this house. A frown crept onto my forehead and stayed as I contemplated my place. Fucktoy. A humiliating name. But with the name came a whole string of emotions. I'd never had a man want me in the crazy way that Klaus seemed to.

"Doesn't that hurt?" I pointed at the cat moving its paws on his leg. I was sure there were claws involved.

"Yes. But I like patting Baxter. He's our pet. I'm willing to take a bit of pain with the pleasure." His smile turned to curiosity.

"Huh." Clearly that was referring to us. I refused to rise to the bait, but I looked out across the sparkling ocean and saw an opening. "There's a difference between him and me. He has freedom." Then I picked up a pebble and threw it out past the cliff edge. "He can go where he wants to."

"True, to a degree." Klaus propped himself back on one arm and contemplated me.

This struck me as so odd—like we were an ordinary couple having an ordinary conversation. The sun warmed my skin and I plucked a stalk of grass to tease the cat with. With my wrists linked, to reach the cat, I had to stretch out both arms. I tickled just next to one ear, smirking when his ear twitched.

"You like playing with danger. Baxter has a mean right paw. He might seem free, but he relies on us for food and shelter and love, companionship, even for help if he gets hurt. Freedom isn't all it's cracked up to be."

*Sheesh. Sure it ain't.*

After trapping it with his paw, Baxter chewed at the stalk but I grinned and tugged it loose.

Klaus nodded, deflecting my stalk when I teased under the cat's chin. "You do like danger." He grabbed my wrist and stopped me pulling back.

"Let go."

The *mean* returned to his gaze. Mr. Predator.

*Uh-oh.* I swallowed around the constricted spot in my throat. "Please, Sir. Let me go."

"Come here."

Then he hauled me over his lap, facedown, arranging me so his right hand nestled on my bottom with his fingers a miniscule amount away from my cleft. I let him, subsiding so my forehead rested on my arm, and waiting. I was too...used to this? Too something I couldn't figure.

Ugh. Too content. Though he'd used some pain here and there, unless I did something wrong, he hadn't truly hurt me for days. Humiliated perhaps, that was a constant, but not so much pain. All the orgasms had rotted my brain, apparently. I sighed as his fingers slipped upward.

"Such a pretty show underneath this red dress. What are you, girl? Hmm?" He leaned in on me, undid the clasp, and took one wrist to the small of my back, then the other, and fastened them together again. "Tell me your name." He left his hand on my back, fingers splayed, warm and heavy.

I did what I'd done so many of the recent times when he'd played with me, I sank into acceptance. I had a small epiphany. That word he wanted me to say no longer meant what it should. I rolled it around in my mind, tasting it, imagining how it would sound on my tongue.

Like the cat they had given me food and shelter and love, at least from Jodie, maybe even companionship before they saw that video, before Klaus decided I needed training. And, if I got hurt, I knew beyond doubt that they'd help me, because Klaus had. That first day he'd marked me, but every day he'd checked them all.

"Tell me what you are?"

"I'm your fucktoy," I murmured.

Silence for a few seconds then he lifted his hand from my back and combed his fingers softly through my hair from the nape upward. "Oh, good girl. That's a very good girl."

I was tempted to thank him, but I didn't. Instead I turned my head to the side and let him pat me while he stirred me down there with his fingers. I moved my thighs a little farther apart.

The crunch of feet on grass warned me of her approach. It had to be Jodie.

"Hello, Steph. You okay?"

After steeling myself, I turned and looked up at her. She squatted nearby, her arms on her thighs, hands dangling between. Casual, yet alert.

What a question. I could go on for hours about that, but then she knew what Klaus was like. She'd let him. I'd dreaded seeing hate, perhaps. Yet unlike in Klaus, where I saw dominance, desire and that contained aggression of his, in Jodie, overlaying everything, I saw an element of kindness.

"I'm good."

"Uh-huh." She nodded. The tweak of her lips at one corner and softness around her eyes—sadness?

Oh boy.

"I think she wants to tell you something, gorgeous." Then Klaus slipped out from under me, standing up before he grabbed me and set me on my knees.

"What do you want to say?" Her denim shorts set off the curves of her hips and her little yellow top formed around her breasts so well I could see her nipple outlines. Her auburn hair draped in crisp curls about her shoulders and her lips were blushing red and pretty enough to make me wish I could climb on her body to kiss her. I sighed and hung my head. Before Klaus could tell me to look up, I did so, meeting her gaze again.

Yeah, sadness was there.

I had my hands tied behind me, her partner had been fucking me in their basement, and yet I felt as if I was in the wrong. Damn. I shook my head, wishing the lump in my throat would take a hike. Maybe I was. Guilty. I'd been a fool, and look where it had gotten me. I cleared my throat.

"I'm sorry, Jodie. That's what I want to say. I know I said that before, but I hope that now you'll accept it. Please?"

Slowly, she nodded. "I accept your apology. You understand that you made me very unhappy? I wonder, does that even matter to you?" The little frown line between her eyes made me want to smooth it away.

"It does." I nodded, with my bottom lip sucked in and between my teeth. How to convince her? "I am sorry. Even though this is…" I shut my eyes for a second. "So very, very weird. I am sorry."

"Okay." She laid her hand on top of my head and stroked me. That simple touch let me breathe again.

"Thank you." Then I managed to knee walk forward and lean down to kiss her knee.

"Oh Steph, baby."

I smiled at her.

"I told you to call Jodie, ma'am. I'll let it pass this time. She has more to tell you. Go ahead, girl."

*Oh god, he wanted me to say that again?* I grimaced. I had said it to him but now, reluctance surfaced. Say it out loud to her? I couldn't do it. "I can't. I'm sorry, Sir," I whispered, keeping my focus on her neck level. Shit. Chicken? He was going to punish me for this but I just *couldn't* say it to her.

"What is it, Sir? What's she supposed to say? Oooh. Wait. I get it. That?" Amusement swelled from her last words. "I love you, Sir, but I can see she's not ready for this. To defy you on this, hmmm. Brave. Are you embarrassed Steph?"

Her fingers tightened in my hair and drew my head back so I had to look into her eyes.

Fuck, fuck, fuck. I squirmed.

She was laughing at me.

"She said it to me. You can say what you want her to do. I like watching you and her with your smaller ways of domming her."

"Domming?" She tsked. "Ha. Guess I am. Shh. It's okay. You don't have to." Her other hand settled around my chin, each finger delicately arranged there as if she was figuring where to put them. Then, while she watched me avidly, she sneaked her thumb onto my bottom lip and brushed along me there, sending a tingle southward.

"You're so pretty. So different to Klaus. I don't need you saying you're my fucktoy because I'd rather have you as my pet. It's cuter, like you," she breathed. Then she took my mouth. Kissing me softly at first then harder, urgently.

I moaned into her mouth, taking in her desire like it was the very air that kept me alive. Wanting her to want me. Loving that she thought I was her pet.

Klaus came in behind me, caging me with his legs outside mine and his big hands above my elbows, trapping my arms even more thoroughly. "You two, doing this, is so hot."

My body relaxed into his grip and I gasped, mouth parting at the probe of her tongue. While I was still lost in the kiss Jodie pressed on me, he bit my neck and growled, "Ours. You're ours. Whatever we call you, that's what you are. Whatever we ask you to do, you will. You're fucking ours, from now on."

I couldn't move at all. I shut my eyes and let them bite and kiss me, rocking my body. The knowledge wiped out my self-awareness, forcing away my thoughts. I was nothing. I was a possession caught between two predators lusting over their next kill. A conquered thing.

# Chapter 19

## Jodie

For all of us, settling back into having Steph upstairs brought a few hiccups. Should we let her in the bedroom again? We did. Klaus even told her to sleep at the bottom of our bed. In the middle of the night, she rolled off the bed. I woke up, startled, with my hand on my heart listening to it thump and wondering what the noise had been. Then her head popped up above the edge and we erupted into small giggles. I helped her back into bed, amazed that she'd not woken Klaus. But he had been working late.

Before going to work in the morning, he made a joke about eliminating the problem by building a cage under the bed.

At least, I'd thought he was joking, until I found a webpage link to exactly that—a cage built under a tall bed with steps leading down from it. The cage even had a mattress inside.

I looked up.

Steph sat opposite me, across the glossy timber expanse of the dining table, doing her old job of picking out relevant research for articles. We were both doing it, except I had the internet connected. Her laptop had all the internet programs disabled and the Wi-Fi passworded. Only a nerd geek genius could get it going again, or so Klaus and I thought.

We hadn't spoken much about the previous week. Yet. I turned my laptop around and pushed it toward her. The picture of the bed was in the center of the screen.

"How about that for a bed?"

She peeked at it, then at me. "Is that a cage underneath?"

I nodded.

"For a person?"

"Yep. What do you think of that?"

"Umm. Different? People do that?"

I retrieved my laptop. "Which? Go into one to sleep? Or tell someone else to do it? Some people in the BDSM community have slaves. Some would do this happily for their masters."

Why had I shown it to her? I didn't want her inside one of these, did I? Though Klaus might. I mulled over my reasons but my subconscious was stubborn.

"Why did you show me that," she asked quietly.

Nail on the head. Why? Maybe because such a bed said permanence, if we had one. That idea tantalized me.

"You know I can't stay." She nodded slightly, agreeing with herself, but her forehead crinkled as if in concern. "He said he was going to have to let me go somewhere far away. Truthfully, that's scary, though maybe, not as scary as going to jail."

"Yes. Jail...I want to avoid that too. He hasn't told me a lot either yet. I don't know what he plans, though I wish things were different."

What a mess we were still in. I didn't want her to go away. A heaviness settled in my stomach. I ran through her words. Both of us seemed to be going off on strange subconscious tangents. Questioning her was risky, but I needed to *know*.

"Steph, you said *can't*, not *I'm not*. Does that mean, perhaps, you'd like to stay?"

The room stilled. My ears strained to hear words she hadn't yet said.

"I..." She shook her head. "No. Just no. Fuck, no. I'm not crazy like you." The heavy feeling in my stomach turned to illness. "Oh! I mean, I don't want pain, like you. I'm sorry, ma'am." As she spoke, her forehead went from smooth to frowning and back again.

Poor perplexed thing. I smiled weakly. "Don't call me ma'am. I don't want that. Just Jodie. But I do expect respect, pet." I gave her a second to think. "Thank you for apologizing."

"It's not you though. It's Klaus. If it were just you, I might. I really might."

"Okay." Was that desire or love I saw in her eyes? Was what I felt shared? Klaus thought I dommed her, but how pitiful was it for a Domme to feel so useless, so infatuated?

I pushed back my chair and went around to her side then hopped up on the table, swinging my legs a little as I contemplated her. I pulled the shoestring strap on my dress into a comfier spot as I thought. What if she wasn't so afraid of Klaus? Would she stay?

"This table," I patted the varnished timber. "Was where Klaus first really tied me up and figured out he liked dominating me. Then we both worked out that he liked giving pain and I liked receiving it, and how much and why and over many months we figured our kinks out. But you're new." I reached out and placed my hand over hers. "You're only just figuring out what you like." I was assuming she wanted to learn. I guess I was assuming a lot of things.

Her mouth was open, her head raised, and she was staring a little crazily. What had I just done?

Clearly, with us, she'd fallen into the submissive role, but where was I going with this argument? It was like I'd found a string on a forest floor and I dreamed it would lead me to some magical place. Now I was following that trail of string, hoping.

"You do want me to stay with you, don't you?" she whispered. "And you know I can't though? There's so many things. To start with, Klaus has other ideas. Then there's…"

She scowled and looked down at her lap then up at me again. "There's yesterday. I'd almost forgotten what the sun looked like. You know? I mean if I walk out into that street now, am I going to be recognized? I don't want to be locked up in a room for my whole life."

Damn. I drew back. I hadn't thought of that. Obvious though. Where could she go if she did live with us? The back yard? Facial surgery wasn't an option like in Hollywood movies.

I squeezed her hand, overcome by a whole lot of regret. "Yes, people would recognize you. There's posters up all over the island and the mainland, and pictures on the news." I heaved out a breath. "Facebook even." Her stepbrother had only flown out a few days ago and he'd stirred up a lot of sympathy for her. Though the papers still speculated that she was a murderer.

"Huh. I thought so, but what I said was true." She looked sideways at me, face tilted in a cute way. "I would stay with *you*. I've been keen on you since uni."

"Oh." My heart lit up. "Oh my, Steph. You never said." From here I could see down the top of her dress and I smiled. The naughty things we could have done if I'd known of her infatuation.

"Yeah." She toyed with a pen, spinning it. "I was a coward. I tried getting you into bed with me once even, when you were drunk. Guess I never learned that was bad. I have now, though." She leaned down and laid her cheek against the back of my hand. "I'm sorry how all this has worked out. I'm so lost that I don't even know anymore how to figure it all out."

Despite the ache as tears threatened, I drew my other hand through her black tresses, separating the locks with my fingers, watching them flow over my skin. "Me too, Steph. Me too. Maybe I could ask Klaus if you can stay? There might be a way."

After a second she answered, "No, don't. It's just a silly dream. I couldn't handle being around him permanently even if there was a way. I'm like a mouse compared to him. He's some feral robotic love machine programmed to make women scream and come. Sorry, but that's my take on it."

"Oh?" Her criticism annoyed me and I tugged at her hair. "You're not gone yet you know, pet. You're to respect him even when he isn't here. Understood?"

She stiffened. "But, I thought maybe you were setting me free soon?"

How fickle. To say she'd stay if she could and yet be so desperate to leave.

"No. You don't go free until Klaus decides to do it. In the meantime, remember your place." I wound a coil of her hair in tight until she winced. "In the bedroom, we're not equals. Even out here, if I decide to get you naked so I can play with you, I will. Understood?" I pinned her hair down to the table then did something I never thought I would. I slapped her lightly on the upturned cheek.

Shock widened her eyes, and I imagined the thoughts chasing themselves in her head. I'd been there. I knew. I wanted, more than anything, to see her surrender to me as I did to Klaus. I didn't break eye contact, I didn't move, and finally she seemed to give in. A change in her expression? A small relaxation of her posture? There was something. I saw it.

"I'm sorry," she squeaked. "I'm sorry, Jodie."

"Good. Now stand up and come here." I patted the side of my thigh.

When she did exactly that I enfolded her, hugging her for a while, soaking up the feel of her in my arms. The day would come when I couldn't do this, when she would go. I arranged her so she was looking at me from an inch away. "I like when you're like this. When you submit to me like you do with Klaus."

"I don't though," she answered quietly. "I don't." Over her pretty eyes, her eyelashes quivered. "I obey him because I have to, because he scares me, and I guess, also, when he uses his strength it's like Bambi versus a wolf. With you, it's different."

I'd seen her over his lap out there. She was so wrong. Klaus had her figured out more than that.

"How am I different?" I kissed her once. "Tell me."

"Do I have to?"

I stroked her cheekbone with my thumb. "Yes. I'd like you to. Is that so awful? Telling me?"

She sighed. The warmth of her breath touched my lips. "No. It's not. I do it for you because I want to."

"Thank you. That's beautiful." I think my heart had done a little skip and dance when she said those words. They were almost as good as her saying I love you. I tucked a stray tangle of hair behind her ear.

"Can I kiss you, Jodie? Please? I'm dying here, being so close without kissing." She wriggled against me. Under her light dress, her pussy was next to mine. Neither of us wore panties but, I contemplated evilness, Klaus had only instructed me not to let *her* come.

The power she'd just given me. I smiled and I kissed her delicately a few times before I said, "You may have more soon, but first, I want you to kneel and apply those lips and tongue between my legs." As I spoke, I pushed the straps of her dress down her arms until I could scoop out her breasts.

*Hell.* I paused, aching at the sight of her. Not playing with her when I could, was like having champagne in my mouth and not swallowing.

When she went to kneel, I stopped her. "Wait." I exhaled, pushing my fingertips along the lower curve of her breasts, just enough to feel the fullness. "You're such a temptation."

Her grin made me shake my head. I could see definite advantages to having her naked all day. Though I'd never keep my hands off her. Fascinated, I circled her silk-smooth nipples until she shivered and they tightened and rose into bumps. Scratching lightly and pinching and squeezing made her skin flush and her breathing hasten. My mouth watered at the prospect of sucking on her.

But, I'd been distracted. I rested my hands on my thighs while I admired the red streaks. She pushed her chest out and whined, begging me for more.

I laughed. "Maybe I should call you little slut and not pet?"

"Jodie!"

"*Shh.*"

After slapping her breasts together, I watched with amusement the small jiggle as they bounced. With finger and thumb, I pinched the peaks hard, flattening them until she both moaned and whimpered, rubbing her groin on mine.

"That's better." I nipped her ear, wetly licking while I toyed between her legs. She was so aroused her clit was easily found, easily stirred. Once I had her in a wonderful senseless state, back arched and writhing, I said, smiling, "Now get down and eat my pussy."

\*\*\*\*\*

Completely withdrawing from contact with everyone outside our house would be both suspicious and bore me to tears. On Friday, I let Adrianna come over to visit. Steph, of course, I locked in the room. Using the excuse of perfect weather, with a pot of tea and plate of fresh scones as lures, I enticed Adrianna out into the back yard. We sat under the small gazebo where there was a white-painted ironwork table.

I quietly admired her, my craziest vanilla friend. Her blond hair was longer than last I'd seen her, and in a ponytail, and she seemed to have added to her tattoo collection somewhere I couldn't pinpoint.

"This always seems so British." Adrianna swept her hand across the air, indicating the bits and pieces on the table. "I mean tea with scones, cream and jam. Next you'll have me playing polo and crocheting."

I just shook my head.

"It's true!" She leaned an elbow on the table, unintentionally showing off a new Japanese-style tattoo of a flock of birds. "Patricia thought you'd been sucked up by aliens and Jess thought it was Klaus keeping you to himself, again. But, moi," She touched her lemon-yellow t-shirt over her chest. "I knew you'd just gone insane and started eating scones and drinking tea. I was so right."

"*You* are insane. Have another scone." The woman was bubbly, as always. And I'd never worked out how she got the blond surfer-chick look down so pat when she never ever surfed. Not that we had any surf near the island.

"Thanks." She stuffed it into her mouth in two bites, chewed, and swallowed. "Yummm. Honestly though, when are you coming out with us? The Island Trekkers are doing a bushwalk to Balding Bay next weekend. Coming to that? Drag Klaus along if you must. We can rag his ass if he isn't fit enough."

"As if. The man's so fit." Though I hadn't jogged with him for weeks, he still went by himself. Another byproduct of our kidnapping venture. I shifted my chair next to hers so I could look out over the sea then sat again with my legs outstretched and my ankles crossed.

She grunted. "I know. He could win the Olympics by himself. I just want to see you again, out doing stuff."

I frowned down at my lap. "I will. I'm having a rest away from everything for a month or so."

That should give us enough time to figure out Steph. Then I could find proper work again, and be me. Be me without her around. Except I'd gotten used to having her next to me while we cooked or researched or joked about things. And we had been doing that more and more. She was even a better cook than me. Not hard to do, but still. It was fun seeing what she made from ingredients I could happily turn into burnt mush. The first time she'd done that Klaus had raised both eyebrows in surprise.

"A month," Adrianna muttered. "Hell. That's a long time by yourself. You sure that's all it is?"

I nodded.

"Sweet thing." She grimaced. "You look sad. If I find out you're hiding something I could have helped you with…"

"I'm not!" I threw up my hands. "We're having a quiet time is all." I scrambled for something to distract her. "Maybe thinking about moving."

"Fuck. No way." Looking alarmed, she put her hand on my shoulder. "Not away from here? I'd miss you heaps. Why?"

I shrugged, lost. Maybe I'd said the wrong thing. Too late though. "I don't know where we'd go. Klaus and I, we're discussing it."

"Oh. Okay." She sat back.

Phew.

But that was when I heard the rattle of the side gate. It wasn't a normal low gate. We had our kinky privacy to protect. On both sides of the house, and partway along the sides where they were climbable, were two and a half meter high fences. The one gate was padlocked.

"Who's that?" She turned to peer back at the house and the continued rattling. "Are you expecting a meter reader or something?"

"No." I rose, and all the way to the gate, I wondered who this could be.

My stride faltered as I recognized the face through the white timber framework. Kat. The basement room was on the other side of the house, thank god. Why was she here? I'd fended off a few recent phone calls from her, said we were busy. I frowned.

Adrianna's car? Had she noticed it and decided I was more likely to let her in? Coincidence surely. Her work with Children's Services meant she visited the island regularly. Maybe it was just a weird coincidence? I slowed, and stopped a yard from the gate.

She was leaning on the thing with her shoulder, patient, dressed in a dark pair of pants and a collared shirt with her hair in a bun. Dark hair too this time. I never knew what color she'd try next, though rumor was she was blond at birth.

"Hi." I put on a stiff smile.

"Hi." She pushed off the timber to stand and face me better. "How are you, Jodie?"

"Good." *And I'm wanting you gone.*

It wasn't that I hated her. It was more that I knew she'd turned against Klaus. More and more as the past year had unwound she'd become unhappy with him. I guess that was the best phrase. She seemed terser and less interested in his opinions on things. I didn't know why, though. It made me feel on edge around her. Because, seriously, she had dommed me so good that one time when we first met that I'd never forgotten her. I seriously melted a bit when she came close. Kat was like a fucking sun to me. Bitch.

Then, like the coming of an Armageddon, panic soared. With Adrianna it was simple, one on one. With both of them near our house, Steph in the basement became, in my mind, as obvious as a neon sign. *Not logical. Not logical*, my mind screamed. But my heart stampeded, my stomach filled with butterflies and all my words got stuck in my throat.

"You don't look so good. Can I come in?" She indicated the gate.

*Oh fuck, oh fuck, oh fuck. No. You fucking cannot.* Panic morphed into full-blown something else so bad I couldn't think straight but it was black and made me feel ill and it filled my head with a maelstrom of nonsense.

*I've been on stage. Handle this. Grow a fucking spine.*

Fuck no.

"No," I said automatically, hating that I'd chickened out the *instant* the words were launched from my mouth.

"No?" She cocked an eyebrow. "Why? I thought we were friends?"

"I can't say."

Adrianna arrived at my elbow. "Hi, Kat." Kat nodded back. "Why aren't you letting her in, Jodie?"

"Christ." I put back of hand to forehead. "I'm sorry, but I'm not. Klaus told me not to." I had a feeling I was digging an ever-deeper hole. Now Adrianna seemed in shock, to some small degree.

"Really? Kat, what did you do?"

The woman shrugged but never varied in her missile-deadly stare that seemed to penetrate my brain.

"Jodie." She wrapped her hands about the timber of the gate and I saw her take a deep breath. "Look. I don't know exactly what this is about…but you are not behaving normally and, knowing Klaus, he has something to do with this. I came to check you were okay. I see that you both are and you aren't."

She didn't know? Truly? *Knowing Klaus?* That phrase burrowed in.

All I could do was stand there with my fists clenched.

"If you need me, or if you need advice, I am here. Okay?" She frowned at me. "Contact me, please. I'm worried about you."

Oh god. What. The. Hell. I was both mortified and pleased, pleased because…I just was. I nodded back and summoned the most noncommittal reply I could think of. "I heard you."

After that, our little afternoon tea party disintegrated. When Adrianna left I leaned back on the front door, head in hands, and I cried. Only I wasn't sure why.

*****

When Klaus came home it took me a minute or two to get the courage to tell him, but I did. He merely hugged me for a long time, with his awesome arms about me, stroking my head, until I closed my eyes and sank into him. Everything was right again.

"I think I messed up."

"It's okay." He kissed my head. "She can't know anything. Maybe she's suspicious because of that one phone call I made to her, but that's it. It will die away if we don't feed her suspicions. Okay?"

"Sure." I let out a last long sigh and looked up at him. "Let's go have dinner."

The pasta marinara was exquisite. Again, Steph had created something stupendous. It was curious having a meal each night with her eating below us to one side. At least Klaus had rescinded his eat-under-the-table order. Before she came, it was me under there, or at his feet. It made me wonder what would happen if Steph was ours forever. Would he eventually make me go back to eating on the floor? It had only been a sometimes thing yet I missed it. I missed being his slave at times, maybe I should tell him so? I made a note in my mind to do that. I was fairly certain he'd find something interesting to do to two slave girls.

The aftermath turned into a relaxed time in the living room with a few glasses of wine, or scotch in Klaus's case, and with the video game console turned on. Once Steph had permission to curl up with me I made sure to make room on one wing of the L-shaped couch arrangement. The black chemise with the leaf pattern that we'd dressed her in was see-through and delicate. It molded to her every feminine curve like the sky fitted the earth. If she'd sat on the floor, I would have followed just so I could pat her.

I'd never had a pet, never had a woman I could call mine, or my girlfriend. If she was leaving someday soon, I would make the most of this time we had.

Though we talked in soft voices while Klaus blasted away enemy soldiers, I noticed her watching him and the TV more than seemed...normal.

She was nestled into me facing outward, so I mouthed her ear and asked the burning question, "Don't tell me you like *Call of Duty?*"

"Don't you remember me at uni?"

"What?" But then I did. "Ahh. You were the one who played the guys at video games?"

"Yeah, and I still love them. Though RPGs are more my taste. Do you think he'd mind?"

"You can ask?"

"I'm not deaf, girls. If you want to play split-screen multiplayer, Steph, the controller is there." He indicated the cabinet the TV sat on.

"Jodie?"

"Go ahead. Not that I want you to get up, but go ahead."

She sat up, sending me a rueful grin before sneaking over to grab the controller. When she came back I sat up too. At least I could still make her cuddle into my side a bit, even if all she did from then on was shoot things and stare at the screen. I draped my arm across the back of the couch and tugged her closer.

"Be aware," Klaus growled. "I take no prisoners."

To my surprise Steph replied grimly, "Neither do I."

She flinched when he turned to look at her but all he added was, "And it's hardcore mode. I'll drop out so we can start from scratch."

"Okay," she said so softly it was nearly inaudible.

"He won't bite you during a game." I nudged her waist.

"You never know," she whispered back.

The game commenced and I watched some of the time, read my ereader one-handed the rest of the time with it perched on the arm of the couch. This setup was cozy and so nearly normal if it weren't for the knowledge of what had gone before...or for the set of black leather cuffs that Steph wore and her matching collar. Klaus had permitted them to be undone, but they were there, and a constant reminder.

Something made me look up, maybe the way Steph was sitting? Whatever, I had due warning. From the way buttons were pressed and from the timing of the soldiers' shooting and running on screen, I could tell that Steph was the man at the bottom of the screen. It was multiplayer and they seemed on the same team, scurrying through abandoned and demolished buildings shooting everyone on the other side.

But then I spotted what Steph was aiming at, or who, and from the surroundings, I saw that it was Klaus. I glanced at her and saw delight a second before she made her soldier shoot Klaus's man in the back.

He put down his controller and looked back at her.

"Oh fuck." She smirked. "You have friendly fire?"

"You knew that. You play far too well to be a noob." He stood, unfolded those long legs then stalked toward Steph.

"I didn't mean it," she squeaked. "It's just a game!"

"No, it's not. That was deliberate. You liked killing me in the game and so you did it. Is that disrespect? Killing your master in a video game?" He angled an eyebrow in a mocking way, held both hands palms forward at his sides. "Spanking time, Jodie?"

"I think so. She definitely deserves a spanking for that."

"What? No, no, no. You're joking. Aren't you?" Steph carefully put down her controller then looked from me to the grinning Klaus and back again to me. "You are joking. Phew. I thought you both meant it."

He stood over her. "But I did."

Then he pounced, wrestled her to the couch and sat back down with her face down over his lap. Due to not wanting a kick in my teeth, I'd sprung off the couch, and now waited a few feet away. Her ohmigods and small shrieks said she was alarmed but she didn't appear game to put up much of a fight.

"Stop wriggling," Klaus said sternly, applying his hand to her now bared ass. The smack of his broad palm on her was closely followed by another screech from Steph, but she stopped wriggling. "Good girl." Then he delivered what I would call a sensual spanking. After every few smacks he slid his hand between her legs. Watching part of his hand disappear between the curves of her perfect little ass made me instantly horny.

I'd never seen him go so light, but then she didn't like pain that much. My man was being kind and playful because that's what she needed. This was why I loved him.

I crept in and kneeled by her head so I could nuzzle her and kiss her while he played with her other end. From the way her eyelids had lowered she was appreciating his efforts.

"Where's his hand going?" I asked her, nibbling the lower part of her plump lip.

"Where do you think?" She wriggled a little. "Why does that feel so good?"

Another round of spanks made her huff and moan.

"You're so cute when you do that. It's good because it reverberates into your pussy. Yes? I'm an expert on this."

"Maybe you need one next?" Klaus asked with that mean glint in his eye.

"I'd rather tease my pet. If I can, Sir?"

"Maybe later." He tapped her butt with one hand. "Listen up. Since I have you both here nice and close, I think I should pass on the news that I've decided we should go to a munch this weekend."

"Oh." I sat back on my heels. "Does that mean Kat will be there?"

He nodded. "Possibly. I decided this before your little encounter with her. We need to be seen and that's a good way to do it. Chris has been saying things that make me worry about dropping out so suddenly. The amount of controversy building around these deaths…it's way bigger than I imagined and will stick in people's memories. We don't need any sort of suspicion falling on us."

"What about Steph? If we go…" I looked at her and saw she was taking this all in though restraining from commenting. "If we go she'll be here. Yes?"

"Yes. We have the apps linking the room's camera to our phones, as well as the alarm systems. You know it's as safe as when you were in there."

"I guess I do." What I didn't say out loud was how terrified I'd been at times. I hadn't even known he was thinking about safety back then though. At least Steph knew. "You'll be safe." I nodded to her. "Okay?"

She nodded back and I patted her shoulder. She didn't have any choice, same as me, but I could see the point in doing this. "Just the once?" I asked him.

"Yes."

Then I considered again how strangely comfortable we all were in this little cameo of BDSM and I realized that maybe we were a whisker away from being able to set her free. All it took was Klaus thinking the same.

"Okay," I murmured. "I wish we could be sure Kat wasn't going to it though."

Seeing her again was not on my favorites list.

# Chapter 20

## Klaus

While Chris helped Jodie hop out of the speedboat into the shallow waves, I checked the sand anchors. Though we'd be able to keep an eye on the boat from the shore, it'd be the height of embarrassment to have the thing drift off. Not least because the sleek red-and-white beast was Jon's pride and joy. Borrowing it now and then from the vet might've been a good swap for doing the man's taxation once a year, but still, I liked to take care of borrowed things as if they were mine.

The rope on the starboard anchor needed a few more turns. Tiny half-foot high waves slopped against the boat—the Great Barrier Reef out there made real surf an endangered species unless a cyclone hit the area.

Steph was, in a way, one of those borrowed things. I smiled and for a few seconds the crystal-clear vista down through the water to the white sand and darting fish faded out. Despite her bobble-headed way of approaching life's decisions, she was growing on me. Like Jodie, I was not looking forward to the day I let her go. And it wasn't just the pasta marinara, though that seemed a damn good reason. It was more the cute way she looked up at me from the floor when I ordered her there—big brown amazing eyes.

If I didn't know better I'd think she was some naïve innocent, but she wasn't. I'd fucked her every which way, introduced her to mild S and m, and showed her what Dominance and submission meant. The woman loved it, but that didn't mean I could keep her if she wanted to leave, and she did.

"You coming?" Jodie shaded her eyes. She and Chris, who carried the basket with our food, had waded halfway to the shore.

I waved to them then jumped into the water. It was cool and reached to the bottom of my board shorts. They waited for me to catch up.

"You coming with us back to the island?" I asked Chris. Wet sand squashed between my toes, turning the water cloudy as a wave washed past.

"Sure, and thanks for the lift. Much faster than catching the ferry to the port and then getting a ride out here."

"Not a problem. We won't go without you then. They're supposed to be having a BBQ around twelve so I'm guessing we'll leave about three."

"Okay." Chris smiled. "If I snag a hot submissive who wants me to take her back to her mansion and whip her I'll tell you."

Jodie chuckled. "If. Good luck with that."

We reached the shoreline and walked up the beach toward the gathering in the park ahead. Color speckled the scene—bright beach umbrellas sprouted above a crowd of people in bikinis, shorts, and t-shirts. Next to a row of council coin-operated BBQs, six or seven big trestle tables were piled with tubs of food and esky coolers.

"Off to a good start!" Chris nodded toward the people. "Food, beer, and women in bikinis, can't beat that."

"Don't rush, man. There's hours yet. If you're too keen, you'll scare off the newcomers."

Not that there seemed many new faces. This munch was supposedly to introduce those curious about the lifestyle to a few friendly faces and to let them talk about their concerns and interests with people who could help them get into kink safely. But, like the last one out here, it seemed mostly the old hands who'd turned up.

Bushland Beach was an idyllic spot but the drive out here seemed to daunt those new to BDSM. The inner city ones attracted more people.

Chris scanned the crowd. "Not much chance of scaring anyone. Can't see anyone new except the tall guy in the cowboy hat. He's not my type. Have you two ever thought of finding another sub to scene with?"

Though Jodie looked discomforted for a second, I shook my head. "No. We're pretty exclusive right now."

"Only Kat, hey? And that's not going to be repeated from what you've said."

"No, it's not."

"She's not much of a sub anyway. She needs a Dom with balls of steel. I'm going to join in on the beach cricket." He slapped my shoulder. "I have to blow all the marching numbers and dollar signs out of my head. Catch you later."

"Sure." I watched the man lope back down to the beach.

We found a shady spot off to the edge of the gathering and chatted to those who came past, and to some friends we spotted. A rule of these was that no one was to get drunk, so light beers and non-alcoholic drinks made the rounds. I tried out the beach cricket for ten minutes and Jodie had a go at an impromptu game of Twister where the subs got to compete against the Doms. A lady switch with a sense of humor tried to get on both teams at once only to be wrestled away by her latest Dom. Mostly things were low key and non kinky. Locals used this park too and it was a Saturday.

Lunchtime meant the BBQs were fired up and soon sausages and steaks sizzled as the cooks tortured them. Jodie went off to find a friend. When I noticed Moghul lazing on a picnic blanket near the BBQs, I went and sat next to him on the grass.

Our mingling and making ourselves seen act was going well. I'd checked the apps that monitored the house a few times. Nothing doing back there.

Moghul lay on his back with a folded beach towel for a pillow and his baseball cap pulled low to shield him from the sun. His big feet were bare and he was toeing up the sand while looking utterly at peace.

"How's it going?" I raised my one and only light beer toward the cook. "Do you know him?"

Moghul tilted the cap and showed one eye. "It's going well. Twister had at least one sub lose her bikini top and the random game of tag had another mostly lose her shorts for all of two seconds. No locals have been horrified though."

I snorted.

"Yes, I do know the cook. Meet Randy Dale. Man of the hour and my employee. From Texas. His mouth, dick and balls are all bigger than life, and I just had to convince him not to expose his thirty-eight revolver to the public."

"You're joking. He brought a gun here?" From where we sat, I could hear the man's Texan accent.

"He did. Bought it illegally after he got here. It's common in Texas to carry, as he calls it. He was horrified we all weren't packing. I convinced him it's only the koalas he needs to be scared of here. If I ever see him with it again, I told him I'd hand him over to the cops myself. Hope he chucks it in the river. He'd never get a license for it."

"Is he a Dom?"

Jodie had wandered over and started talking to Randy. The man certainly seemed to amuse her.

"Yes, he's a Dom. He's doing porn for me. D/s and bondage. Brilliant rigger. But hell, what a bragger. The women love him, though." Moghul adjusted his cap again, shading his eyes with his hand as well. "I hope he can cook as well as he fucks and talks."

I couldn't help chuckling. "Okay. You got me though. What the hell is it with you employing a man to film porn. True?" I squinted down at Moghul. "I never knew."

"It's true. How do you think I made all my money? It's a lucrative business. Like all BDSM it's consensual, only you get paid a shitload." He searched blindly for his drink, found the bottle and took a swig. "I think I owe you the truth. Kat's got it in for you and seeing she's my second cousin twice removed or some such, I had to come clean. You need to watch her."

"Oh?" More news—I'd not known Kat was related to Moghul, even distantly.

"I've told her to be careful. Being in the lifestyle she should know not to talk about people without having facts."

*Fuck.* "What's she saying?" Now the Texan had tipped back his cowboy hat and was smooth talking Jodie while going on about how Aussie banana prawns were almost as good as the shrimp from back home but the laws about firearms were crap and the beer wasn't half as good. "Are all Texans like this?"

"Not the others I've seen. Randy is a whole special case."

"I see."

Moghul waved his drink bottle toward Randy. "You want to go rescue her?"

"No. If he goes too far she'll just kick his balls in. Chris and I have been teaching her some good martial arts moves."

"Okay. Well, back to Kat…she's just going on about you not being the squeaky clean guy everyone thinks you are. Which is so nebulous and basically nasty that I told her to get facts or say nothing. So, now you know. I'm sorry I steered you toward her. I would never have thought she'd get jealous like this."

"You still think it's her lusting after Jodie?"

"What else?"

"Don't know." I shook my head. "I don't know."

"Well, be careful. She's like a terrier after a rat when she thinks she's right."

"Sure. Will do." What the hell. Not good. "I might go see the guy in action."

"Don't get too close. He's got a ten inch prick and isn't afraid to use it."

I grinned. "Thanks. I'll be careful."

On the far side, Chris was leaning on the wire fence with Kat next to him, talking. Shit. But the man was loyal, completely. I couldn't stop her talking to people.

As I walked up to the BBQ, Randy was drawling about all the Aussie words he was learning that meant different things like trucks and thongs and how what we called an egg flip was really a spatula. To demonstrate he waved the mentioned device and turned over a sausage. He didn't seem dangerous but then a spatula cross egg flip was less lethal than a thirty-eight.

After lunch, even though I had a stomach full of hamburger, someone I barely knew convinced me to join the next round of beach cricket.

"Go!" Jodie gestured from her comfortable position on a towel under an umbrella. "Be brave. I'll watch the app. Would you like a token of mine to tie round your arm? I saw the knights get those at that medieval festival. I could find a table cloth from the picnic basket?"

I tossed her the phone. "No, but thanks for sacrificing me. If I get a mouthful of sand your backside will pay."

She scoffed. "Just don't get sunburnt."

Easy for her to say, she was in the shade of an umbrella.

But I jogged down and joined in—diving for the tennis ball and fetching it from the water when it was batted in by a giggling woman in a green bikini. At least I got to watch the women running about with all their bits jiggling. Not bad compensation. By the time the game finished I was well toasted and my neck felt hot. Sunscreen never ever covered the bits you thought it did. I flopped onto the towel beside Jodie.

"Excellent running!" She grinned. "You sure have losing down to a fine art."

"Brat."

I stared out over the mostly flat blueness of the ocean. Sea gulls cruised in on the wind and trotted about the beach with wings outstretched while they squawked at the other birds. The ever-present background roaring roll and surge of the waves had to be the most peaceful sound in the world.

"Beautiful."

Jodie crept her hand into mine. "Yes, it is. This was a nice day. I'm glad we came."

"Yeah. Me too." I looked over at her. "How much longer do you want to stay? Where's Chris? Does he want to stay much longer?"

"I think he left with someone else. I haven't seen him for an hour or so."

"Really?" I sat up. "He was supposed to say if he left with anyone." Why would he do that? Chris was normally so reliable. Danger seemed to prickle up my spine. Cold, distant, but there waiting.

"I'm pretty sure he has. I saw him walking toward the car park with someone, and then after that, nothing."

Christ. He'd been talking to Kat. "Have you been looking at the camera app?"

"Yes, last was fifteen minutes ago. No alarms though. Here."

But as she handed it to me the phone rang. The text message sent a chill through me. "The burglar alarm's been triggered."

"Oh no."

"I'll check the cameras." There were three internal ones including the one in the room. The front one showed no movement. The back one was black. Shit.

"The back camera isn't working." The prickle sharpened to ice cold.

"Might be a power problem, or it's broken?" Jodie leaned in, frowning.

"Might be broken. A power surge?" No, the other cameras were working. The fire alarm was too and it hadn't gone off. "Steph's still in the room."

"Maybe reboot the app? You know some of these things have bugs."

"Maybe." Coincidence.

I did that, waited a few seconds then restarted it.

But all I saw was black. I stood and searched the crowd. No Chris. I couldn't see Kat either. Crunch time. Decide what to do.

"Right. We both go look, and we meet back here after we do the left and the right of the crowd. Ask one or two people if they've seen him. If not…" I stared at Jodie. "We head straight home."

After blinking for a second or two, she nodded. "Okay. Or I could phone him?"

"No." If he was up to no good, that would only warn him.

But as I walked up the bank, I was checking the room camera again. I grabbed Jodie's arm. "Stop. Now the room camera's black. We're going home. Now. If he's here somewhere he's going to have to catch a lift back."

A few minutes later we were in the boat heading back. "Nothing?" I shouted above the throaty roar of the engine

She checked the phone again with the wind blowing her hair backward. "No! Nothing."

Things had gone bad. Maybe. I couldn't be sure. Maybe it was a coincidence. On the other hand, maybe someone had turned off the cameras and she wasn't in the room anymore?

"I changed my mind. Phone him."

"Okay." Mouth tense, she quick dialed and waited with the phone clamped to her ear, before giving up. Her expression grew ever more worried before she finally lowered the phone. "He's not answering."

# Chapter 21

## *Stephanie*

No one ever said that kidnapping was half the time terrifying and half the time boring. And the rest of the time wondering what evil plans Klaus had in his head. Though evil was a little too far. Jodie was right. He wasn't all bad, just a fraction, and it was a fraction which seemed to shrink with every extra day that I knew him.

Right now though, what I wanted was for them to come home. How wrong was that? No matter how many times Jodie said she had been in this same situation and come out unscathed, I would never stop worrying. I was locked in, for fuck's sake. If the cliff crumbled and the house slid off into the sea, I would be inside this room, dead, at the bottom of a pile of rubble being washed by the waves. Why couldn't they trust me? And let me go?

Then I heard the crunch of footsteps outside the window and I froze. It must be them. It'd been hours.

But when they returned from anywhere, they never came around this side of the house. They came in through the front door and the gate entry was the other side anyway. Who was out there?

More footsteps. Foolishly, or maybe wisely, I kept still and quiet. There was the *spang* sound of metal being tapped and a scrape, and a cell phone was thrust into view through the blades of the outside shutter. Whoever held it had to rearrange their grip when the phone knocked into the window glass. Distantly, I recognised the click of the phone again and again as the phone's owner took pictures.

Of me, staring back.

*Shit.* I hovered, fingers clenching, torn between running to a corner, or under the window, or waving my arms madly and screaming. Terror tightened its grip on my stomach. Whoever was taking photos of the room, they were not Klaus or Jodie. They couldn't know I was in here, could they? Maybe the picture wouldn't turn out. Maybe they planned to come in here with an axe and chop me into bloody pieces. Maybe they meant to free me.

My eyes seemed stuck in the open position. What should I do?

I was nervous. So what? I *did* want to be freed. Who wouldn't? *I'm normal.*

With my senses tuned to high alert, standing in the middle of the room, I listened.

The sounds were muffled but I knew them. Someone climbed the back steps—one person, deliberate, and heavy, perhaps. Someone unlocked the back door, came inside and prowled about for a while before making their way down the internal staircase, toward me. There was nothing else down here except for storage, I was pretty certain.

The owner of the foosteps stopped outside my door. The key hung on a cord out there. The handle jiggled then a moment later the key scraped in the lock, and slowly, the door opened.

*Crap.*

The man who entered was taller than Klaus, more muscular, though his eyes were somehow kinder. Black board shorts. Red t-shirt. The smell of sunscreen. The whitest blond hair I'd ever seen in office-worker hairstyle. He hesitated, murmured a somewhat surprised, "Hello," then, as carefully as he'd opened it, he shut the door behind him. *He shut the fucking door.* The key was in his hand.

What was this? He could get out again, but I still didn't have a key. Why had he shut it?

Fear snuggled in next to my heart, cold and scrabbling. A little desperately, I studied his face. Friend or bad guy? What the fuck was he? Who was he? As he drew closer, I backed away into the wall, then waited, shivering, as he came to within a yard of me. His eyes were the lightest of blues, like the blue of a dry summer sky seen through glass.

"Who are you?" I croaked.

"First I need to hear who you are." Deep assured voice—the opposite to what I'd expected. Hannibal Lector had a nice voice.

Should I say? I opened my mouth to reply and was stuck on the words. Say the wrong ones and Jodie and Klaus might go to prison for a very long time. Maybe me too. "I don't think I…" I shook my head. "Look, just leave."

"Leave?" He sounded incredulous.

"Yes. It's not your house. Leave the door open, and go, and I won't tell anyone you've been here."

"You won't? But you want the door open. Nice of you. And naughty of you, hey?" He tsked. "You're Stephanie."

Not a question. A statement. I swallowed past the thick lump in my throat and nodded. *Naughty?*

He nodded back. "Good. I knew it was you from the picture."

I dredged up some courage again. "Then open the door, please. I'm being held here against my will."

"Oh?"

I'd learned ever so well what a man could do to me over these last few weeks. This guy looked stronger than Klaus and his quiet attitude bothered me. Maybe I had a problem with my concept of what was normal—but this was not it. My creepy-crazy detector was going off. He should be jumping up and down about now going, oh my god, it's you. Are you okay? Let me call the police—all that and more.

But all he did was go over and sit on the BDSM implements chest. "I can see you're scared of me. You don't need to be."

*Sure I don't. I'm only locked in with you.*

"Let's say I know Klaus. I'm a friend. Actually, I work for him."

Damn it. Relief flooded me, and that was so, so fucking wrong. Relief? Everything was inside out and back to front. He knew Klaus.

"You know Klaus. That's such a great fucking recommendation mister whosiewhatsit. So you know he put me in here?" I gestured.

He chuckled. "Call me Chris. Yeah, I do. It's his house." His eyes brightened. "I wondered if it was true. Someone told me they thought you were here and they asked me to check. Now that I know though…what do I do about it?"

My reply tumbled out. "Let me go?" Yay, a normal response from me. Gold star.

"Not so easy. Sit down while we talk."

He pointed at my mattress.

It seemed safer to obey. So I sat cross-legged and tried to look confident. They'd be back soon, and rescue me.

*You're fucked up.* Then I answered myself, seeing I was being dumb. *Yes I know that, shut up.*

*And* I was being pitiful. I'd automatically trusted Klaus and Jodie more than this guy. But, when I thought about it, I understood their reasons, even if Klaus had done things to me that weren't done to…that were done… *Simply because he wanted to do them to me? Yes, that.*

A frisson of arousal ran through me swift as fire.

I shook myself from my crazy introspection. This guy, Chris, might look handsome and nice, but nasty oozed from him in some strange under-the-surface way.

"Stephanie, you need to tell me what happened so I can figure out if I should open that door for you." I guess I looked incredulous because he went on. "Like I said, I'm his friend. Look here's my business card." He tossed it like a little Frisbee and it skidded to a few feet away.

I leaned over and retrieved it. There was a picture of him on a card and he was listed as Klaus's partner.

"He must have his reasons. Let me understand why I should release you. Come on. That has to be easy. Unless…what did you do?"

I'd never ever been good at lying. What should I do? Crap, crap, crap. He's a *friend*.

He'd wrapped his hands over the front edge of the box he sat on and now he drummed his fingers. When I said nothing, he added, "You did something bad, didn't you? I guess maybe I should leave you here." He went to rise.

"Wait! No. I mean I did, but it wasn't that bad."

After he sat again and waited, I tried to decide what was best. I didn't know how to say this but I had to try. And I needed to keep in mind that one likely explanation for this man being here after they'd left me alone was that he'd been sent to test me. However not saying anything meant missing an opportunity to go free and I wasn't doing that.

Damned if I did, maybe damned if I didn't.

I looked up. "Where do I start?"

"It happened at Leon Edante's house? The night he died? There."

I took a breath. "Okay."

Then Mr. Blue-eyes Chris began to extract my story from me. Though he didn't threaten, after a while he wore me down and I answered most of his questions. Not in full—I held some facts back. I tried to tell what helped me and yet I also tried to explain how Klaus and Jodie had been involved without making them too terrible.

If I'd said the wrong things, Klaus would be so unhappy if he found out. If I was still trapped in here…

Unhappiness gnawed at me. Maybe I should have held my tongue. But I'd never been good at that.

"Thank you, Stephanie. Now I understand. So. If I open that door, what would you do?" There was genuine curiosity in that question.

Oh. This was promising. "I'd walk out."

"And? Call the police?" He leaned forward with his legs apart and his arms propped on his thighs in that posture that said male through and through.

That was the zinger of a question.

"Don't you want to send them both to jail? After all they've done to you? Klaus at least?"

I so wanted to tell him to shut up. But instead, I stared at the floor. What did he want me to say? What did I want to say? What should I say in case this was a test? Complicated, so complicated.

"I don't know."

"What if you weren't at risk of being charged, and believe me when I say I think you'd get a big exemption considering what you've gone through here."

I would? Yet how did I know that was the truth? And there was Jodie also. I liked her…a lot. My thoughts ran in circles and I stayed mute while I tried to pin down the right answer.

"Ah. I see. That confusion I can see on your face is fucking amazing."

I scowled. Creepy bastard. "You're not letting me go, are you?"

His phone rang and he held up his hand, gesturing sharply to stop me talking. Each of his next growled words struck fear ever deeper into my flesh. "*You* are small. *I* am big and nasty. Believe me when I say that. Don't speak a single fucking word while I answer this."

I blinked at him in full Bambi-mode. So much for not being scared of him.

He smiled grimly.

"Hi, Kat. Yes, I've looked. I got inside with my key. No, there's no one here." He eyed me. I looked at his large thighs and the bulge of his biceps, and I recalled his instructions.

I didn't need any further incentive. I knew pain, intimately. If I yelled I had a feeling this man would make me disappear yet again, only more permanently. And, oh my god, this wasn't a test, and from what he'd said he never intended to let me go. I'd spilled everything. If he found out, Klaus would be angry.

"No, you can't have the key so you can look too. You're going to have to trust me. I've done as much as I'm willing to. Look, I'll agree to talk again about this tomorrow, but that's it for now. Bye."

When he hung up, he leaned back against the wall. "So. Now you know. You're not getting out. I have to say, I'm in awe of Klaus."

I didn't care anymore. I was so worn out I just wanted to curl up in a corner and pretend he wasn't here. Except there was one last question—why was he here?

# Chapter 22

## Jodie

The boat ride back with that damn camera screen blacked out whenever I checked was one of the worst experiences in my life. If it was Kat and Chris who'd done this it was bad for us, but if not? I imagined her dead or assaulted or terrified, when I should be worried about a team of cops waiting for us at the house. If I'd wondered at the depth of my feelings for her, now I knew. I was besotted. Stupid but true.

Police… Okay, that worried me also. As the car wound up the road toward our house I tried to shake off a feeling of imminent doom. Despite the heat, I had to tuck my hands under my armpits to stop my trembling. "Do you think," I swallowed, "It's Kat and Chris?"

"I don't know." He reached and tugged my hand out then squeezed it. "Wait, please. Wait until we have facts." Then he held my hand whenever he wasn't changing gears.

The familiar shadow-dappled drive up the winding road had never taken this long. I wanted this over. I wanted our life back without all this drama. Only I wanted her in it too. I wanted to tell her she was mine, just like Klaus had to me. Which was so crazy. All those ebooks I'd read with capture fantasy stories had warped me somehow, irreversibly. Why else did I want to keep someone I adored by my side by tying them up and telling them to sit and stay?

I sighed. Eyes unfocused, I recalled how she looked when repentant. So many possibilities.

*Snap out of it. We're here.*

The gravel under the tires popped and crackled as we rolled to a halt. There were no cars here before us. The engine cut out. No noise. I listened hard again, noticing Klaus doing the same.

"There's no cars." I ventured a smile. "Maybe it is a false alarm? If there were police, we'd know by now."

"Probably. But I saw Chris's car farther down the road. He parked it mostly out of sight. He must have come over on the ferry."

"Oh. Fuck. Then…" By now, he'd found her. This was still bad.

Klaus shook his head. "I'll go in and see. I imagine he's inside. He's a friend. Maybe we can get time from him before he tells anyone. A few hours."

I frowned. "You don't think he'll have told the police yet."

"If Kat's here, yes. But…" He tapped the steering wheel. "We don't know who's in there. There could also be police. We may have to face up to what we've done. If we do, sweetheart, I'll try to take most of the blame. So follow my lead. Okay?"

I did not want to go down this path. "Klaus…"

"Okay?" he insisted.

"Yes, but I'm coming in with you."

His sigh was so long and wrought with tension that I sniffed and put my hand on his shoulder. "Please."

He patted my hand. "Sure, but if there are cops, or any signs of violence, stay out of the way. Do as you're told. We aren't fighting this."

"Of course not. I know."

With sadness and fear plucking at me every step of the way, I followed Klaus into the house, watching his broad back muscles move under his shirt and wondering if soon I might not be able to touch and kiss him or draw comfort from him when I needed to.

The back door was unlocked. The webcam in the hallway had black paint sprayed over the lens. Simple yet effective. The police wouldn't do that, would they? My heart pounded faster. We wound down the stairs to the room.

As we neared it, the door opened.

"Hi." Chris smiled suavely. "Only me. I've been waiting for you."

After the first frightened lub-dub of my heartbeat, I inhaled, resurrecting some calmness. Only him? What had he been doing?

Past him, I saw Steph sitting on her mattress in her cream dress, small, vulnerable, her feet tucked under her, her eyes glassy. I nudged by him, doing a swift check of the room as I walked to her. No one else was here. Thank god. I kneeled and ran my hand over her hair then down to her nape where I cupped my palm on her. "You okay, pet?"

"Yes." But her voice shook.

"He hasn't done anything to you?" I didn't know why I asked that. Chris was a Dom and had always been a gentleman at all times to me.

"No. Nothing. Nothing really."

I leaned in until my nose brushed on her neck. I breathed in. "You smell so good." Then her hand came up to my face and she gently pulled me close so she could kiss me once.

"I'm so glad you're here." She blinked, owl-eyed. "I'm sorry. I told him things. He said he was your friend and that he might let me go if I did." Her focus darted about for a second or two before she settled on just looking into my eyes. "I know I'm a fool, but he scares me."

"It's okay." I smiled. "I'll make sure Klaus understands."

I sat down next to her, putting my arm about her shoulders, and turning to the men who'd been watching us. "Well. What's this about?"

Klaus looked from Chris to me then he strolled over, saying, "Yes, why are you here, Chris? I assume Kat is involved?"

"She is. The woman's suspicious of you. Convinced that you have something to do with this girl's disappearance. I don't mind telling you everything." He held out both palms. "Full disclosure here. I came here because I was intrigued by her theory. I figure I know you pretty well, Klaus but I'd never have picked you for a man who would kidnap her." He nudged his chin toward where we sat huddled together. "Anyway, I agreed with Kat to investigate."

"You did. Huh." Klaus squatted beside us and studied Steph. "You okay?"

Quietly, she nodded, but behind my back, her hand tightened in my shirt.

"Good." He patted her leg, squeezed. "Chris wouldn't have hurt you, but scared was pretty much engraved on your face when we came in. You two stay there. I'll sort this out."

He rose and went back to Chris. "What have you told Kat?"

"That there's nobody here."

*Oh thank god.*

"She knows I copied your keys—I got them from work. You leave them on your desk sometimes when you go down the street for lunch. Sneaky of me. Sorry." He pulled out a key ring, unlinked some keys and gave them to Klaus. "Here. I don't have other copies. I admit I was torn for a while when I discovered her in this room. But..." He sucked in a deep breath, shook his head slowly from side to side while meeting Klaus's gaze. "No. No way. I couldn't."

"Couldn't what? Give us up? Why?"

"Why?" Chris asked.

I glanced at Steph and melted at the way she'd cuddled in and laid with her head in the hollow of my shoulder. She peeked up when she realized I was looking.

"Thank you for being so sweet," she murmured.

"Me?" I kissed her forehead. "It's nothing. Only, my heart was in my mouth when we arrived here. I was worried about you."

"Oh." Her smile warmed me then she wriggled to look at the men. "Klaus is so sunburnt."

"Yes, he is. It's a side effect of beach cricket." Wow. With all this, she'd noticed that. It made me wonder about how she regarded him.

"Yes, Chris, why the hell are you risking yourself helping us?" Klaus's shoes scraped the floor as he shifted his stance.

"I don't know exactly." Wonder flooded Chris's words. "Fuck it. No, I'm lying. I'm lying to me as much as you." He clasped both hands at the back of his head for a moment. "Give me a second."

I'd never seen this man so discomforted.

"Okay. I guess I admitted this to her—your little captive girl. I'm in awe of you, Klaus. I know why this whole kidnapping thing happened, but I'm still in awe. I...I would have done...the same thing, beyond any doubt. I might have hesitated but once I decided to do it, zero to a hundred. If not faster. Respect, man." Chris frowned. "Not sure it's right to say that, but I do. I am."

He was really on our side. I realized I'd been holding back. Worried. Tightness left my muscles.

"Respect?" Klaus rubbed his face. "I'm not sure I'm comfortable with getting respect from you for this. You know we plan to let her go? I'm just waiting for the time to do it." He looked over. "For when we trust her enough."

"I see. You're waiting for that? Trust? If I was a cop, you'd be in trouble. She did just spill it all to me. Though I have to admit I showed her our business card with my photo. That swayed her. Plus I'm a bloody good interrogator—I've practiced on way too many subs. The curious and cute thing is—she described what you did in a way that made it seem almost sensible."

"She did? That's good then." For a second, he eyed Steph as if he'd found an unexpected treasure. "Let's go upstairs. We'll all go up, the girls included, and we can have coffee while you tell me what Kat's doing."

After arranging the coffee for them, and one for me, I sat on the floor rug in the living room with Steph and listened to them. After Klaus had Chris repeat what Steph had told him, he asked about Kat. It had been the phone call on the night of the party that first made her suspicious, but whatever had kept that hunch ticking over, Chris wasn't certain. It made me wonder if even he knew everything.

"Bottom line." Chris slapped the table next to his coffee mug. "She's not giving up easy and wanted to come snoop for herself when I said the room was empty. I told her she couldn't have the key, though. I'll say I no longer have it. Stands to reason I'd not keep it if I was honorable, and I am." He looked at me and at Steph where she lay with her head in my lap, getting stroked. His gaze sharpened. "Except maybe when it comes to this. I never thought I would be okay with this, even though it's a scene I love to role play with subs when I get a chance."

That wasn't the first time he'd looked at us that way. Chris was more than a little attracted to this, maybe to Steph herself. But, really, that was good, wasn't it? It meant we had him on our side. Meant he was unlikely to go the police, or to Kat.

"So she's going to chase us about this still then." Under the table, Klaus's feet were ever-moving, just the tiniest bit. He was worried. "If it had been her and not you... I think I may need to take the option I didn't want to and go overseas."

"She's probably going to chase it, yes. I have an idea. You need time to sort things out and time away from here where no one can see what you do, or who is with you. My brother has a rundown house on a private island in the Whitsundays. Just a spit of land. But no one goes there. He can't sell it and you can't live there all year. Cyclones have wrecked the bungalow a few times. Right now it's safe enough. Take some equipment and you can sit there away from any snooping that Kat might do, and you can think about where to go from here. At seven knots it's about ten hours' sail from here. If storms come you can duck into the coast."

"Interesting. If I can get internet access, I might do that."

I looked down and, to my amusement, Steph had fallen asleep on my arm. If nothing else, I could enjoy this moment and so, mindful of not waking her, I caressed her soft skin, rearranged her hair strand by strand, and just by being with her, I inhaled her scent. I took pleasure in the feel of her body as she breathed the unworried sleep of the innocent. It was us who were to blame now. She'd done her penance. We owed her. We owed her freedom.

What a pity, though. My eyes moistened at the thought of that day which must come soon.

I raised my head. The men had decided something. Klaus was thanking Chris while shaking his hand.

"Let's go with Wednesday. We'll get packed and wait for you to arrange it. Thanks for this."

"Sure. It won't take more than a phone call. You have to get a boat to get down there. I can't do that part." Chris pushed back his chair, looking ever so tall as he rose to his full height. "Happy to do this for you. If it's okay I might join you there on the weekend if I can get away. I could leave Friday night if I can take Saturday off?"

"Do that. Take Saturday off. You need to think about if you want the place. Maybe I can sell it to you somehow. I don't know. It might implicate you if I do."

"Uh." He rocked back on his heels. "Sure. I'll have to think."

Selling the accounting practice? He was thinking of really leaving here then. *Suck it up. Put on those big girl panties.* If we had to leave, we had to.

I watched Chris walk from the room with some relief. We were going to his brother's island? Yet whatever they'd arranged it was far better than the scenarios that had played out in my head when the door downstairs had opened to the room.

There might have been violence. We were messing about with a very important law that governed people's freedom. Historically, when laws like this were broken, people got hurt.

Chris was a martial arts expert and had beaten Klaus at least once. As much as I hated to admit it, I thought Klaus would lose in a fight. I didn't want to see a face-off between them, ever. Watching my Dom get the shit beaten out of him would be sickening.

I thought back on what had just happened. The way Chris had looked at Steph bothered me. It was partly why I'd stayed on the floor with her. I couldn't shake the feeling that she needed my protection.

It made me think about how I felt about her. Last night I'd been talking to Klaus about our relationship—me and him. He'd been worried he'd been neglecting me and vowed to pay me more attention from now on. He had been neglecting me, but it was obvious why. Besides, we were in love. I knew it even if he didn't. I'd trust him to the end of the world. He'd thought I might be jealous.

Only now, I was cuddling Steph like he had me a few hours ago, and the feelings I had for her were almost as strong as they were for him. I adjusted where my nose rested, inhaling her pretty scent, and wishing I could keep her like this, forever in my arms.

# Chapter 23

## Klaus

Like Chris had said, the entry to the one safe place to anchor in the lee of Rat Island was difficult to navigate, but I managed. With the sea calm, I wasn't concerned but in a choppy sea it'd be difficult. Though going outward looked to be a little easier, I'd need to keep an eye on the weather. If I had to leave in an emergency, the port at Bowen wasn't far away. The whispering of the hull slicing the water lessened then silenced. Once Jodie and I tossed the bow and stern anchors overboard and cinched them in, I straightened.

We were in the middle of the ocean with nowhere to run if a police helicopter arrived overhead. Chris knew precisely where we were. Not for the first time I searched myself for reasons to worry and came up with nothing. I'd trusted him with my business and my livelihood, and with the money of thousands of my clients from the moment I'd employed him. He'd proven himself many times. I doubted my mother more than I did him.

I let out a long breath and smiled at our surroundings.

Rat Island might have had rats but it looked like a little bite of tropical heaven had fallen from the sky. Against the blue, the silhouette of palms and a few heavier trees was utter green. The beach was on the western side, and small. The *shush* of the waves shifting the white sand back and forth had no accompaniment apart from the creak and slap of the boom and the sail and the indignant caw of a crow.

I shaded my eyes to see if the bird was visible in the one tree that stretched branches over the beach.

"Is that a crow?" From her seat near the midships hatch, Steph also searched the trees. "The nasty things go everywhere."

"Nasty? Crows have a bad reputation but they're amazing birds. Beautiful plumage and they know how to survive."

In that cute way of hers, she wrinkled her nose. "Like you, Sir?"

"Uh. I have beautiful plumage? Or did you mean the bad reputation?"

"You're...pretty, yes." She grinned.

The outdoors had revived her cheekiness. On the short voyage here she'd increasingly come out of her shell. She interested me more this way. Like a trinket that you find has secret layers.

I lifted my eyebrows. "Brat."

The blush that followed revived me too. I examined her. Both her and Jodie wore bikinis and if any clothes were made for quick access and for admiring the female form, it was the bikini.

I'd been planning to keep my hands off her from now on, a plan that was looking shaky. I scrubbed my fingers through my salt-stiffened hair. We were going to part ways soon, though imagining that tore me up inside. Why the fuck that was...I wasn't sure. I'd abducted her, for god's sake. Maybe my reasons had been good ones, but what I'd done since then was far beyond what I had to do.

This was a good island for me; I had the morals of a rat, lately. Or a dog that'd scented a bitch in heat. Not that Steph was a bitch—just a woman who made me want to tie her up and do nasty things to her...and lately, to hug her gently. When I saw Jodie doing that, I yearned to be there, holding both these women in my arms.

But, keeping my hands off her? My libido had other ideas. Memories arrived, the details of scents, tastes, sounds—her mouth wrapped around my cock, the way she gasped and shuddered when she came, and afterward, when she was sexually exhausted, the feel of her body against mine.

No. I simply couldn't resist. I growled out a command, pointing at the deck, "Kneel up, toy. You too Jodie, beside her."

When they were both kneeling facing me, I assessed them slowly, lingering on the swell of their tits where they spilled from the bikini tops. I stepped up to them, reached out, and lifted their faces higher. "You're both hot enough to make a man want to bend you over the nearest boulder. I think I'll have to make a sacrifice to the maker of the bikini. After we find this bungalow, you're going to do this again and I'm going to use your pretty mouths."

Jodie's grin widened as her gaze travelled lower. She let her tongue swipe across her lips. "Yes, Sir."

From her, that response was par for the course, but the way Steph also dwelt on the bulge in my pants with widened eyes, made me pause. On both women, I let my fingers trail down their necks, across the edge of the silken fabric then lower again, circling around and sometimes bumping over their erect nipples. They breathed a little faster, except Steph looked downward while Jodie maintained eye contact.

I kissed Jodie's mouth then made her look at Stephanie, who still had her head down, as if hoping I'd ignore her. "Doesn't she look desirable? With that pout on her lips and her hair hanging over her face." I tugged on one black curl and was rewarded by the flash of Steph's eyes.

"Desirable, Sir? Yes. May I touch her? Please?" That determined answer from Jodie and the way she stared at Steph—my oh my, my cock liked that.

"Jodie!" she whispered.

"Well you are!"

I laughed. "Not yet. Later." Then I kissed Steph also, a little rougher, tasting her mouth until she opened to me. "Both of you are gorgeous. We're done here. Find yourselves your beach shoes and we'll check out the island."

The island could be walked around in five minutes. Once past the beach, you had to clamber over rocks on the eastern side. The bungalow turned out to be visible from the beach, though disguised by the trees and the shadows. Since the center of the island rose into a low rocky crag, there was no other place to build, if you could call the two-room shack a building. Chris had said his brother rebuilt it each year atop the concrete foundation, after the cyclone and storm season passed, and I could see the signs of repair in the grafted-on timber. The roof was corrugated iron and had no insulation. In the middle of summer you would roast in here. On the boat we had water, a toilet, a shower and cold storage. Here we had four walls, a roof, and a couple of inches of sand on the floor. Also two distressed wooden chairs and two wooden bed bases. The bed slats looked solid if in need of removal of, yes, more sand.

"I suppose, you ladies would like to sleep on the boat tonight?"

Jodie shrugged. "I guess."

"Umm." Steph swiveled on the spot, the sand grating under her rubber Croc shoes. "I've never camped out. Could we try one night here?"

My eyebrows must have shot up. "Never camped out?" The shake of her head made me tsk. "Sure, we can do one night here. We'll bring over lights, water and sleeping bags, and the inflatable mattresses. What have I forgotten? Bear in mind there won't be showers here. And we all have to keep watch on the weather reports. We can't afford to wake up to a storm."

"Thank you," Steph said. "Food, you forgot that."

"Right. Food. Let's go fetch all that. Jodie you want to sweep out the sand?"

"Sweeping? Here? Jeez. Even in a deserted hut I get to sweep." She'd put her hands on hips while she surveyed the mess. "I'll need a broom."

"Let's go then." I cracked my palm sharply onto her butt, smiling as she hissed at the pain and swung her head to glare.

"Ow! I mean, ow, Sir."

"That grin makes me want to spank you again. Go! How can I watch your butts if you're not both ahead of me?" Steph was already in the stark sunlight halfway down the beach, though she'd stopped to observe Jodie's antics.

"Well, in that case, watch this." Then she put on an exaggerated sway as she walked away.

The deliberate grind of her hips made me sigh, but I followed. "Paying for that later, sweetheart."

I glanced up. Steph seemed fascinated by our banter. I guess she hadn't seen much of my frivolous side. I eyed her too. Maybe it was a good idea to show her more? As she turned to stroll across the sand, the seductive lower line of the t-shirt she'd pulled on over her swimmers tantalized me with glimpses of her butt cheeks.

I adjusted myself. Noted. More joking. After I use her ass.

Tomorrow I would start checking my emails for feedback from a certain contact who knew illegal exits from the country, and where to go afterward, as well I'd begin talking about and thinking about what to do. Hard decisions. Maybe sad ones. Tonight would be for something else.

\*\*\*\*\*

I'd been going to line the girls up side by side to use their mouths, but there was always that temptation to do something kinkier to Steph. There was something unique about her that made me crave doing despicable things. Luckily, Jodie also delighted in this. Using persuasive words and bondage, and sometimes a little force, we could make her perform.

Our little lustful sex puppet. I swear the room heated when I thought of things to do to her body.

I'd told her some of my plans before we tied her up. There'd been only one episode of her biting the corner of her lip until it twisted out of shape. After a growl from me she subsided. That little bit of fear in her was what drew me. She'd never lose that. I could play with her for a year and still find that in her when I wanted. Oh the fucking attraction of that.

I forced calm on myself.

As Jodie pulled her wrists behind her back, her breathing hastened. When Jodie undid the bow on her swimsuit top and pulled it away, Steph bit her lip and watched. And when I grasped Jodie by the hair and made her suckle on each breast, her mouth fell open and she looked so amazingly aroused that I gripped her by the hair also then took her mouth. When Jodie crouched and shifted aside the scrap of material over her mound, Steph parted her thighs.

The girl was so into this. Orgasms were clearly a good persuasive tool.

"Would you like me to lick you here?" The lamplight showed Jodie already tonguing her clit with the very tip of her tongue, teasing, flicking.

"Yes," Steph begged, squirming her groin closer.

I chuckled as Jodie pulled back and teased again. Each dab made Steph tense her thighs and hitch her breath.

"Please, more. There, just there!"

And yes, the more we did, the more she moaned. Her first orgasm happened a minute later, at most. I held her hair at the roots while she shuddered through it with Jodie still lapping at her.

Getting Jodie to undress was easy, and getting her to undress Steph the rest of the way was amusing. She was so enraptured in pulling down the bikini bottoms and yet willing to slow down the whole process by following the slide of the material with tens of tiny kisses and licks.

The lamps we'd set up lent a decadent ambience to the scene—shadows flickered across the women's naked skin, painting them like slave girls from some jungle harem. Naked, voluptuous, and ready for a man to force them into acts of depravity.

I smiled. That, I could do.

After I had, at last, used her mouth and Jodie's, until I came in hers, I made our toy stand before me in the hut. Some shibari would make her breasts stand out like swollen fruit, would make her feel what I did next exquisitely. Simple bondage, since the light was poor.

Using her wrist cuffs, her arms were pulled sideways by ropes that attached to the frame of the hut. With a stick and more rope, I fastened her legs shoulder-width apart. A spare pile of rope lay coiled on the beds we'd made up and shoved against the walls of the bungalow. The shibari was in the chest tie which looped from her collar O-ring to her breasts, between them and around her chest twice, then the rope ran down between her legs in a double trail that, after running up the crevice of her ass and the length of her spine, joined to the back ring on her collar.

"Do you know what I'm going to do to you now?" I walked sedately around her, watching her body's responses and scratching my fingernails as I went across the skin of her back, her breasts, her belly. It was too dark to see the thin red lines but I could imagine them.

The last piece of rope I'd tied, doubled up, across her mouth in a perfunctory gag—it was more a decoration than a gag, a very dark disturbing decoration. Rope was so ugly, yet so alluring and sexual parked there, between her lips and teeth, pulling the corners of her mouth back. Like I'd defiled an angel. It made me want to fuck her mouth again and I didn't even have another hard-on yet.

I watched her, watching me, as I circled her.

I was grateful that some pristine carpet wasn't beneath our bare feet since the insides of her thighs already glistened with her moisture.

"What's this, little fucktoy?" I crouched to run my hand up her thigh over the wetness then entered her and finger fucked her slowly. "Before I end this tonight, you're going to be dripping on the floor. I promise." Though she wiggled, I held her around the waist and made my fingers penetrate her as far as I could go, stretching her opening. She moaned a little as I moved them inside her. Hot, so fucking wet. My dick resurrected. Miraculous that. Hah.

I pulled out then moved in with my chest against her back. The rope was harsh on my skin, which meant she'd be feeling it too. With my moist fingers clawed into our toy's ass and my forearm across her throat, I called Jodie over. My voice next to her ear, and no doubt my firm hold on her, sent a shudder through the girl that even my cock felt. I stiffened at the prospect of putting it in her. Later, I told myself, after we mess with her body.

"Do you remember the day she came up from the room and we bit this girl everywhere until she was begging us to make her come?"

Jodie nodded. "Yes, Sir."

"I'd like to give her pain, but I can't see well in this lighting. So we're going to use our teeth and fingers on her. If she comes, that's okay, but make her work for it."

Then I went round to her front and took both Steph's nipples between finger and thumb. I squeezed them then pulled them outward by an inch or so, until she mewed and struggled to get loose.

"No," I said harshly. "You can't get away. The perfect curve of your tits begs me to torture them, you know that? One day, if I had you, I'd pierce these with metal. I'd make you mine by right because you'd have something of mine in you, permanently."

How true that was. My mind rendered an image of these parts of her that I held submitting to me pushing steel into her. An ultimate sadistic thrill plus that sexual element. Nipples felt so much, hurt so much, held so much potential for torture in a woman. The light was good enough to see the change when I squashed my left finger and thumb down firmer. Barely a morsel of an inch separated them.

She whined, her hands twisting in the bondage.

Her darkened eyes stared up at me and her lips moved on the rope as if she were biting it. Already, below where I stood, Jodie had begun to nip her and pinch, including right over her clit. Her whimpers became mews then gasps as Jodie sucked on her clit, making wet noises. I let go of her nipples then twisted them, tugged again, over and over. I moved my pinching onto the skin around her nipples. Enough of this and they would be on fire.

Orgasms tempered by pain could send the pleasure level through the roof.

"I know you don't like pain that much, but I do. When I see you whimper, it makes me want to fuck you sideways until you can't walk straight. Luckily for you, toy, I have an idea as to your tolerance now. I can give you pain or pleasure…when you need it most."

I leaned in, squashed her now-engorged breasts together then bent and took her nipples into my mouth, sucking and chewing on them, making her wince and moan, sometimes almost at the same time. With my hands clasped around both her breasts and the bondage she'd be feeling like she had nowhere to go. Jodie always loved that. When her arousal escalated rapidly, I suspected this one did too. Though she strained at the ropes, and tried to writhe against my grip, her pants and groans became louder and desperate.

"Shove some fingers into her, Jodie." I smiled around my mouthful of breast when she almost immediately tensed and bowed her body forward. Another orgasm wracked her.

After giving her time to recover, I started on a full-on biting assault, covering her front then her back and her ass in small nips and, here and there, large bites that let me take a chunk of her ass or shoulder or back muscle between my teeth. She was so eminently biteable.

Then I stood back, admiring our sweaty captive as Jodie kissed her face. I moved so I could see her mouth over Steph's with the rope gag between them. That Steph was answering the kiss or trying to was inspiring.

I checked her hands and feet. Good. Warm. Her fingers and toes moved well when I tickled her.

Hand on my cock, I contemplated which of my beautiful women to fuck.

I pulled off my shorts, seeing that they were the most uncomfortable things in creation when I had a full erection, and found a condom from a pocket and rolled it on.

"Wish I could do your ass again, pet, but it's too hard to clean up here."

She grunted at me then whined a little, shaking her head. Sweat flicked at me from her hair. In the low light I could see trails of it running down the sides of her face.

From behind Steph, with one arm anchoring her body to me, and the other holding one butt cheek and the rope aside, I probed upward. My cock knew where to go in all that slipperiness and I thrust up and up, sliding in, grunting in satisfaction when I knew I was in all the way.

Smooth gentle strokes seemed to do little for her so I undid the rope at the back of her neck to get it out of the way. Sanding off my dick would not be a smart thing to do. I grabbed the other side of her butt so I held her properly open and I rammed in over and over until she squealed and bounced on her toes. Her back arched, her chest jutted forward and I could feel her legs try to open even more.

"G-spot?" I smirked and tried hard to get the same angle and depth.

If she'd thought she couldn't climax again Jodie soon proved her wrong by wringing one out of her. Her little gasping screams gradually petered out.

I'd withdrawn in time, barely keeping it together and not coming inside her. Best to use a new condom. I found another in my shorts.

"Your turn, Jodie. Come here."

Leaving Steph panting, with her bedraggled hair across her face, she walked the few feet to where I'd sat on one of the chairs. When she arrived, I pulled her over my lap, facedown. I stroked her ass, getting a feel for her flesh, remembering the many times I'd done this.

"You have such a great ass."

"Thank you." Her voice was husky and I grinned. Playing with Steph had wound her up.

Then I began to spank her. Each slap made her shift a little—her legs, her thighs, her waist twisted, and at the harder ones, she threw back her head and tried to look at me. But I kept her there, on my lap, trapped as I slowly increased the force. By the sound of her moans and her panting, by how she dug her toes in the floor, or by the writhe of her hips, I could tell where my girl was at. I slipped my fingers inside her when it seemed a good time, or rubbed on her clit, then spanked her some more. When I finally stopped, I rested my palm on her skin, spellbound in the heat radiating off her.

"Sit on me sweetheart, but facing outward. I want Steph to see your face when I make you come."

"Okay." She kissed my thigh once then shakily climbed to her feet.

She stood between my legs and while she slowly lowered herself, I held my cock upright and still. Her ass wiggled. In. Fuck. The cupping of her warmth around the head made me arch my head back for a second. Then she slid further. At halfway, I put my hands on her shoulders and made her sink all the way down.

"Fuck, fuck, fuck. Oh, that's good." She swallowed. Her head fell forward as I thrust a few times.

"Now ride me."

I found her clit and stroked her with the rhythm that would get her off if I did it for long enough, biting her back and nape here and there, and making her thump herself down on me harder when I wanted it. But I didn't let her come.

When she was close, I stood with her impaled on me, and slipped to my knees while she went to hands and knees. It was gritty on the floor but I was too interested in getting my cock happy to worry. Then I settled in with the thrusts while I kept at her clit until she gasped and came, squeezing onto my cock hard. The sensations rippled into me like a minor seismic event.

I gasped once and let myself rest for a second. Earthquakes had nothing on sex.

I kissed her shoulder then started to fuck her in earnest. Feeling that aching pressure reach its peak, I put my palm in the center of her shoulder blades and forced her to the floor. My knees would hate me for this but I didn't care. Bursting to come, I slammed in a few more times, spurting into her hard enough to make me gasp through my teeth and wonder if my balls had imploded. I hugged her a while, for she was still breathing fast, still clamping onto me now and then. Her head turned into my arm. For a minute we stayed there. Her hot breath stirred the hairs on my forearm.

I rolled to take my weight off her then clambered to my feet. I had to free Steph.

She was so tired I had to support her or she would have collapsed. "Stay up here with me, sweet girl. It's not worth getting all sticky and gritty on the floor."

I kissed her hair and patted her, seeing Jodie's bright eyes watching us from where she lay. I suddenly realized what I'd called Steph—sweet girl. An endearment, maybe the first I'd ever called her. I sighed and smelled her hair. She did feel sweet in my arms. Then she grumbled and I felt her small tongue lick at my chest.

"You're all hairy," she complained. Her words slurred and she sounded half-asleep. "But...I like it. You taste like a man should. Nice." She sighed.

Oh hell. I held her tighter, frowning down at Jodie. This was meant to be a night to show her what she'd be missing when she left us. I meant to fuck her brains out and to give her so many orgasms she'd never in a million years forget us, but instead, she'd made me wonder if *I* could ever forget her. I'd grown...fond of her.

Eventually, Jodie got to her feet and I drew her into the cuddle.

"I'll get you both a drink, then we can go down to the beach and rinse off. Okay?"

Jodie nodded. Steph whispered from her place in the middle of the hug, "Sure." Then she added something that near stopped my heart. "I know this is odd, but that was amazing. Thank you, Klaus."

But it wasn't the thanks that hurt my heart; it was her saying my name.

# Chapter 24

## Steph

Klaus had pushed the two beds together and, after drying off with beach towels we'd piled in together. I'd drunk what seemed gallons of water before collapsing on the bed and snuggling into my lovers.

My head was fuzzy. My body seemed to have fires lit on my skin in so many places. I throbbed with aches and stings and yet I floated toward sleep, somehow strangely content, despite the sadist sleeping behind me with his hand on my thigh. A few lame mosquitoes whined in my ear then I was gone into dreamland.

I awoke to the sound of the waves surging and the trees rattling and whispering above, and to something scratching on the floor. Puzzled, I shifted up onto my butt with my arm out, and rubbed my eyes. The lamps were turned off, though a tiny blinking red light showed where Klaus had left something on. Sitting up gave me a better view. The floor was moving.

What was it? Dreaming still? The bedclothes were real. Jodie lay before me curled up and spooning to my front. The pale moving things scuttled forward. I blinked then I shrieked.

"What the fuck?" Jodie sprang awake, sitting up and staring up at me.

"What is it?" The bed shifted as Klaus also woke. His baritone reassured me, even if he sounded confused from being hurled from sleep into reality by my scream. His hand settled on my waist and he squeezed lightly. "Have the Martians landed?"

"There's something on the floor!" I pointed frantically, half expecting whatever it was to leap onto my extended arm then crawl up it to smother me and rip out my throat.

"What?" She turned and peered over the edge. "Oh shit." Jodie giggled. "Crabs! We have an invasion of crabs. Well, three or four. Silly. You know the door has a hole." She lay down again then pulled me on top of her.

Though the soft warmth of her female body instantly reminded me of sex. I had to look. From closer, I could see the little creatures making their way across the floor. Two nearer ones had frozen in place. I guess I'd scared them.

"Fuck. Sorry. Though ick too. What happens if I need to go to the toilet?"

"Not a problem. Mostly they skedaddle faster than you can step on them, but I can shoo them outside and put something in the hole in the door." Though clearly amused Klaus patted my hip. "Poor girl."

"It's okay." Jodie drew my face down to hers. She nibbled on my lips, slowly fading it into a true gentle kiss. I couldn't resist poking my tongue between her lips and pressing down on her, taking more of her mouth. I moved my legs to go outside hers but she spread hers instead and ground her pussy up into mine. Pleasure surged and I moaned as I exhaled.

"You're hot for it already." I felt her smile against my lips then her hand groped for the hair at the back of my neck, gathering it.

Already she was trying to take control. Slightly annoyed, I shook my head to get loose but she firmed her hold.

"Uh-uh. Stay there. Didn't we exhaust you, pet?"

"I…" The night's meager light outlined her face with silver and dark. Her hair spread about her pillow in a wash of tendrils. I traced her cheekbone, swallowed. "You're beautiful, my goddess."

Jodie chuckled. "Am I? Maybe…maybe I can be a sex goddess."

Her pelvis kept moving, circling upward, stirring me, and heat flooded in. I heard the rustle of plastic tearing and wondered if that was what I thought it was. Every part of me was awake now and aware of where this was heading.

"We should go back to sleep," I whispered, hoping, and not hoping, but mostly there was that dark and new need of mine to be made to do something I might not want. Pet. Fucktoy. Depravity had found me.

"No, we should not." As he spoke, Klaus settled himself above my body. His heavy thighs pushed mine apart. His arms propped either side of me.

He must have pulled down his pants and I had none on, only a t-shirt. I could tell his cock was precisely where it should be. My entrance spilled wetness and opened. I couldn't help myself. I couldn't help anticipating the delicious slide. Transfixed by the knowledge that he meant to fuck me at any second, I waited, enthralled. His first thrust entered me, slick, hard, impatiently driving in and in until his groin thumped onto my ass.

Eyes slamming shut, I grunted at the invasion, wanting more, needing *more*.

Oh god. So full. So amazing being used like this. No asking if or when. No nothing. Though still sore, I so liked this.

"Damn that's pretty," Jodie murmured. "Are you in her, Sir?"

I opened my eyes and saw her studying me.

"In all the way." He laughed. "She was ready for me. Kiss her while I fuck her."

"Yes, Sir."

I braced my arms on the bed, and was rocked forward by the power of each of his thrusts. My neck strived to curl downward, my lips opened, and Jodie licked at my mouth.

"Come back down here."

Our kisses ended up being wet and sloppy as she took over that part of me while he took me with his cock. I couldn't concentrate on one or the other. Soft woman under me, breast and devouring mouth, her hand clawed in my hair, and him, hard-muscled, powerful, and heavy, thumping in deep. Possessed by the two of them at once. I groaned and writhed.

When I was at the point of wanting to scream at him to drive into me harder, he withdrew. I almost cried and fisted the sheets. A second later I knew what he was doing as his hands fumbled at my back and rearranged us. Jodie grunted under me and gasped. He'd entered her. She shifted back and forth as he plowed her instead. So did I, caught in the middle of their lust. I smiled despite my ache to have him in me. Watching her enthralled me.

When he at last climaxed, Jodie's eyes rolled back. My own pussy clenched in a sympathetic wish to feel what she did in that moment. I imagined the swell of his cum and pulse of his member. Him fucking her like this was amazingly arousing.

When he pulled out, she whimpered. He lowered himself more and I had no choice except to snuggle half my face into the angle of Jodie's neck and shoulder. With one eye, I watched him kiss her gently.

"How was that, gorgeous?"

"Good." She smiled. "Good, mister sexy beast."

"I figured it was your turn to have me come in you."

"Mm-hm. Great minds think alike."

This fascinated me—seeing how loving he was with her. Yet also it bothered me. I wasn't sure I was a part of this. I wasn't sure why I wanted to be. I shoved that away and shut my eyes and felt my breathing slowly synchronize with theirs.

I hadn't come. I didn't need to, and I could have stayed there under him forever. Man-weight squashing me. *Mmm.* The fog of lust made me happy to just *be*. At last, I shifted. Klaus moved away and lay next to me. I was drooling on Jodie. I huffed as she kissed my cheek and stroked my hair.

"I'm sorry. I think I dribbled on you."

She chuckled. "Sex is messy. We can swim in the morning. Nothing's perfect on an island with no showers. Go back to sleep, pretty one. I want to just cuddle you."

"M'kay." I snuggled in, still mostly on my belly with my hand curled on her shoulder. I was halfway to sleep when Klaus spooned up to my back.

"What about the crabs?" he whispered from close to my ear.

"Forget them," I mumbled. With both of them warming me and stroking me, I faded out into dreamless soothing black.

For the next two days we luxuriated in our tropical paradise. I hiked around the island with no one holding a leash or telling me to beg or lie down or spread my legs. Though at other times, that happened. I discovered the fun, crazy side to Klaus as well as the way he could protect when called to. We spread sunscreen on each other and mocked the redness that showed when we'd done the wrong thing and sat in the sun too long anyway. And we administered pain-killers and Band-aids when someone stepped on a rock and scraped themselves.

I even did this to Klaus while he watched—smoothed a Band-Aid onto his knee. His bemused expression pleased me. I liked him like this—fun yet wise, yet an amazing lover.

It was when he threatened to stick metal through my nipples and torture me that I cringed. He was smart to tie me up at those times. I would have run. Sad but true. He was so close to perfect yet he'd never be right for me. And soon I would be freed. Why was I so sad then? Too much ecstasy, too much attention paid to me, I guessed. I'd wallowed in them treating me as their treasured thing for so many days that the good things I'd loved overwhelmed all the pain and humiliation. I had to admit to myself—I liked being their sex object.

Soon, I'd have withdrawal symptoms.

And so we swam and splashed each other, made sand castles, of all things, and Jodie and I ran away shrieking from Klaus when he found something dumb to do, like chase us with a bucket of water with a crab in it.

On the Saturday, Chris arrived. He'd hired a speedboat and come out from Bowen after driving there overnight. His casual nod when he sauntered onto the beach, chilled me. The sun dimmed a notch.

At times, that day, he and Klaus sat discussing what they should do. I heard raised voices, or more raised than seemed usual during a measured discussion. Later at night, with the campfire crackling between us, they came to a decision. The teriyaki steak he'd brought with him was marinated perfectly. The bought salad was also no doubt delicious, but all I could think of was their final words. My last bit of food went down as a gray, tasteless lump. Tomorrow I was to return to the island with Chris so he could free me. If Klaus scared me, Chris fucking terrified me.

"Let's go for a walk." Jodie took my hand and tugged me to my feet.

We strolled, arm in arm, past the circle of brightness, our eyes adjusting to moonlight as we trod the cold sand. We couldn't go far anyway and the only predators on this island were the mosquitoes and the men behind us.

I stared up at the crescent moon and leaned my head in toward Jodie with my arm sliding about her waist.

"Friends still?" she murmured. "Even after everything?"

"Yes." I was miserable and didn't know how to fix this.

The coldness at the pit of my stomach was to do with my dread of travelling with Chris, or so I told myself, and nothing to do with leaving Klaus and Jodie. I was sure of that, until she pulled me up against a sun-warm boulder and kissed me.

Jodie tilted up my chin with her fingers. "I'm sorry this ends you know, though I guess to you this is a victory. You know that I love you?"

I rested my forehead on hers a moment, struggling with my answer. "Yes, I do. Because I love you too."

Then she sniffed and curled her arms around me, hugging me in tight. I began to cry, silently, trying not to let her notice because it was so dumb.

A tear rolled onto her arm from my cheek.

"You crying?"

I sighed, and nodded. "I'm stupid, aren't I?"

"I have no idea. Guess we both are. Let's just hug a while before we go back."

"Okay. And…" My hands were at her hips and I moved my fingers and resettled them, squeezing, playing with her as the cotton dress slid on her skin. I wanted to somehow implant a memory that would never fade of her warmth, her exact shape, of the sound of her voice, and her scent. I never wanted to forget this night. "Jodie, I'd like to kiss you again. If that's okay?"

I felt her laughter in the shake of her body. "Sure. We can do that. This, pet, should be our goodbye. I want to make it now and not tomorrow when the guys are watching."

"Yes. I want that too. Though I wish…" *You could come with me.* But that was wrong, she belonged to Klaus more than to me. I was a late extra.

She paused for a long shuddering inhalation. "Oh my, though. I don't know where Klaus and I are going. Maybe he'll say after you're gone?"

Here we were saying our goodbyes and she was worried more about where they were going? Somehow that said this, us, didn't mean as much to her as it did to me. The story of my life.

"Maybe. Maybe you can somehow send me a message and I can come visit you? In a few months? A year?"

"Maybe." She didn't sound hopeful. That was yet another blow to my ego. Here I was, willing to follow her to some unknown place and to risk being near Klaus, dealer of pain, and she rejected me?

*Get over it.* My mind didn't listen too well to its own instructions. The hurt stayed even if I managed to push it to the back.

I caressed her side before I drew back to look into her eyes. "I won't give you up to the police. I'll manage somehow. I'll lie. I'll make up stuff. I will."

"Thank you." I could see the vague upturn of her mouth that said she smiled.

"There's just one thing. Can you ask Klaus to double-check what happens after I go? Follow the news or something? Chris scares me even more than he does."

"I will. Promise. Though, girl, he's trustworthy. He might be a little kinky and crazy like Klaus, but I trust him. Whatever Klaus tells him to do, he will. Be happy. Don't worry."

I nodded. I wasn't convinced, but I nodded. No point in concerning her over something that might be nothing and that I couldn't alter.

"Now," she whispered. "Kiss me like you said. We got moonlight and a deserted tropical island and we really shouldn't waste this night."

"Sure." I leaned in and met her lips chastely, with feather-light kisses that roved over her mouth, her chin, her nose, and then the slender curve of her eyebrows.

When she growled and dragged me up hard against her, I melted into her embrace. That was my Jodie.

# Chapter 25

## *Steph*

In the morning, after an awkward breakfast on the beach sitting on the driftwood logs we'd been using for days, Chris rose to his feet and looked across at me. "Time to go. We have a boat ride then a fairly long car drive. Klaus." He put out his hand and they shook.

I didn't move. The bowl of breakfast cereal hadn't been to my taste anyway with the strange milk we used. Trying to stay calm, I placed it in the sand. "You haven't told me anything. What is happening?" Jodie's comforting words seemed to lose their effect in the sunlight. "I don't know that I want to go with him."

"Stay there, Jodie." Though she hesitated, she stayed. Klaus came over, the sand squeaking underfoot. He squatted in front of me. "Steph, what's happening is what I said would weeks ago. You're being set free. Except not overseas, because there's no way I can guarantee your safety there. And I see no point in releasing you far away somewhere else in Australia because you're very likely going to be found out for who you are. Chris will let you contact the police on the island after we have time to fly out. With Kat adding to the chances of this going wrong, I've decided this is the best answer. He was going to tell you all this." Klaus lowered his head for a second before continuing. "But that's it in a nutshell. We no longer need you to lie, except about one thing."

"One thing?" I stared over his shoulder at Chris. "But you trust him."

His hand came up under my chin. "Look at me." Those gray eyes. I quivered. I needed to grow a fucking backbone. "Yes, I do trust Chris. He's been honorable in this except that he's helped me. The one thing is that you need to help protect him. Otherwise he may be charged with being an accessory. Okay? So say what he tells you to when you're asked questions."

"I guess I can do that."

His explanation was so reasonable that the knot of anxiety low in my chest lessened.

"What about me though? You told me I would get charged. How has that suddenly vanished?"

"What Chris said to you is most likely correct. You'll get an exemption providing the cops think you're co-operating, because of what we did to you." In his smile and his eyes was a hint of the sadistic man I feared, and I blinked and forced myself not to look away.

"Okay," I croaked out. "I see." *Most likely. Shit. Better be.* I was the one who had to go do this.

He gripped my jaw firmly enough that it was close to pain, in the V of his fingers and thumb and his next question was said in a dead-level tone. "Stephanie, what if I said we'd get you out too? We're going out on regular flights, but…if I put my mind to it, I can get you out anonymously. Would you stay with us? Would you like to continue to be our pet and our toy?"

Dead serious. Oh god. He meant it and just him asking this aroused me, I could feel my body responding, feel myself dampening, my nipples peaking. Insane. I shut my eyes. "No. Please no."

"Please?" he murmured, laughing a little. "That you say please tells me a lot. I wish I could force you to stay with us, little fucktoy. But I can't."

I willed him to let me go but he didn't for several traumatizing minutes. He was looking at me but I simply could not open my eyes.

But I watched him walk away. My emotions were a fragile mess—a mess of joy, despair, loss. How in the world did saying goodbye to him mean loss? I rubbed the ache from my forehead. Just having him do that, talk to me like that, had drained me.

But it made me wonder if Jodie had mentioned my idea of visiting to him.

I said my farewell to her without crying though I could see a hint of them in her eyes. We simply held each other tightly but said no words apart from a whispered goodbye.

As the boat pulled out into the open sea, she wiped at her face. I waved for a few seconds before letting my hand flop to my lap. The lush red seat of the speedboat was padded but my teeth rattled as we hit waves.

Klaus hadn't even said goodbye. My last sight of him was of a man with sternness carved in the lines of his face like he'd turned to rock.

But…I hadn't wanted a hug or anything. I just wanted *something*.

From my kidnapper. Yeah. I shook my head.

"Not far to the mainland!" Chris yelled back. He smiled. "Cheer up. You'll be free to do what you want soon."

I nodded. True, except I felt numb. Emotionless. As if someone had died, only I couldn't figure out who to mourn for.

Chris acted like a human guide dog, he didn't put a foot wrong, telling me what would happen next and why, asking me to hide under a baseball cap and scarf inside the car as we crossed via vehicular ferry back to the island. I wasn't sure why we had to go back there, but then he explained his house was there. Of course, how else could he hide me while Klaus and Jodie caught their plane to wherever in the world they'd headed?

I wondered how long they would remember me. A year? A month? A day?

His house was a neat modern rendered-brick, two-story thing perched on a hillside on Horseshoe Bay. Ironic really, considering where this all began.

I barely glanced at the outside as we pulled into his garage. My borrowed sunglasses, cap and scarf came off—how un-suspicious wearing a fucking scarf in this climate. My collar and cuffs were still on. Chris didn't have the key to the little padlocks and, besides, I was meant to have escaped, so I'd still be wearing them. Made sense, though it also made me uneasy.

In a blurred state of emotional exhaustion, things happened, and a room was found for me. I flopped back on the single bed and stared at the white ceiling wondering what the hell I was doing.

Late afternoon, from the sun on the wall. I drifted into sleep curled up at the bottom of the bed.

Someone's hand shook me and I burst into reality, gasping, scrambling backward across the bed.

"Hey. Hey." It was Chris. He held up his hands. "It's okay. I don't bite. If you're hungry, I came in to tell you dinner will be ready soon. Toilet's down the hallway." He backed up. "Look, the door's open and you can come and go."

My heart slowed to less than jet plane speed. I gulped and let go of my hold on the quilt. "Thanks."

"Why not come out and watch me cook?"

"Sure."

I waited for him to go. The door might be open but the man had steel grates on his windows.

Ah. Course. Stupid. They were burglar proofing or something. Even though I'd been a total zombie on the trip back he'd done absolutely nothing bad. Chris had a corner on the being a gentlemen thing.

In the kitchen, I found him preparing to cook a Moreton Bay bug. Yum. I realized I was starving. Nothing was better than these lobster-like critters on a plate. My cooking antennae refused to let me stay back. "Need a hand?"

He peered over his shoulder at me. "You can cook one of these? I buy them sometimes but they turn out tough."

I heaved out a sigh. This I could do. Cooking calmed me. "How you can make one of these tough, I do not know. Like to have it with garlic butter?"

"Sure." He stepped aside. "I may have garlic somewhere. Butter is for certain."

Bugs were sweeter than lobster if done right. "All you need is a frying pan at the right temp and that garlic and butter." I frowned. "Seriously, this is the easiest thing."

"Go. I'm at your mercy. Cook it how you want to."

My frown faded. What had I been afraid of? Chris was, if I subtracted his initial odd behavior in the room, sexy and big and one of the squarest-looking men in build, but he was plain *nice*. He'd been gorgeous. Just, yeah, I wouldn't want to be a fly he swatted. *Maybe that's what set me against him from the start?* Big equaled scary.

I smiled. "Let me at that fry pan. But…" Go for it, like he says. "Can you tell me everything, please? Like, what and where am I going to the police?" I shut my eyes a second. "All that."

"I can. Sure." He leaned against the kitchen counter and crossed his ankles.

And he did, while I made a light stir-fry of vegetable to go with the bugs. It was simple. I only had to stay with him a while, then I'd be gone. Like he'd shown me, the doors were open. But to walk out now would betray him. I needed only to wait.

I checked him out, whistling as he set the table. I was such a dork. Not everyone was Jack the Ripper.

The bugs turned out wonderful. As we ate at the dining table, me sitting on a chair at a proper table for the first time in almost a month, I felt a split in reality. The floor beckoned me.

I shivered, remembering being at *His* feet, under his body, Jodie holding me while *he* did things to me. Lust. Sex. Pain. I breathed in some oxygen only to find Chris looking at me strangely. Shit. I was going to need a shrink after this.

For some reason the expression on Chris's face reminded me of how he'd looked at me in the room—like I was something special, as if letting myself be trapped in a room had bestowed me with some unique quality. He'd said he was in awe of Klaus. If he was in awe of the man who'd abducted me, what did that make him?

I checked him out as I took another forkful of my meal. He was as normal as ever here. In the room had been surreal. I couldn't count that against him, could I?

Yes. Yes, I could. Trust had become a precious commodity to me.

In the dark, later, I reassessed what he'd told me. Two days with him, then he'd let me go near the house Klaus owned so I could make my way to the police station and say I'd escaped. All I had to do was pretend I'd never met Chris before. I'd checked his front door and it was unlocked. That had been so amazing I'd smiled. A few days more, that was all. Easy.

I stared at the ceiling.

So alone.

No one else warm and solid to hold me.

No one to tell me what to *do*. I was free. For a second I panicked. Get a fucking grip. It's just Stockholm or lost puppy syndrome or some such crap.

When I awoke with the sun in my eyes and slanting across the wall, I found myself curled at the bottom of the bed where I used to sleep when I was with them.

Damn.

The next day passed, slowly and agonizingly, as I angsted over how things would play out when I walked into that police station. After harassing myself for ages, I discussed it with Chris.

His reply buoyed me. "You can only do your best. I don't expect miracles but if you do your best, I'm happy. But, just to help you. We'll practice." Then he pretended to be a police officer interrogating me.

If it wasn't so serious, I would have laughed. He was right, though, rehearsing my story over and over gave me confidence. We varied the precise words too. Real stories rarely used the same words while made-up ones tended to be learned by rote.

It helped, until the night brought back to me the past few weeks. I woke up frantic, sobbing, and had to sit clutching my pillow to get my breathing back to normal. I stared at the shadows of trees washing across the walls. For an adult, I was pitiful.

Shrink, remember. Afterward, after I spilled everything to the cops, I'd get a shrink and fix this problem.

At five in the morning I gave up on sleep, and sat cross-legged in the middle of the bed, with my head stuck in my pillow. I wept silently as the dawn light crept in.

I hoped Chris didn't notice the soggy patch in the middle of his pillow.

What distressed me the most wasn't the crying, or the sleeplessness, but that when I had awoken it was often in the middle of them making love to me. Awake, I recalled the pain he had made me take. Asleep, I recalled the love. Then I was stuck in the middle of nowhere, longing for something I could never have. I wanted to be able to hold and kiss Jodie again. I even, in some damn weird way, flip-flopped between wanting him and hating him. Was there some psychological clue there? I had no idea. I just wanted someone to tell me where the hell to go from here.

On the third day, early in the morning, Chris drove me up to the house and let me out. I looked up at the swaying trees and the fine blue sky. This here had been my prison. I'd never seen the front of the house. It appeared so serene, so normal: a garage, a gravel driveway, trees, and a pretty garden. Butterflies floated about from one flower blossom to another.

After he went in and made the room door stick open with a small bit of scuffed tape that he'd showed me, as if it had fallen from somewhere and been kicked along the floor, Chris came back outside. He shook my hand.

"Good luck, Steph." He bent and kissed my forehead. "You'll be okay. Just remember the story. Stick to that, please. For my sake."

I nodded. "I will. Thank you for all you've done."

"No worries." His gentle grin and thumbs-up lifted my heart. "Take care out there. There're some crazies on the road."

His car passed me as I set off down the winding road.

My legs felt odd taking these long strides and I had to check myself a few times when I almost skidded on the loose gravel. Somewhere, deeper in the trees, a kookaburra laughed in its lunatic bird voice, as if mocking my lack of hill descending skills.

I'd been inside for a long time and even on Rat Island the world was small. Here, under the shade of the trees, I was truly free. I smiled. I could do this. Fuck all that had happened. It wasn't my fault that things had gone down the gurgler for these last weeks. I'd do as Chris asked and tell my white lies. I'd even try to show Klaus and Jodie in a good light if I somehow could.

Walking as exercise had never been my favorite. I had to walk all the way to the cops? All the way down this hill? It was hot and already sweat was rolling down my back. Maybe I could get a lift? Or maybe not. Hitchhiking after all that had happened to me? Not wise, girl. Not at all.

A small rock that ended up in my Croc shoes made me hop about and grimace and rethink that vow. Who invented damn rocks anyway? If only I had gym shoes, but there hadn't been much use for those in the room.

I continued but the farther I went, the more something pulled on me, and the more I slowed. I stopped and looked up at the sky with my eyes shut. Yes, that was it. I was between two worlds. Behind me was the strange fantasy world of Klaus and Jodie where I was their sexual toy to be cherished, and made to perform and, at times, to scream. I shuddered at the thought of the latter. Even Jodie had relished that. My cruel girlfriend who even now made me ache. My girlfriend who'd gone somewhere far away without me. I wrapped my arms around myself imagining she was here with me and grieving that she wasn't mine anymore…and that I wasn't hers.

Ahead of me, down this road, was the normal world where I would have to explain where I'd been for these past weeks. How I'd gotten myself into the situation in the first place. Damn, that was going to be difficult. Then, once that was done, I had to go back to work. To the gray world. Money, clients, rent, filling out papers, driving cars, arguing, forever and ever.

I opened my eyes and stared down the slope of the black asphalt. But also movies, parties, talking to friends, achieving things and, best of all, being me, for myself and with no one to order *me* about, except for my bosses at work. The pluses were definitely on that side of the scale.

Then why was I miserable?

Because, I told myself. Just because. I'd come out of the maelstrom back there, unscathed, sane, and with the most amazing sexual memories ever. *Be happy, girl.*

I kept going.

My chest tightened as I went past a house—the first one since Klaus's. The silver-gray SUV in the driveway looked safe. Yet again, I hesitated as I wondered if someone in there could give me a lift. What exactly were the odds of encountering a serial killer in the average posh car? A thousand to one...surely? I sighed and continued.

But when I heard the engine approaching from behind me, I stuck out my thumb. Bugger walking. I turned. It was the silver-gray vehicle. I glimpsed a man with a baseball cap as it rolled past. A man. The vehicle slowed and stopped in front of me and I walked toward the SUV as the passenger door opened.

A lady would be safe, not a man. My stupid instincts nagged at me. *Do not get in.* I swallowed and stepped up, ready to brush him off with a lame-ass explanation.

Klaus. Lunging at me. Halfway across the seat, with his hand already reaching. My mouth gaped, I started to backpedal.

His fingers clawed onto me.

"No!" I squeaked, as he hauled me in by the front of my shirt and my armpit. My knees banged on metal, and a split second later, my mouth had his hand across it. I bit down.

"Shit." He slapped me and shoved my face into the seat. "Behave."

The fight left me. Three weeks before I would have screamed more, struggled more, but not now. I knew him and what he might do. Ashamed at myself, I realised I'd also snapped back into that submissive mode he'd trained in me.

His arm flattened on my back, squashing me. I felt him wrap some new leather about my elbows then came the distinctive sound of a belt being cinched in and fastened. He clipped together the wrist cuffs. Last of all, he leaned over me and did up the ankle cuffs, and pulled my legs in so he could shut the door. After working a gag between my teeth and buckling it, he turned me over.

Tears ran down my cheek. Whether from the pain of the slap or from shock, I couldn't tell. Fear had mastered me, as had the unknown. Why was he doing this?

"Welcome back." The rasp in his voice betrayed his passion. I trembled, confused, and overwhelmed. With his fingers, he roughly combed my loosened fringe away from my eyes. "Welcome back, toy. I decided we should keep you after all."

Then he frowned—that tiny corrugation of his forehead I knew so well. He brushed away my tears with the back of one finger. "Hey. *Shh.* It's okay. I was just getting you to be still. Stay there while I drive back up to the house. Lucky for me the Dysons are away on holiday."

The quiet patter of his words in his steady voice helped me to calm down. He was doing this deliberately. He knew the effect it had on me. My breathing slowed and I looked up into his eyes, searching for something in the gray-green depths.

He stared at me for a while longer, as if memorizing my face before he started the engine and drove the SUV back up the hill.

My head was in his lap. When the vehicle went over bumps, the hard denim of the crotch of his jeans rubbed my face. I could smell him. Familiar. A man who'd had his hands on me, in me, many times. Now I was at his mercy again. *Oh god, I'm sick.* This was arousing me.

# Chapter 26

## Klaus

I'd crossed the line here and I knew it deep in my guts. As I hauled her out of the car and kicked shut the door, I knew it. As I walked down the stairs with her over my arms, I did more than *know*, I exhilarated.

I could have taken her here at the house before she set off down the road, except Jodie had a thing for car abductions and her eyes had glittered at the possibility of Steph being picked up this way. It had certainly added to the excitement and the risk. But, some risk seemed fair considering what I was doing and planning—my last bit of fair play to Steph. Now, the gloves were off.

Methodically, despite her wrists and ankles being linked, I ripped off, or cut off, or unbuttoned, her shirt and tiny black shorts and underwear. When I strapped her against the wall, using the wall anchor points, I figured an observer would notice my eyes burning bright.

Jodie had known that this was crossing the line, but she'd begged me to do it, then she'd hugged me with tears streaming down her face as I left her for the plane flight back. We both knew we were being bad, but we also both had a craving to make this woman ours for good.

As a result, I was so jet lagged my brain was possibly in another state or time dimension, but I still comprehended there was no way I would qualify as Dom anymore due to the small misdemeanor of abducting Steph. Consent was nowhere in sight. If Moghul found out, he'd be the first to condemn me.

I surveyed my gorgeous nude woman pinned to the wall. I wasn't Luke Skywalker with right on my side. I'd turned to the dark side. Apparently, they didn't have cookies like someone had once told me, but they did have hot women.

"Let me guess, you have some questions for me?" I undid the ball gag from her mouth and tossed the thing aside so it bounced across the floor.

With her hands fastened to the O-ring above her, with one thick leather strap beneath her beautiful breasts and another above, as well as various other straps designed to keep her in place while I did my work—she was exquisite. Her glossy, night-black hair hung in delicious tendrils about her shoulders, with one strand long enough to curl across her nipple.

"Let me get that," I said, roughly, and I tucked the offending strand of hair behind her shoulder. I pressed a kiss on her luscious mouth, and another on that nipple then I played with it with one fingertip until it popped upward.

I noticed her reactions in detail—the huff of breath after I kissed her, then the licking of her lips and the flutter of eyelids, even the slightest tremble of her body.

With my arm laid on the wall above her head, I leaned in to admire her. "You must have questions, my toy."

She blinked and pushed against the leather before answering, making her breasts bulge out even more. "Why have you done this? I was...I was free." The last word trailed away.

I caressed her cheek, feeling wetness. "More tears? You need to accept what you need. For the last few days I've had reports about you from Chris. I flew out of the country with Jodie but I left him with instructions to report to me. When he told me how you were crying at night and calling for us, and for Jodie especially, that made me wonder. I wondered if I should do what I've been wanting to since

I first saw you. And I listened to Jodie. She wants you back. She's been begging me. It's hard to say no to the woman you love."

*Love. Shit. I'd never said that before. But maybe I do.*

Vigorously, she shook her head. "No. No. You made this up to get what you wanted. I never did that."

"You think?"

"I'd never cry out *your* name. I didn't want you back."

I stroked the underside of her breast. So soft. So giving yet heavy. "Untrue."

"Fuck no. I did not." She sucked at her lip.

"Don't swear at me." I hardened my eyes. She froze. "The rules are back. Take care."

Steph swallowed a few times. "I'm sorry, Sir."

"Now you're uneven. Not teasing your other nipple would be unforgiveable, though here is beautiful too." I traced around the intricate shapes and whorls of her ear while she watched from the corner of her eye. "You're breathing harder, girl." I smiled as her tongue tip flicked out and back in. Worried. I liked that. "Why do you think I've strapped you up here like this?"

She shook her head the tiniest amount.

"Why do you think I need these to stay in place?" I brushed my palm over each breast, circling over each nipple until they were both taut, then I moved my hand onto her belly, over her belly button, watching her contract her stomach muscles as she gasped.

Her clit was poking out enough for me to find it unerringly with my forefinger. I toyed with the tiny button, then I caressed from low down between her legs where her labia had swollen out nicely. Her moisture came along with my finger as I traced a warm wet path from her entrance, up her cleft, to her clitoris again.

She hadn't answered, but I guess I'd distracted her, judging by her closed eyes and the way her pelvis bowed outward seeking my finger.

"Why, little toy? Why would I want your breasts still? Can't remember?"

"Hmm?" She moaned as I increased the pressure on her clit, making ever smaller circles on top of it.

I chuckled. "Never mind."

I pushed off the wall and brought over the little table that held what I needed. "I'm going to move us all to another part of Australia, perhaps Western Australia." I raised an eyebrow. "Somewhere no one is likely to identify you. After being on Rat Island I can see that we need to let you out to see the world now and then. Once you can behave, you can do that."

I picked up the long metal piercer with the hollow stem.

Her gaze focused on the instruments and her brow wrinkled. "You never meant to let me go."

"I did. I struggled with this. I did intend to leave you be."

I'd sat up late arguing my way out of this, only to have Jodie and Chris show me that the alternative was possible. "Chris has found a way to stop Kat chasing us." That had been the key. With her off my back, we could stay in Australia.

"What is that?" She licked her lips, staring at what I held.

"It's a special piercing needle. Don't you remember my vow to use metal to claim you? I'm going to pierce your nipples and put bars in them."

"No," she whispered. "Uh-uh. I don't want that."

"You have no choice. This is what I'm doing."

Precisely this—almost putting a needle through Jodie's nipple—had been what made me doubt myself and my sanity once before. I'd never have pierced Jodie without her consent, but with Steph, it called to me in a way that connected straight to my balls. The need to pierce and claim her was overpowering. It was my *right*. I owned her. She was my property to do with as I chose.

I ignored the rest of her protests. I placed the clamp on her nipple to hold it utterly still and she stiffened and keened quietly. After swabbing with antiseptic, I assessed how I should do this again. The long fat needle needed to go right to left just outside the center of each nipple. I settled the tip in the correct spot.

"Take a deep breath."

That hesitation of hers said in bold letters how much this scared her.

"*Now*, girl."

She inhaled, expanding her chest outward. A half second later, I sent the angled tip of the needle a fraction of an inch into her nipple. Her gasp turned into a tiny scream as I squeezed the needle further into the flesh, watching her skin swallow then embrace the metal. Her little ragged whimpers enthralled me. As if by magic, the point came out the other side.

The weird joy I extracted from causing pain was at its utmost. Seeing that piece of metal projecting either side and knowing I'd just tunneled it through her nipple. Seeing the rise and fall of her breast as she inhaled and exhaled with her flesh embracing my metal.

Sexual possession, sadism, power—all rolled into one. I think my gaze was as sharp as the point on the needle. I had to count backward to ten before I could go on.

"No blood. Pity." I kept the timbre of my voice low as I stroked her shoulder, admiring her minutely as she huffed out a series of shallow breaths to control the pain. I was struck by a need to both reassure her and to do this again. "Good toy. You're behaving beautifully. I'll be quick."

Then I did the other nipple. I was quick, but I still couldn't help being absorbed in that moment as it slid through her. The penetration of her with a needle seemed to echo the intimate pleasures of sex.

I was breathing harder at the end too. Two pieces of metal in her. I checked her face but every few seconds I was drawn back to look at those embedded needles. Just for the pure sensation of holding her, I cupped my hand under one breast.

"How do they feel?"

"It. *Ssss*." She sucked in a gasp. "It hurts! They're throbbing. What do you think!"

I smiled as I carefully inserted the short bars through the hollows then withdrew the needles and screwed on the bulbs that kept the bars from falling out. "I think you're brave. And…" I leaned down and kissed the top of each nipple once. "I think you're ours now, whether you want to be or not."

She summoned courage from somewhere though her reply was squeaky. "No. Never. I'm not."

"Oh?" That was defiance if anything was. Deliberately, slowly, I unstrapped her from the wall. I watched her fidget as if wondering what to do with her hands. I kept my voice low. "You're going to show Jodie and me how good you are. You're going to give us a gift to show that you are hers and mine. What do you think you should do?"

Then I took two slow steps back, folded my arms, and I waited.

Eyes dark and wide, she stared.

Strange, after all that had been said and done, this moment had become everything. If she refused, I would doubt my convictions. If she refused I found I had abruptly grown a ludicrous need to let her go. Though I wanted her to be mine, I *needed* to see evidence she had some tiny inkling of that same desire within her. A desire for submission. A desire to be mine. Though it might be colored by fear, I needed that. Right now, I needed to see.

Seconds ticked past. I made myself be still even though mentally I was willing her to submit with every atom of my being.

When Steph bent her head for a while, then inch by inch shuffled to her knees, put her hands on those knees and raised her head to look up at me, my balls tightened and inside my head a roar blanketed all thoughts. *Yes. My god, yes.*

"Put your hands behind your head."

Though she winced at the pull on her breasts, she did so, lifting her tits perfectly.

*Hell, yeah. Mine.* She'd also gifted me with an especially rigid erection. "Thank you." I nodded as if this were entirely as I'd expected. I pulled out my phone and took a picture of her with her breasts outthrust showing off her new piercings. "Now cup them with your hands."

This time she did it straight away. I took another picture. The longer I examined her the more her face softened, the less focused her gaze became, and the more dilated her pupils. My quietly stated, *good girl,* resulted in her eyelids fluttering down for a second, as soft and amazing as a petal falling in slow motion.

Beautiful. Everything...I saw everything there that enthralled me—serenity, acceptance, a willingness to give, but also a willingness to take whatever was given her. I inhaled raggedly. Submission, deep, deep submission.

I let Steph see the photo before I sent it, and also let her see Jodie's text reply of, *Thank you, pet. You look beautiful. I'm going to be home tomorrow to kiss you. Stay safe. Trust Klaus.*

Moisture glistened on her lower lids and she clutched my thigh as I patted her head. My next act came so naturally it surprised me. I went to one knee, cradled her face in my hands and kissed her deeply. Then I whispered to her as I looked into her eyes. "We own you now, but you are also our most precious possession."

She blinked slowly then nodded.

I rose to my feet.

"Wait there, pet." I sighed looking down at her, feeling a surge of that protection Jodie had told me to make sure to use. This had been hard on her and for the first time I truly understood Jodie's use of *pet.* I figured I'd be using it a lot.

"I'm sorry, Sir," she whispered. "I'm sorry. Don't leave me. Please, don't leave me. I'll be good now, always."

Damn. I stared down at her, wishing I could put aside everything on the instant and do more to her, but I only ruffled her hair. "I'm not going to leave you. Be good. I have to ring Chris."

This was the last of it. I prayed he'd done what he said he could.

He answered on the second ring. "Hi. How did it go?" I kept petting Steph, deriving as much comfort from the feel of her hair under my palm and her arms wrapped around my leg as she probably was from my caresses.

"Good." Chris sounded a little breathless. "All's good. You don't have to worry about Kat anymore. I have her phone with that photo. I doubt she made copies after Moghul and I told her not to throw accusations about without being one hundred percent certain."

"Thank you." I closed the phone and stood with my eyes shut and my head bowed for a minute.

*May whatever deity might be up there in the heavens please forgive me for what I just may have done.*

# *Epilogue*

## *Chris*

I slipped the phone back into my pocket and swiveled on my shoes to look again at what I'd wrought. This was something new for me. At least it was in real life. For a long, long time, I'd wanted to do this. The craving had become so excruciating that seeing the result was close to orgasmic. Hands on hips, I stared down at her.

Helpless. No safeword. No friends. Just me and her, and each day from now on, whatever struck me as a good thing to do to her, I could do.

I pulled out her phone and had another peek at the offending photo. Taken from a boat off shore, like she'd said. Only it was so fuzzy I had no idea to how she'd used it to decide anything. Three people, yes. Klaus and Jodie, maybe, but the third was only vaguely identifiable as female. I put the phone away.

Kat lay on her side curled backward with the zip ties fastening her wrists and ankles behind her. One lady who abso-fucking-lutely wasn't getting loose until I cut those ties. She still growled at me despite the huge gag. Her glare wasn't stoppable with a gag. That needed something else. I dragged the duct tape from my pocket.

I stepped up to her and went to one knee, yanked the back of her head toward her nape by a handful of her bright red hair, so she was compelled to look at me. I tapped her nose with the hand holding the tape. "I need to cover those pretty eyes of yours."

Her look would have melted the sun, but I only grasped her throat.

"I'd kiss you and knock some of that fire out of you here and now, Kat, but the gag is a bit of an obstacle." I thumbed the hard ball sitting between her teeth while she breathed moistly and scowled. "You need to think about where you are, woman. I'm going to make you beg and cry and fucking crawl. When I'm done, I'll be your oxygen, and the very blood in your veins, because I'm going to get into your head right there." I pressed my finger in the center of her forehead. "Where you can never ever get me out. You hear me?"

She shook her head angrily and growled.

I chuckled. "You think you're a tiger? Maybe. Maybe you were. Not now. You've haunted me forever, woman. You've been so unreachable, so sure you can't be tamed. But I like challenges, and you are my ultimate one. Here's how it starts."

I took out the duct tape, settled a couple of pads over each eye, then I wrapped the tape round and round her head, covering her eyes, while I talked quietly. "You're going to be blind for a few days. When I take this off, you'll be somewhere far from civilization. There will be no one who can help you. There will only be me."

*The End*

# Glossary of US and Australian terms

In the interests of not jerking most of my readers out of the story with some unfamiliar word usages, I opted to sometimes use the US word instead. However, since I completed the book, I've been told by many American readers that they'd rather I use the Aussie words.

I'm not entirely convinced. Since I think I have far more American fans than Australian, I may still be tempted in Book 3, "Make Me Yours, Forevermore", to use some American terms. If you want to tell me otherwise, feel free to pop a comment on my facebook wall.

This example is why I hesitate:

Klaus put on his thongs and strolled out the door to take his daily walk on the beach.

**US word vs Aussie**

Cell phone = mobile — *US term used in the story*

College = University or Uni — *Australian word used*

Dishcloth = tea towel — *I used the US word*

Flip flops = thongs — *This was explained in the story*

Cooler = esky — *US word used with the Australian word*

Popsicle = ice block — *US word used*

Shrimp = prawn — *This was explained in the story*

Spatula = egg flip — *This was explained in the story, and it's a regional Australian term that isn't used nationwide, I think*

SUV = Four wheel drive — *US word used*

There may be others I substituted but missed seeing. I have become so used to doing this in my stories that it's almost automatic. I have also used US spelling throughout. Though this book is self-published both of my earlier publishers, Loose Id and Lyrical Press, used US spelling.

Visit CariSilverwood.net

Look for Cari Silverwood on Facebook and Goodreads

# Books by Cari Silverwood

**Pierced Hearts Series**
*Take Me, Break Me*
*Bind and Keep Me*

**The Badass Brats Series**
*The Dom with a Safeword*
*The Dom on the Naughty List*
*The Dom with the Perfect Brats*

**Cataclysm Blues Series**
*Cataclysm Blues*

**Rough Surrender Series**
*Rough Surrender*

**The Steamwork Chronicles Series**
*Iron Dominance*
*Lust Plague*
*Steel Dominance*

**Others**
*31 Flavors of Kink*
*Three Days of Dominance*

# The Dom with a Safeword

## Book 1 in the Badass Brats series

*Late at night, on an amateur ghost hunt, Sabrina and her best friend Q are caught trespassing by the gorgeous, blonde Jude. The embers of attraction between them sizzle when they discover Jude's kinks match their own. Jude is a Dom on his last summer of freedom before starting the prison sentence that is med school. Q is a badass bi switch who knows what she wants, and for years it's been her cute, doe-eyed straight friend Sabrina. But the only way for Q into Sabrina's heart and panties may be with Jude's fist wrapped in her hair.*

*Domming the bratty Q and mischievous Sabrina isn't going to be easy but Jude relishes the challenge. At the end of the summer, will they find a way to stay together when everything is tearing them apart?*

\*\*\*\*\*

"Do you think he's ever going to take his pants off?" Sabrina whispered in Q's ear. "Maybe he shares his penis with another guy and today wasn't his day to use it."

"I kept the jeans on so I wouldn't rush things," Jude replied, slapping Sabrina's ass.

"Well it's not exactly rushing anymore. Both of us are naked, so how is this fair?" she retorted, gesturing at the offending article of clothing.

"I'm the dominant, so I get to make the rules." His head tilted in a look of smug amusement.

"Fuck that!" Q knelt up on the window seat, leaned over Sabrina and pulled at the button of his jeans. "This is a mutiny, Captain!"

After wriggling free, Sabrina tried to hold him still while he batted away Q's hands. They had just managed to get the button untied, when he dragged both of them over to sit on his lap. They didn't quite fit, but he didn't give them the option of getting up.

"Hold your hair up, both of you," he ordered.

Looking askance at each other, they complied. The sensation of his breath rippling over Q's neck sent shivers up into her hair. His mouth latched onto the place where her neck and shoulder met, and Q sighed in contentment. Sucking and nibbling on their necks and shoulders, he held them still for his enjoyment. Eventually he let them go so they could participate.

Sabrina sucked on Q's bottom lip then trailed tiny kisses down to her chin, past her neck, to her breast. She paused as though she was having an internal debate. Slowly, she backed off Jude's lap onto the cushion. She shifted onto her hands and knees, grazing Q's nipple with her lips and making her groan. Her pink tongue darted out, licking the very tip. She looked up at Q mischievously, her ass wiggling.

Both she and Jude eyed Sabrina's backside with interest, smiling at each other when they realized they were doing it simultaneously. Q's smile became a gasp as something warm and wet engulfed her nipple. She watched in fascination as Sabrina's sucking and nipping mouth alternated between her breasts. Her tongue investigated Q's piercings. Enraptured, Q ran her fingers though Sabrina's silky hair, the slide of it through her hands sensuous. The elastic that had been holding it when they were painting hung tenuously onto the bottom of a lock of hair, and she tossed it aside.

# Lust Plague

### From Loose Id

### Book 2 in the Steamwork Chronicles

*Saving the world should be easier.*

*With her airship gone, Kaysana must rely on Sten, a human clone, a man who has fought all his life to master himself. She despises his kind and detests Sten's growing hold on her. Though he never takes no for an answer, surely it's the lust plague that makes yes slip from her tongue like melted butter? Or should she blame her own traitorous heart?*

*Hordes of slavering zombies await them. Sten and Kaysana unlimber weapons, don goggles, and set a course for the origin of the plague. Yet their victory will be hollow if they cannot also solve the puzzle of their hearts.*

*Publisher's Note: This book contains explicit sexual situations, graphic language, and material that some readers may find objectionable: anal play/intercourse, BDSM theme and elements, exhibitionism, spanking, strong violence.*

\*\*\*\*\*

The shop had everything, and all of it was ridiculous. Slave Costumes Galore, the gold embossed business cards said. Well. If she wanted to traipse around as a harem girl or squeeze into a corset with her tits out, she was in the right place.

"Let's find another shop." She tapped the card on the marble shop counter.

Without an internal light on, the place was lost in the subdued yellowish light filtering through the front window.

"Nope. Here's your clothes." Sten emerged from the aisle between the clothes racks and held up a skimpy leather outfit on a hanger.

"No way." She shook her head. "Nothing that jeopardizes my air fleet standing. Walking around in that"—she backed away—"would do so and therefore end our agreement."

"Uh-uh." Sten grabbed her elbow. "It won't. Who's to see? Zombies? Wear it, and this." He had a tan half mask hooked on the hanger—with little catlike ears pricked up at the top and gold tabby markings striped across the leather. "Nobody'll know it's you."

She opened her mouth to speak, paused, caught up in trying to figure out their agreement. "No. There may still be some normal humans. Hell, Sten. We have a world to save, and you want me dressed up like a cat?"

"A big, lickable pussy cat, yes." His voice was hoarse. His eyes gleamed with lust. "Obey, remember?" He tossed the clothes onto the counter. "You can't do this every time I come up with a new twist you don't like."

"Sten, this is just one of those sexual urges. Block it out. You can't be making up new—"

Without giving her time to react, he pulled her to him, then picked her up around the waist.

"Hey!" She struggled, but his big hands grabbed hers and gripped them tight at the small of her back. "What are you doing?"

"I'm going to spank you." He hooked a timber chair with his foot and sat with her across his lap, head down.

"What? Why?" She spluttered, still thrashing, but the hand at her back pushed her firmly onto his lap, held her easily. Awareness of their size and strength difference left her suddenly floundering. She was small, and he was so damned big. His other hand pushed up the shirt, smoothed across her bottom. Toes shoving at the floor, she tried to rise. The first blow fell with a whack, reverberated through her, sent a liquid message into her flesh. Shocked, she stiffened.

"No," she said in a hushed voice. "You can't do this."

"No?" In quick succession, he struck her again and again, alternating from one ass cheek to the other. His large hand gripped and pressed her wrists into the small of her back.

Ohh.

Kaysana made one last frantic squirming effort to free herself. If she moved her legs, he hit harder. If she stayed still…

Warmth built, turning hotter and hotter. Panting, hair falling across her eyes, she stayed put—half-afraid to move, half anticipating the rush of the next blow. Each smack seemed to force a louder gasp from her mouth. Her bottom, of its own accord, rose up to meet his hand.

"Good." Sten's spanking hand slid down her cleft, and his finger dipped inside her just enough to make her close her eyes. "You're very wet, Kaysana."

She could hear the wry amusement in his tone but didn't care, too lost in the mesmerizing slip and slide of his fingers between her folds and the stir of heat whenever a finger forged in deeper.

"How far will you let me go, Kaysana? Hmm?"

"No fa—" She jerked as one finger delved into her vagina, inches deeper. Her walls closed on him, tight, then let go. The floor under the chair, Sten's feet, met her fogged gaze. Upside down on his lap, with him probing inside her. She groaned. "This isn't kissing."

"No?"

He shifted. She felt him bend, and his lips met just above her nether hole, his tongue licked a little way into her ass crack.

"Nooo." Her whispered word trailed off as his fingers moved in, three into her pussy. Then his thumb nudged against the other circle of muscle, swirling saliva from the trail of his tongue and her juices around the hole, lubricating her. She tugged at where he gripped her wrists, felt the steel in his grasp. Inescapable. She wriggled. "Mmm."

"You like that?" His words, spoken as if into her very skin, sped straight through her like a steaming arrow.

Her clitoris throbbed, the little nub standing out so high and hard she knew he would feel the movement on his thigh. The heat from her bottom sent a warm message flowing everywhere, softening her thoughts, making it nearly impossible to think.

"Ahh, you do."

Every sensation screwed up inside her so tight she could barely breathe. She shoved her ass up onto his fingers as much as she could, writhed. Her last resistance fell away. She wanted him inside her— fingers, cock, tongue, anything would do as long as it happened soon.